I0553024

Monster

by Jeff Drummond

Copyright © 2013 Jeffery Phillip Drummond

All Rights Reserved

ISBN 9780989344319

Illustrations by Brittany Rollins

This book is a work of fiction.

The names, characters, places, events, and theories/processes are either products of the author's imagination or have been fictitiously used and are not real.

Any resemblance to real people, living or dead, actual events, locations, theories/processes, or organizations is purely coincidental.

Table of Contents

Monster

Being Born

It was like I was being reborn.

Except that's not quite right because I didn't know what born was so how could I redo it? Because it was all new to me.

It was like I was being born.

Whatever born was, because I didn't know what it was.

Everything was out of focus, white, fuzzy. But I could hear a voice calling to me. It sounded far away, echoing across miles and miles. The voice. It wasn't calling my name. But even if it were, I wouldn't have known it. So maybe it was calling my name.

Or not. I was being born. Whatever that was.

I didn't have a name. Or know what one was.

I was thinking, but didn't know how. Didn't know the words I was thinking. Words? English? What's that?

Confusion reigns…rains? Reigns and rains.

There were bright lights, everything was bright white light and blurry and fuzzy soft. Even my skin felt fuzzy soft, like I was encased in fur or down. I tried to keep my eyes open, but they started to close. I slipped back into the darkness again, but I could hear the voice from far away.

"Everything is fine. Relax. You'll be fine…"

As my eyes closed I saw flashes, orange lights flashing, red light glinting off broken glass on wet, black asphalt. I was lying in a road somewhere, a broken heap, night pressing in, pain pressing in. Enormous pain, crushing pain, obliterating everything. And darkness beginning to press inside, nighttime taking over inside, spreading outward.

Pain without; darkness within.

And someone was crying, saying "I'm sorry, I'm sorry, my God what have I done" over and over again. Sounding like the voice talking to me...and as I came back to the present, I went under the darkness again...

———

Ouch.

Pain or something like it.

Everything hurt. Or so it seemed. It was like pain, but not pain. I was cold, I was freezing. Ice water flowing through my veins. I shuddered and shook. Warmth seemed like a distant memory, except since my memory was blank maybe it wasn't. Arms and legs were blocks of cold, cold steel, heavy lead that I couldn't move and could barely feel, only cold, cold pain or something like it.

What's steel? What's lead???

I opened my eyes and heard the voice again. Closer this time.

"Try to relax. Your body is...adjusting. You've had a medical procedure, a very...ah...difficult surgery. I had to use some...radical treatments and you're responding to them...well, differently than I expected. Everything will be fine."

It didn't feel like everything would be fine. It felt like I was going to turn into an ice cube, a living block of ice with legs and arms. Living? Couldn't be sure of that. The voice made it sound as though I were alive, but maybe that was an illusion...

And the flashes again...lying on the cold hard ground...lights shining in my eyes...the incredible pain, feeling like I was torn apart...

Right before everything goes dark again.

———

Fuzzy. Hazy. Murky. Thinking, not seeing. Darksight. But not as dark as before. But thought is fuzzyhazymurky.

Getting better, though.

Sounded like birds. And wind. And I knew what those things were now, what they *meant*.

The not-quite pain was nearly gone, the dark is gone. For now. And I could hear a light, slow *thud-thud-thud*.

"Good, you're awake." I jerked, shocked and scared. "It's all right, it's all right. I'm sorry I startled you." That voice again, so calm, so reassuring. The same voice from before. And before that. When I was lying in the dark with lights in my eyes. I'm lying in the dark again, except it's because there's something across my eyes. I can feel it stuck to my face.

"Uhhhh..." What was that noise? I instantly froze, thinking about what kind of beast could make a noise like that.

"Don't try to talk, just rest. You've been through quite an ordeal." A deep, deep voice that could have been a bass if he were a singer.

"Ahhhh....mmmm...." Wait. Was that me making that noise? Was that me? I sounded awful!

"Relax and trust me, you'll be fine. Don't try to speak, just rest." I felt a hand on my shoulder. It was hot, burning hot against my skin. I jerked away from it. "Sorry, I must feel very warm to you now. You're cold, but you'll get used to it. There's going to be a bit of adjustment, but we'll need to take it slow. Your eyes are covered to help with your...healing process."

Healing process? Trying to sit up. Straining.

"No, don't struggle. I have you strapped down to the table so you won't injure yourself. As I said, you've been through quite an ordeal and you need to heal. Struggling will only make things worse."

Strapped down to the table? What for? What table and where? Who does the now-familiar voice belong to?

"Aaack. Ngoh." Why can't I talk? What's wrong with me? Why am I healing?

"It may take some time for you to regain control of…yourself again. Your speech will be affected, so don't panic because you can't talk. You might find that your thoughts are a little confused as well. It's to be expected after something like this. Please try to relax and I'll answer your questions when you're feeling better. I've given you a mild sedative to help you sleep. OK?"

Can't talk – how do I respond?

"OK?"

"Nnnng…"

A soft chuckle. "Sorry, my boy, I've gotten so used to talking to you that I've been interpreting your speech a little. I'll take that as a yes. Sleep well."

"Uhhh…"

"Oh don't worry, I won't be far away. I'm sorry I can't share more, but perhaps tomorrow. For now, sleep."

All too easy…

Being Re-born

So since I was born a short while ago, maybe now I'm being reborn. Or re-reborn. Opening my eyes slowly, I could see light. Things weren't as blurry, but still out of focus a bit. I was staring at a ceiling of dark wood, lying on my back. My thoughts were making a little more sense. I could name things a little better now. I could *think*.

"Hello again." He sounds like Alec Guinness, only an octave deeper. But who is Alec Guinness? Seems like I still have some blanks to fill in. "Good to see you awake. I've taken the bandages off your eyes, but you still might not be able to see properly."

Blinking, trying to force my eyes to focus, I could only see a dark form of a big man sitting on a stool looking at me. I could barely make out his face: a black beard streaked with gray, long black hair also streaked with gray. He was tall, very tall. But maybe that's because I was lying down. He was broad-shouldered, and broad in general, but not fat.

"You can try sitting up if you'd like. Let me help you." He stood up and came over to the table. Putting his hand on my arm, he slid his other hand under my back to help me up. But his hands were hot again, burning hot.

"Nnnnhhh..." I pulled my arm away, rubbing it.

"Yes, I know, my hands are a bit warm to you. That's one of the things you'll have to adjust to. Your...injuries have left you with sensitivity to warmth because you've got a lower body temperature than most humans. You're not being burned; it only feels that way. You'll find it's not really pain you're feeling if you focus on how it feels."

His soothing voice reassured me. He was right. As he reached back over to help me up again, his hand wasn't really very hot. It felt like it was burning, but it wasn't a painful burn. I tried to sit up, but fell back down again. I moaned in frustration.

"I know, it's going to be a little tough get around while you adjust. Let's try again. I'm sorry I didn't have a very good grip. It's been years since I've worked with an actual patient. All of my work for the past couple of decades has been in a lab, so my patient handling is a little rusty."

His hand felt firmer, his grip stronger. He helped me sit up and I was immediately sorry. My body felt weighted down with iron ingots on my arms, chest, and head. My shoulders slumped and my head dropped slowly to my chest.

"Here, let me help you." He placed his hands on either side of my face and lifted. "That's better."

His face came into better focus. I was right about the beard and long hair. He was wearing glasses with dark gray, wire frames and smiling at me gently, like a father. A kind face.

"My name is Devin. Devin Burroughs. I checked your personal items, but didn't find any identifying information, so I don't know your name. We'll get to that later, after you've had some time to adjust. Let's get you into a chair so we can talk a bit more. I'm going to help you off the table."

He put his arm around my shoulders and held my arms crossed in front of me with his other. He eased my feet to the floor, where I thought I'd wind up in a heap. I weighed a thousand pounds; no, a hundred thousand pounds. Devin's strong arms, however, gave me the support my weak legs needed.

"Easy, one foot in front of the other. Into the chair, there we go." He slowly moved me across the floor and into a chair. My vision was getting better. It was leather, overstuffed. The chair, not my vision. I still felt so confused, thoughts jumbled in my head, tumbling into each other. But things were coming back to me, words started to have more and more meaning.

I shook my head a little to try to clear it and things came into focus a little better, but I felt myself sliding a little. Devin was sitting on the stool again, smiling at me. He reached out and righted me a little. I turned my head slowly to look at the room. Dark oak floors, dark gray walls, granite counter tops, stainless steel sinks and appliances. The ceiling I was just staring at was the same wood as the floors, with exposed beams and giant, black metal plates connecting them. A kitchen? No windows except for very high near the ceiling, easily 20 feet above us. Bright light fixtures lighted the room and sunlight streamed through the windows high above us.

"This is my lab. I brought you here, after the…accident." He shifted uneasily in the stool and his smile faltered a little. He flushed, looking at his hands and rubbing his fingers across the pads of his thumbs.

I frowned at him and opened my mouth. "Uhhh. Nnnh." Words were coming a little easier, but I still couldn't speak. The words were somehow getting trapped between my brain and my mouth.

He looked up and his smile wasn't a smile. His lips were pressed together too tightly and the corners of his eyes were too crinkled. "I'm sorry. All this is my fault. I tried to help you, though, but you may curse me for doing so after you hear me out. Or you may question my motives."

Confused, I frowned. I still couldn't talk, so I had no idea how I could question anything.

"It was late at night and I was driving home." He got up slowly from his stool and walked over, kneeling on one knee on the floor next to me. He looked like he was in pain.

"I couldn't see very well, I was tired. I hadn't been drinking, but I had been working late into the night. I shouldn't have been driving. I thought a drive would help clear my mind a little, refresh me. Driving is one of my passions outside my work," he chuckled nervously, running a hand through his mussed hair.

He put his hands on my shoulders, gently squeezing them, looking into my eyes. I could see tears forming in his eyes. His voice was rough as he continued. "I came around the corner, struggling to stay awake. And I saw you in the road. I don't know where you came from or what you were doing. You were just standing there. And it was too late. I couldn't even brake."

He got up and turned his back on me, wiping his eyes as his voice evened out a little. "I ran you over. At over 60 miles an hour, I ran you down and ran you over. I stopped the car and got out, hoping against hope. Hoping you were still alive."

He paused, cleared his throat a little, and went on, looking up at the ceiling as if for guidance or strength. Maybe both. "You were alive, but barely. I must say, you were a mess."

He looked over his shoulder at me and I could see the pain in his eyes as he remembered. He looked down, as if he were ashamed to meet my eyes. "I brought you back here to take care of you. I swear to you, I worked hours on end just to keep you alive. It was three days before I could get you stabilized, but you didn't get well. You weren't healing. In fact, you were getting worse, not better. I needed to take drastic action."

He got up and walked slowly over to what looked like a refrigerator. But it was huge, all shiny steel, with dials, knobs, and gauges on the side.

Words came more easily...understanding was much easier. It felt like something was just beyond my reach. Something that would help me clear my thoughts a little and start to make sense of my jumbled mind. If only I could remember more, figure out what happened. An accident?

Devin opened the door and pulled out a large tube of clear liquid that had a blue tint to it. But not just blue – like electric neon blue. The fluid sloshed around as his hand trembled; he gripped the tube tightly, steadying his hand.

"I had been testing out a new...compound...I developed for a pharmaceutical company. I hadn't tried this on a human. I'm sorry. I couldn't think of anything else to do. Of course I couldn't get your consent to try out an untested and unlicensed drug, and for that I'm sorry. I could go to prison for what I did, but I would do it again to try to...save you."

He put the tube back into the refrigerator and walked slowly back, looking at me with pity in his eyes. "And I'm sorry for the changes it's made in you. Perhaps I should go to prison, if for that alone."

I frowned when he said that. I didn't know what he was talking about. Having just been born, or reborn, whichever, I had no prior knowledge of who or what I was. I shook my head.

Whoa, where did that come from, I thought, surprised at my head shake as much as Devin apparently was.

"Did you shake your head at me?"

I nodded. And like that, a small spark went off, I started remembering simple actions. Like the beginning of an avalanche, smaller things came back, like handshakes and milkshakes, nodding and shaking.

A joyous grin broke through his serious face. "Amazing! You're communicating. That's a great sign! That means your motor function is returning and your cognitive abilities are improving. Maybe the compound is doing more than I hoped it would." He clapped his hands and rubbed them together.

I looked at him, mouth open. He was right. Somehow, I knew what to do, but I was still confused. I was thinking about moving my head, and it just moved.

As I looked at him, I saw his smile fade and he looked serious again.

"But you must see to believe." He held up a finger and walked toward the back of the lab. When he returned, he was carrying a mirror, looking concerned. He hesitated, then he held it out to me and I took it, trying to curl my hands around it. They felt like claws wrapped in towels. I was so focused on holding the mirror that I almost forgot what I was supposed to do with it.

Then I remembered to look into the mirror. As I looked at the person in the mirror, I couldn't understand what I was seeing. The image...

"You see, the drug is supposed to repair damage done." He was speaking faster, in a higher-pitched voice. He started pacing back and forth, his hands clasped behind him as he seemed to talk to himself, more than to me. Or lecturing in front of students. "During your recovery the first three days, I had to repair extensive damage to your body."

He stopped pacing and looked at me. He sighed heavily and stood up a little straighter. "Including your heart."

I almost dropped the mirror as I snapped my head up at him. I knew what *that* particular body part was. My heart – I knew that was important.

"You have an artificial heart. But more about that later." He stepped back a little, wincing as he watched my reactions. "I was able to mend some of the damage, but I'm afraid there was nothing I could do for the scars. The compound helped you heal at a tremendous rate, but the cost it exacted…well…," he trailed off as he watched me with the mirror.

Artificial heart, he said. My mouth gaped.

I looked back at the mirror and stroked the side of my face, cold, hard, unyielding. I could see a wide, pale scar running from my right temple, down my cheek just in front of my ear, then thinning away to nothing halfway down my neck. A thinner, darker scar started on the left side of my nose where it connected to my eyebrow and ran down just under my left eye, down my cheek, ending abruptly at my jaw line.

There was a series of smaller, crisscrossing scars on my forehead over my right eye that resembled a weave pattern. I had a similar pattern on my chin. But the worst was my mouth: I had a scar on the right side that hooked down into a semi-circle and one on the left that made my mouth look grotesquely wide, as if my lower jaw were almost torn off. The lips themselves were scarred with cruel vertical slashes of light and dark skin.

But beyond all that was the cold, hard, unyielding flesh. It wasn't soft or pliable. My nose might as well have been leather stretched over steel.

"The scars you see are the result of the accident. But the changes you see to your skin color and texture are the results of overdosing with the medication I created. I originally intended it to be used in small doses, but large doses were required in your case."

He walked toward the counter and leaned over it, cupping his forehead in one massive hand. "The trials I had done were with small animals and very small doses, comparatively speaking. Even adjusting the dose for humans, I was giving you roughly ten times the dosage I administered during the animal trials."

He looked up and moved his hand to his mouth, as if to cover the expression on it. But I could see the horror in his eyes. Horror at what he had done? What he had...created?

"I didn't see...couldn't have foreseen...what would happen to you. I'm so sorry," he whispered as his voice failed him.

I stared in the mirror. The pale gray skin with the texture of leather that didn't give at all when touched – it felt like it was part of an over-inflated football, a frozen baseball glove. It was smooth, except for the scars.

My skin.

The murky, gray eyes, nearly colorless irises that were so light they were almost white. The pupils appeared like dark gray dots in the middle, not fully black but darker than the irises. The corneas weren't white, either – they nearly matched the color of the irises, with a darker gray outline separating the two.

My eyes.

Devin interrupted my inspection by clearing his throat, his voice more authoritative, again as if he were delivering a lecture. "The chemical...made changes to your body. It first started with your blood, but then rapidly moved on to the rest of your body. As I made test after test, I found that your blood cells were changing – then it started affecting the rest of your tissues, slowly at first. What you're looking at is a result of that changing. The mutating."

I looked up at him again. Mutating?

"A few days later, the tissues of nearly all of your organs had been changed. Very few areas of your body were untouched. Your respiration slowed. Your heart would have, too, if it weren't artificial.

"Since it was artificial, it continued pumping, pumping what I thought was poisoning you, my miracle drug. A couple of weeks later, all of your organs had changed, every part of your body was affected. Your blood—"

He stopped and stood up straight to look at me. I looked back at my reflection as I brushed my hand against the smooth skin. Was it skin?

"Your blood was no longer blood, so to speak. Your heart only continued to pump because it was mechanical."

I almost dropped the mirror. I put it down and tried to stand. "Ohhahhh..."

He rushed over and held my arms steady as I stood. I put my arm on his shoulder and squeezed. He winced and I released, pulling my hand back quickly.

"It's all right, it's OK. You've just been strengthened a bit because of the medication. I intended it to be used for patients who were gravely injured, especially those injured in combat. I wanted to heal patients, but also strengthen them more quickly to get them back into action, to limit the loss of a team member during combat. Because of the dosage, however, it took you over. Instead of speeding your recovery and returning you to your strength, it augmented your strength. It took over your body and gave you extraordinary abilities."

He looked at me, in pain again, as if he were afraid to continue talking. Afraid to reveal something.

"But it also took things from you. As I said, you have no blood. Your organs are intact, but most of them are...nonfunctioning. Your heart continues to pump, but it is a machine. You can see and hear, but I think that's because those are connected to the brain. The compound seems to

18

augment electrical processes, so your thought processes could become enhanced. You're probably already finding that your thoughts are clearer. But I can't be sure of anything, really.

"Your brain function was severely impacted after the accident and I can't even guess how long it will take you to recover. If you will ever fully recover. Preliminary tests look fine, but I can't begin to test your mental function. It's way too soon. And we need your speech to return. I can only hope that it will with a little work."

He stopped talking and took a deep breath, exhaling slowly.

"Your body—your organs—don't need oxygen through respiration, but the fluid in your body needs oxygen. Without oxygen, the fluid will start to coagulate. And although you won't get wounds or infections like everyone else, I have no idea what would happen if the fluid stopped circulating.

"As I said, the fluid helps you think. That much I know. It helps speed the chemical and electrical processes in your brain. Speeds them beyond normal human thought, so once your healing is complete, you'll probably think faster than most people. And I anticipate your reflexes will be faster. Your brain isn't like the rest of our organs, because it still functions.

"But, you're not…technically…alive."

Then I did drop the mirror, shattering it into several large, jagged pieces. I saw my reflection in the pieces, seeing myself reflected in several slivers, but not as a whole.

Not alive? What *was* I, then? What did that make me?

"I'm truly sorry. Your body, by strict definition, is no longer living. I know this is a lot to consider, if you can even conceive of what I'm telling you. If you can process what I'm trying to say – I realized this is too much, too soon, but I need you to know.

"You are...animated. I don't know how to explain it or what to call the state you're in, because it's definitely not in any medical textbook. In fact, I wouldn't be surprised if you were the only person of your kind. I've heard of drug-induced fugues where victims were poisoned and made into something like a living zombie, but their hearts still functioned, as did their organs. They had blood in their veins and were alive. But you..."

He broke off, obviously frustrated, stricken with what he'd done and unable to properly describe it or understand it. He took off his glasses and rubbed his eyes, sighing heavily, pausing several minutes before continuing. He put his glasses back on and looked at me sadly.

"I do not know how or why you continue to be, but you do," he whispered, shaking his head, as he bowed it to his chest.

I reached out and patted his shoulder. He looked up, tears in his eyes. I tried to smile.

"Annnk..." I shook my head and tried to clear my throat. It sounded like I was growling. I scowled and shook my head, trying again.

"Annk...ooo..." I shook my head and shrugged my shoulders. I pointed to my heart and pointed at him. I held out my hand to shake his, trying to hide my amazement as my human instincts took over again.

"Are you—are you thanking me?"

I nodded. I couldn't stand to see the pain. I didn't understand most of what he had said, but he had saved my life. Or maybe not, since he said I wasn't alive. But I didn't want him to be in pain, not after he had worked so hard. I would deal with the issues later – for now, I couldn't stand to see Devin in pain.

Pure joy spread across his face as I tried to smile with him. He reached out and grasped my hand. I tried not to squeeze too hard, but could see him wincing anyway. But he was smiling. "And you're smiling! You are, aren't you?"

I nodded again. His smile was infectious.

"I'm sorry I'm explaining so much to you so soon after you've regained consciousness," he said, taking off his glasses and wiping his eyes. "I know you must have many questions, all of which you're not able to verbalize. But you will," he said. "I know you will. I thought it would be best for you to hear everything from the beginning so you'd be better able to understand your recuperation and the changes that have happened to you."

I put my hand on his shoulder and gently squeezed. He smiled weakly and patted my hand. "OK, no more long faces, I promise."

Take It Slow

The next few weeks went very slowly. My thinking improved, as did my speech. But I was still often frustrated. I also broke a few more things other than the mirror – my strength was increasing and I was still learning control. I managed to snap off the entire faucet in the bathroom one morning just trying to turn it off. Luckily, Devin managed to shut off the water before I flooded the bathroom.

I also broke one of the lab doors. I was carrying some books for Devin and tried to push it open with my foot, gently. Not knowing my own strength, things didn't go as planned. The door swung open violently, punching holes in the wall behind it, shattering the glass in it, and splitting the door in the middle. I dropped the books and tried to grab the section of door that split. I managed to catch it, but the bottom was still attached to the other piece with the hinges, so I managed to yank the door out of the frame and split the door frame in the process.

"Seems you're stronger than you know," Devin said, smiling with real glee. "Amazing, my boy, amazing. Just put the pieces in the garage – I'll have Louie get a contractor in here to fix it."

Louie was Devin's property manager, so to speak. I cringed at how much my little "accident" would cost.

Sometimes I'd have a little setback, like trying to remember how to tie my shoes. Devin showed me time and time again, but I still couldn't get it.

"No, bring the other piece around," Devin said, coaching me one day. "No, wait, you're going to—"

And I winced as the shoestring snapped off in my hand. I waved my hand impatiently and took off the shoes. I could go barefoot anyway, since I didn't ever leave the house and my feet never got cold. I finally figured it out a couple of days later, though: I simply made two bows to tie them instead of using the wraparound method. It seemed a lot easier.

I also continued to learn a little bit more each day – simple things, like reading. I had started with the newspaper, but was beginning to work on novels. I had followed Devin's advice and started with books for younger readers: Call of the Wild, Tom Sawyer, Johnny Tremain. I had read through a few more classics for young readers and was stepping up to read more difficult material: Pride and Prejudice was my current undertaking. I could follow the story easily enough, but I often put it down to rest my mind. It got easier to keep up, but I still needed to take it in small doses.

I was also listening to music, but found Devin's tastes a little too tame: classical, jazz, and the occasional soft rock album were all he had. I was learning to navigate my way through the web and found heavy metal, to Devin's chagrin. He bought me an iPod and I quickly filled it with music by Black Sabbath, Iron Maiden, and Judas Priest. I also found my way to lesser known bands like Walls of Jericho and Children of Bodom.

"You honestly enjoy that noise?" Devin asked, shaking his head.

I smiled, not trusting myself to a verbal answer. There was more to it than just listening to music. I couldn't express myself yet, but I felt…powerful. When I listened to that music, it made me feel invincible. I could identify with the angry vocals, the shrieking guitars, and the rapid-fire drum blasts. Sounds corny, but it spoke to me, the same, angry language I spoke: nearly inarticulate screams.

I still struggled with *what* it was saying to me, though.

Groceries

Weeks had passed and I was…convalescing, for lack of a better term. And then one day…

I knew Devin had something on his mind, because he wasn't in the lab. He had to have something planned, because he wasn't sitting on his stool, staring into a microscope or looking at one of the numerous computer screens and flat TV monitors sitting on benches, desks, hanging from overhead, and mounted to the walls. I found him in the kitchen, holding a set of keys in his hand.

Uh-oh.

"I know it may seem a bit early," Devin began, clearing his throat a little, "but I think we should take you out in public at some point."

True, it was several weeks after I first started moving on my own without his help, but I still wasn't sure about this. For the first couple of weeks, I walked around with one arm around his shoulders as he guided me from room to room. I then moved on to holding myself up with furniture and I could walk on my own at this point. But how would it look if I collapsed in the middle of a store?

"Public? So soon?" My voice was raspy and my speech was still a little stilted. My thinking was fine, better than fine. Devin was right; I was improving faster than even I expected. But for some reason, my thoughts got trapped somewhere between my brain and my throat. Most days, my moods were caught between intense frustration (at not being able to do the most basic of human functions) and intense anger (at, well, not being human). Anger about what had happened to me and…well, anger at the world, basically. There's no better way to describe it. The anger would abate, but often the frustration stayed.

"Like I said, I know it's early, but I think it's important to get you acclimated to the world outside the lab. I know it will probably be difficult because people will stare," Devin said, looking at his feet in embarrassment. "Rude, I know. But the sooner we do this, the sooner we can get you back into life."

"Not missing much. From what I've seen," I mumbled. I was still trying to get used to speaking and hearing my voice. Every time I heard it, I cringed. And it sounded like Devin wanted to increase the audience.

"You've got a bleak outlook," Devin said frowning. "This is for the best. You need to have social interaction. You need to be in public."

"Why?" I asked.

Devin sighed and looked at me intently. "You don't really expect to live out your life in the lab, do you? You can't be a hermit. You need social interaction."

I turned my back as I frowned. My frown must have been audible because I heard Devin sigh again. "I don't want to upset you, but I didn't save you for the express purpose of having a lab assistant. I know it sounds cruel, but I don't think you'll be happy with a life stuck inside these four walls. Living an easy, safe life really isn't living."

Resigned, I shrugged my shoulders. "OK. When?"

He walked toward the garage and opened the door. "No time like the present." I stood in the kitchen, staring at him.

"Now," I croaked.

"Yes," he nodded. "Listen, I know this is—"

"You. Don't."

He frowned. "I don't what?"

"You don't. Know."

"OK," Devin nodded, slumping slightly. He seemed to visibly droop as I let the wind out of his sails. "You're right. I don't know how you feel or how hard this must be. But I do know this is the best thing for you. Please."

"Hate it when you beg," I growled.

I lowered my head and walked toward the garage. He decided to take the HHR, since it had better storage than most of the sports cars in the garage. And it had better gas mileage than the array of trucks and SUVs. Even though Devin had more money than most small nations, he was still reluctant to waste it all on gasoline. As we wound our way down the driveway, I could feel the tension start building, starting in my shoulders. I could feel my shoulders starting to hunch.

I knew there would be staring and whispering. And pointing. People gawking at the odd-looking creature lumbering through the aisles. Goody, goody, yippee, hooray. I'd read enough and seen enough on TV news shows to know how I'd be viewed in public. With every mile that ticked by, one more muscle in my shoulders would tense up. After all my shoulder muscles seemed to have tightened, up, my neck muscles started.

We didn't even get to the grocery store before the first staring episode started. We were at a stoplight and the guy in the car next to us kept glancing over at me. Eventually, he gave up all pretense of glancing and just stared. So I eventually gave up all pretense of ignoring him and stared back.

"Easy," Devin said, putting a hand on my arm. "Just because he hasn't any manners is no reason to—"

I opened my door before Devin could finish. "Do I. Know you?" I raised my voice, knowing it would startle him:

my voice is damaged, raspy, and nothing like human speech. And I wasn't wrong about startling him.

"No," he said, clearly shaken. "I'm s—s—sorry."

"Should be," I said, getting nearer to his car. The words weren't coming very well. "Next time you stare. Think." I lifted my foot and stomped the front quarter panel, leaving an impression of my foot. The guy shrieked, pushing himself backward in his seat. I slammed my fist onto the hood of his car, denting it slightly in the middle. Not satisfied, I slammed both of my fists onto it and made the dent larger. "Next time, might be you." I grabbed the edge of his partially open window and yanked it toward me, shattering it.

The light turned green and I walked back to the HHR, muttering "sorry" to Devin as I buckled up again. The driver's tires screamed as he sped off as quickly as he could.

Devin sighed. "I'll call the police when we get back home. I doubt the man will file a report or want to press charges, but it would be best if they heard it from me."

"I'm sorry," I said again. "Staring. Made me angry. Control…is tough…"

"Yes, you'll need to work on that," Devin said mildly as he drove us to the grocery store, though I could hear his concern. We rode in silence the rest of the way.

After he pulled into the grocery store parking lot and picked a spot, Devin turned off the car and sighed. "People are going to stare," he said evenly. "You are probably going to get angry, but please don't break anything." He smiled at me weakly.

"Try not to," I said, getting out of the car and steeling myself for the onslaught of stares and turned heads. And I wasn't disappointed. I kept my head down, trying to ignore them, clenching my fists tightly at my sides. I heard excited voices and even some broken glass as a shopper dropped the bags they were holding.

"Relax your hands," Devin said quietly. "People are starting to...scurry, I suppose you'd call it. Why don't you grab a shopping cart. That will give your hands something to do."

I grunted as I picked a cart and pushed it through the whooshing doors, squeezing the handle tightly as I did. The plastic grip shattered into pieces and I bent the metal handle. Just a little. I frowned and shook my head in disgust.

"Good morning and welcome to..." The woman standing at the front door trailed off when she saw me, completely forgetting that she was supposed to be greeting me and reminding me of the store I just entered. She gasped and let out her breath with a little squeak.

"Thanks," I said sarcastically, smiling at her.

"Well done," Devin said, chuckling. "You didn't even smash the stand she was using for the sales circulars."

"Close," I said, staring at the bottom of the cart.

"It's OK to look up and make eye contact occasionally," Devin said. "You might be surprised."

"Right. I'll get cereal," I said, pushing the cart ahead of me. I walked toward the aisle with the cereal, trying to meet the stares and shocked looks with what I was hoping was a light smile. Luckily, the cereal aisle was deserted, so I could drop the façade and continue with my moody grimace.

As I was looking through the cereal, I realized the stares were bothering me more than I thought. I thought about all of the self-help crap that's on TV and "human interest" news stories that make you feel good about a disabled person who's getting along in life. News shows always seem to capture people standing around a person with a disability or ailment and everyone is smiling, extending a helping hand. Accepting.

And I realized the only reason those people on the news don't stare is because they're on camera. Take the camera away, and they'll stare, too. Take away the camera, and you take away their acceptance. They'll whisper and point. Speculate about injuries, missing limbs, and scars. Feel pity and maybe even sympathy, but not empathy.

I wanted *none* of it.

While I was staring at a box of Lucky Charms cereal, the anger building, I felt a tug on my pant leg. I looked down and there was a little boy standing next to me. I raised my eyebrows – kids usually run screaming the other way.

"Hi," I growled as evenly and as softly as I could.

"Want dat," he said, pointing up at the Apple Jacks on the top shelf.

"That," I whispered quietly in my broken voice, pointing at one of the boxes.

"Yes," he shouted, smiling at me and giggling.

"Trent, no, don't bother that poor guy," I heard a voice calling from down the aisle. He started jogging down the aisle, his sneakers squeaking on the clean, gleaming floor. He smiled a little, obviously unsure if his son was bothering me or not. And also unsure about how close his son was to me.

"OK," I said, smiling. "Don't mind." I reached up and pulled a box from the shelf and handed it to the boy.

The guy slowed to a walk, clearly embarrassed. He was turning a hilarious shade of red, which made an interesting contrast with the green Red Sox t-shirt he was wearing (which had a "Green Monstah" logo on it). "Oh, sorry...I thought...well...," he started, trailing off.

"...I couldn't speak," I finished for him.

"Wow," the guy said, smiling sheepishly. "I put my foot in my mouth and didn't even get to finish my thought."

"It's OK," I said. "Happens. Most people don't talk. To me."

"Dave," the man said, sticking his hand out. I shook it lightly, or so I thought. I could see him wince a little. "Good grip! And that's Trent."

"Hi Trent," I said, waving.

"Hi!" The boy yelled as loud as he could, making me laugh – a throaty noise that sounded like a good-natured growl from a bear. Seeing me laugh sent him into high-pitched giggles again.

"Happy. Little guy," I said.

"Listen, I'm sorry—" Dave started, but I stopped him.

"No problem. Accident left me this way."

Dave looked embarrassed again and muttered another apology.

"No, I'm sorry," I said, sighing. "Had to relearn speech. And…public behavior." I smiled ruefully at him.

He nodded and chuckled. "Well, as you can see, I'm not very good at it myself. My wife has been trying to train me for years, but I'm a horrible student. So when you figure it out, let me know."

"Sure."

"Have a good day," he said. "Come on Trent, let's go find Mommy so she can keep us both out of trouble."

"Tanks!" Trend yelled as he walked away, waving, hugging his box of Apple Jacks.

I laughed and waved to both of them. I picked a cereal Devin liked (something with twigs and bark in it) and turned to go, only to see Devin smiling at me at the end of the aisle.

"How's that?" I asked quietly as I walked toward him.

"Spectacular," Devin said, patting me on the back. "You're a natural, my boy, you really are. Easy on the handshakes, though."

We walked through the rest of the store, adding things from Devin's list. We continued without incident, until we reached the checkout. I should have figured that's where the worst of the staring would be. Standing there among the racks of tabloids, I looked like I belonged on the front cover of one. 'I Married a Monster!' 'Quasimodo is the Father of My Children!'

And the talking, no matter how hushed, always carried.

"Do you suppose it's a birth defect of some kind?"

"I don't know but there has to be some kind of operation for that..."

"...do you think he's in pain? He looks so angry..."

"Maybe he's dangerous, I mean look at the scars on his face!"

More than one voice, multiple voices, male and female. I could hear kids, the middle-aged, the elderly. All of them standing and staring. I kept my head down, staring at the laces on my black boots. Looking at my jeans, trying to focus on the patterns in the denim, faded streaks, and white patches that would turn into holes in a few washes. How tight they were, how I seemed to be outgrowing them, but...

But I could still hear the voices.

All of them talking about me.

And I'd had enough.

"Stop! Stop staring! Stop whispering!" I wasn't shouting, but I was close. I could feel myself shaking, trembling.

"Easy, son, easy," Devin said, putting a restraining hand on my arm. I shrugged it off violently and stepped away from him, colliding with a magazine rack and sending it toppling over amidst little squeals of surprise and shocked murmurs.

"No, Devin! Not the one with the problem. They are." I pointed my gray finger at all of the staring faces. I saw one of the store workers in the customer service area slowly pick up the phone, staring at me with fear.

"Sure," I growled at her, "call in the cops. Call in the troops because you're scared."

"Wait," Dave said, shaking his head at the woman in customer service. He was standing in the checkout line next to ours. He stepped forward a little, looking at me, embarrassed. "He's right. Leave the poor guy alone. You should be ashamed of yourselves, just like I was after talking to him. He's had an unfortunate accident that left him this way. Have the decency to keep your comments to yourself."

"Poow guya," Trent said, tugging on my pants again. I smiled at him as he reached both of his arms up to me, opening and closing his little hands.

"Up," he demanded.

I bent over and picked him up, ignoring frightened comments of the onlookers as Trent squeezed my face and nose.

"Hawd face," he squealed as he tried to dig his little hands into my cheeks.

I laughed and nodded as I heard the conversations start up again.

"He's going to hurt that poor baby…"

"…he looks like a monster, someone should stop him…"

"No one needs to stop him," a woman standing next to Dave snapped at an older couple near the door. She smiled at me and didn't appear at all anxious. "Trent doesn't go near other people, ever. This young man is the first person outside of his Mom and Dad that he'll go near."

She lowered her voice a little, talking only to me. "Trent's had stranger anxiety with every person outside of his parents, including grandparents and aunts and uncles. So badly that we thought he might have development problems or issues." She stopped talking and looked at me again, almost reverently. "But he doesn't have any anxiety with you. If Trent says you're OK, you must be." She smiled at me as I handed over her son. "I'm sorry for the way you're being treated."

"No need to apologize," Devin said, patting her hand. "Let's go, son, before—"

"Break something," I finished. I waved to Dave and his family again, taking the cart from Devin, glad to be away from the voices at least. I was squeezing the cart handle too hard – I could feel the metal bending in my hands again. The stares continued in the parking lot, so much so that there was a minor fender-bender near the entry of the store.

I got a slightly sadistic chuckle out of that.

Realizations

Animated.

An *animated* corpse. Not really alive, but definitely not dead

Animated.

It was early morning and I was done resting. I didn't need much rest time, but I normally confined myself to my bedroom in the late night and early morning hours, if for no other reason than to allow Devin time to sleep. But like so many mornings lately, I was thinking about my state of being.

I stared at myself in a mirror in the bathroom. I had finished showering and put on my jeans, but stood in front of the mirror, staring at the scars on my torso and arms as if for the first time instead of the hundredth – or thousandth. My left shoulder had a huge scar, about half an inch wide, running from the top, down the front, and well into my arm pit. Other thinner scars radiated down my arm like stripes. There were several scars on my chest and abdomen, some large and some small. There was an odd-shaped patch in the center of my chest, a darker gray than the rest of my skin, that Devin told me must have been a burn from the exhaust from his car.

I stopped looking at the scars and stared at my changed—and changing—body. My chest was widening; I could see that had happened over the past months and even over the past four weeks. My biceps were growing larger, my shoulders bulkier. Even my legs seemed to have gained mass: my quads were more developed (which could be seen through my jeans) and my calves had definitely filled out.

I looked at my face, trying to see past the scars. I didn't need to shave and hadn't since the accident; hair stopped growing on a corpse. I'd never need a haircut, either. Devin thought he might be able to do a procedure to implant longer hair if I ever wanted to, but I told him not to waste his time – hair was the least of my problems.

I was never hungry, never thirsty. I never had any of the normal biological needs of a human. I didn't breathe, sneeze, or cough. (I was especially thankful that I didn't get hiccups.) No headaches, no joint pain, no muscle aches. No flu, no colds.

I forced a sigh – "forced" because I don't breathe, so it was a little exaggerated. Shaking my head, I put my black Slipknot t-shirt on (one of the few I owned that Devin didn't find offensive) and frowned at how tight it was.

I sighed another forced sigh again. My thoughts were still confused, but they weren't getting any clearer as I considered the changes I was still seeing. And it had nothing to do with my accident this time.

I didn't remember what my life was like before the accident, so I don't remember what my body used to be. But I could certainly see changes occurring weekly – almost daily.

The contrast of my light gray skin against the dark gray slate on the walls and floor made me realize how my skin must look to other humans. "Other humans" – as if I could categorize myself as human. My skin wasn't as white as the cream-colored sink or the white bath towels hanging on nickel-plated wall racks, but the pale gray certainly wasn't even close to normal skin tones.

I stepped out of the bathroom, letting the issue of my skin tone fester a little more, with all the other differences and changes. I walked slowly down the second floor hallway, trying to muffle the sounds of my footsteps on the hardwood floors. I didn't know if Devin was up yet, so I treaded quietly down the oak steps, trailing my hand along the banister, feeling the wood under my hand – warm, to my touch.

I walked into the family room and sat on the brown leather couch, picking up a magazine and flipping through it without reading anything. I saw ads for medication for illnesses I'd never have: allergies, high cholesterol, and diabetes. I saw pictures of people who had skin that was olive, peach, brown, black, or tan. But not gray skin. I saw people with eyes that were green, brown, blue, and hazel. But not colorless, nearly clear eyes that looked…well, dead.

I angrily tossed the magazine across the room, chalking my appearance up to one more huge difference between me and the rest of the world. Let that one fester, too.

I didn't look right, I didn't move right, and I didn't sound right. I couldn't go out in public without being stared at, couldn't talk without people gawking and whispering to Devin, "What's wrong with him?" Right in front of me, as if I were so oblivious that I couldn't hear them. I usually just shook my head and scowled as meanly and scarily as I could. Most people took the hint and scurried off pretty quickly. "Scurry" was quickly becoming my favorite word.

I thought the trip to the grocery store would have been enough for Devin. I was wrong. The first trip we made to a mall should have been an indicator to Devin that things wouldn't go well. I made a few little kids cry and their mothers held them close and looked at me as if I were about to steal them away. *Great, they'll be getting their torches and pitchforks any minute,* I thought to myself, *just like the villagers did for Boris Karloff.*

My speech was frustrating me. Those first few public outings were horrendous, making my first excursion to the grocery store look like a spectacular success. I couldn't ask people what they were staring at or if they had a problem. My meeting with Dave was my most lucid, but my anger usually got in the way of my words.

A few people took me by the hand and tried to lead me to the front of the store. "Don't worry, we'll find your mommy or daddy – whoever you're with," a seventy-year-old woman at a mall said as she tugged on my arm. Luckily, Devin caught up with us in the food court and assured her there was nothing wrong with my mind, just my speech. Of course, I was angry and embarrassed, so I couldn't talk very well at that point. The woman blushed and apologized; I smiled as politely as I could and patted her on the shoulder, trying to focus on how hard I did it so I wouldn't knock her over.

Devin started to work on my speech a little more after that and almost every day since, but it wasn't going well. I still couldn't fit my mouth around the words. And then there were the tests. His tests proved that my cognitive abilities had been damaged very little in the accident. Aside from amnesia, I seemed to be thinking OK. Better than OK – as he suspected, the compound he was giving me that robbed me of so much had also given me quicker thinking, an ability to think through choices or sift through current memories very quickly. But speech still eluded me, as did my long-term memory.

I got up from the couch and walked through the small archway that led in to the hall between the family room and the kitchen. I glanced at the Dürer print on the wall on the hallway – Knight, Death, and Devil. I looked at the print on the opposite wall, depicting The Four Horseman. I stood in the shadows of the hallway between the two sunny rooms, looking between those two works of art, feeling in some ways like the knight and in other ways like the rider of the white horse.

I broke out of my reverie and pushed open the swinging door, walking into the kitchen, one room in the house I hardly ever used. Hunger never bothered me; Devin gave me periodic injections to keep the fluid in my body at a constant level, which was something like my form of nourishment. He had also mentioned the possibility of a transfusion at some point, but he didn't seem to think it was a pressing concern. Like a car needing an oil change. He was also working on a drink of some kind that I could supplement for the injections, but he didn't have anything finished yet. I didn't need food – somehow, the fluid in my body created the energy I needed and maintaining the level of fluid was all I required. Even the drink wouldn't be for refreshment or energy; it would just be absorbed by my body and replace the injections I got.

As I sat on one of the stools at the breakfast bar, I looked out into the rising sun coming into the backyard, pushing the darkness away and lightening the shadows. And I considered all of the other issues I was currently struggling with.

Of course, one of the big ones was, would I ever die? *Could* I die? Without a heart that could stop, when would the pump stop? Would the battery give out some day? Devin had said it had a virtually unlimited supply of power, but every battery runs down. Ten years? Fifty? Five hundred?

What do I do when Devin is gone? Fade away? Will I be gone in a decade or 50 decades?

Since that one was too big and too messy to consider, I tried one of the smaller ones. Almost everyone faces mortality and no one knows if the next day or hour will be their last. Better to focus on some of the issues that are less philosophical and more practical, more immediate.

Like what I would do. I wasn't concerned about not being able to speak well or looking the way I did. Plenty of people use sign language to communicate and there are even more who don't look like everyone else. That said, as a reanimated corpse (a phrase which Devin clearly loathed), I imagined my job prospects would be bleak; I doubt I'd ever get hired as a preschool teacher, I mused ruefully. My prospects were even bleaker than someone with similar differences and speech limitations because I'd never pass a physical. And Devin was aware of that.

"We need to be careful about you…being in public," Devin explained one day.

"What about the malls and stores. They were your idea," I pointed out.

"I know you've been out, but we need to be careful about…other things. People will stare at you because of your appearance, but that's not my main concern. We can't allow you to have blood tests or physicals. We can't allow anyone to know your true nature."

By that, he meant my dead-ness.

Dead.

I could move, think, interact. I could *be*. But I wasn't alive.

Knowing that, I began to understand that I'd never lead a normal life. Never be married, never hold a job, never try to realize whatever potential I may have had before the accident. Or the potential I might have in my new existence. I'd never live a life because I wasn't living – I was being, existing.

And there was my old friend again: anger. Closely followed by rage.

I could feel the anger starting to build again and I got off the stool and walked toward the sliding glass door in the kitchen. I opened it and walked out onto the patio, staring at the flagstones, trying to contain my anger. I slid the door closed silently and carefully, not allowing my anger any outlet, yet.

My anger.

My rage.

My fury.

Anger, stemming from the knowledge that I was dead, froze me as I thought about it. Not truly alive. Little more than a robot. My thoughts turned to the same subject they always do at these moments, pointing my hate toward one group: criminals.

Humans who wasted their lives or spent their lives trying to extort from others, exerting their criminal power over innocent people for control. Thieves. Drug dealers. Rapists. Pedophiles. Murderers. Child abusers. Wife beaters. So many categories used to describe human depravity. I watched them on the news and read about them in newspapers and magazines. I even researched them on the web and had read a few books on criminal psychology. And even after reading those books, I was still no closer to understanding how a criminal could do what they do.

Sometimes, after reading and hearing some of the horrible stories that criminals had perpetrated, I would lash out violently, breaking furniture in the lab or smashing equipment. I cracked the granite countertop of one of Devin's benches one day. I placed the offending news article (regarding the recent arrest of a serial pedophile) on top of it by way of explanation when he came home. Devin sighed and patted my shoulder, apologizing again for his mistakes…

I started to seethe again, gripping the back of a wrought iron patio chair. I closed my eyes and could feel the chair start to give under the pressure of my hands...

...I was furious at the people who were throwing their lives away...

...people who could speak clearly and who had normal human skin tones and normal eye colors; people who had hearts instead of fluid pumps and blood instead of blue "compound"; people who had all of the regular functioning organs and followed the basic laws of nature.

I clenched my hands tighter on the patio chair, listening to the metal groan in protest as I tried to release some of my pent-up anger.

And I started thinking the same thoughts I'd gone over a hundred times before. I wondered why I *was*. What was my purpose, why was I here? Why did Devin bring me back? Was it to save me, or was it to save himself? To nurse his remorse and make himself feel better about killing me?

I felt guilty for feeling the way I did, ashamed of how I felt and how I saw Devin, but I couldn't help it. Because even though he tried to save me, he killed me. I may have come back for a bit, struggled to stay alive a little longer, but his miracle drug finished the job that he started with his car on that lonely road late at night. Poetic, I thought, since he set me on a different lonely road by trying to save my life.

All of these things and more swirled around in my head, locked up inside me because I couldn't express it, couldn't speak it. My fine motor skills weren't good enough for me to write or even type – I had already mashed a few of Devin's computer keyboards before giving up. I used a pencil to tap the keys whenever I wanted to do something on a computer. Still, I couldn't find answers, couldn't think of any conclusions to the problems I was facing.

I felt in constant conflict, at the end of my inhuman tolerance...

...and I tossed the chair.

Except that maybe 'toss' is too mild a description of what I did. I had picked it up with both hands, raised it over my head and, taking a gigantic lunge forward, threw it across the yard as hard as I could, uttering a deep bass growl as I did. The chair hit a small dogwood tree and warped around it, splintering the trunk and bending it at a drunken angle. One of the legs detached and flew into the woods, whipping through the underbrush with a whistling sound. The rest of the chair fell and rested at the base of the tree in a twisted hulk, a malformed lump that barely resembled a chair.

"I like what you've done with the chair," Devin said quietly from behind me. "Very postmodern."

I opened my eyes and looked down. I still held a bent piece of the top of the chair, a misshapen mass with impressions of my fingers in it.

"Hmm," I grunted.

"Angry again," Devin said, looking up at me with sadness.

I jerked my head forward, once, too angry for words.

"I'm sorry," he said.

"Doesn't help," I said, ashamed of myself for voicing my opinion.

"I know, I know. I wish..." and he trailed off, lost for words. Devin dropped his head and walked back into the house, shaking his head.

I felt guilty for making him feel bad. I couldn't imagine how he must feel, with me as a larger-than-life, constant reminder of his past mistakes and how horribly wrong it all went when he tried to make it better. His life-saving efforts had life-taking consequences, robbing me of my humanity.

But I was also still feeling the emptiness of being alone; the anger at people who waste what I didn't have; the feeling that my destiny was decided by forces outside my control. Feeling like the world held nothing for me.

And then I saw her.

The Neighbors

I usually ventured into the backyard only at certain times, after the service staff and ground crew had left for the day. I preferred to stay indoors when the groundskeepers were working to avoid the stares (and occasional screams) when new workers were added to the crew and not warned (sometimes I swear it was done as a cruel joke). But Devin's lawn and landscaping required minimal upkeep – he loved the desert southwest and it showed in his landscaping. Stones rounded by rivers and streams, aged driftwood, dilapidated wagon wheels, wooden barrels with rusted iron straps, and sand were the primary materials in his motif, though he did have small, immaculate patches of Kentucky bluegrass.

Devin's house was on a secluded back road, surrounded by pines. He had purchased almost all of the homes around the property before I even came into the picture. He then had the houses leveled, driveways torn up, and pine trees planted to build a forest around his land.

Part of his reason for doing it was to provide him with more privacy, so he wouldn't have nosy neighbors wondering about all the flashes of light coming from the mad scientist's lab at one in the morning. It also helped when he received shipments of supplies and materials. Delivery trucks and vans were constantly pulling in and out of our driveway.

None of the deliveries were illegal in any way, but it would be best if neighbors didn't know about the lab equipment. They might then try to have ordinances passed or zoning laws changed to prohibit some of the things Devin was working on. It had the ancillary benefit of providing me with more privacy, so we wouldn't have the same nosy neighbors walking past the house to get a look at the scary gray guy living with Devin.

He had purchased all but one home, one holdout, a house near the back of the property. A single mom with a daughter. The mother very politely, but firmly, declined all of Devin's offers, no matter how outlandish. At one point, he had even offered her ten times the market value of her home.

"This is my home," Lilly, the mother, had said.

The last time the subject had been discussed (shortly after I was reborn, so to speak), Devin was throwing out extra incentives while sitting on a stool in her kitchen. He had given me a detailed description of the discussion because it troubled him a little. He had repeatedly pushed Lilly to sell, but stopped because of what he had learned. On the particular night that he found out her reason for staying, he was finishing a brownie and a glass of milk Lilly had coerced him (not too strongly) to accept.

"But I would be more than happy to help you relocate—" Devin had begun.

"Absolutely not," Lilly had said firmly, interrupting him. "Even if I were to accept your offer, I could never accept that kind of generosity. That would be too much from a stranger."

"But I'm not a stranger," Devin had protested. "We've been neighbors for years. And I have no ulterior motive – I truly want to help you, should you decide to move. And I would expect you to visit often. I don't want to push you out of our lives. I just think, given the nature of my work and…other things…it would be easier for you to—"

"I can't," Lilly had said quietly. Devin said her voice was quavering a little at this point and he wondered then if he had pushed her too far. "And it has nothing to do with your generous offer or some stubborn need to feel independent or some power trip—"

"I assure you," Devin had said, reaching across the table and clasping her hand gently, "I wasn't thinking those things at all. I assumed there was a very good reason for you to refuse. One that was probably very personal and none of my business."

"You're right. There is a good reason, it's personal, but I don't think it's none of your business. My husband passed away when Tessie was little, so I try to provide her with a very stable home. I try to make everything very constant and steady for her. I know I probably don't need to and she would probably not mind moving, but this is the only house she's known. And she has memories of her father in this house. If I sold it, I feel like…"

"Like you were selling her memories," Devin had said. "I apologize – I won't press the issue any more. Besides, at least I have a very agreeable neighbor. If you ever change your mind, please let me know – the maximum offer will always stand. In the meantime, if there's anything I can ever do for you, please don't hesitate to ask it!"

But Devin rarely waited for her to ask. He would often send our groundskeepers and maintenance crews to their house to prune trees, mow the lawn, plant flowers, repair the house, and do whatever might be needed. "A plateful of your excellent brownies from time to time is all I ask in return," he'd say when Lilly offered payment for their services.

Curious about our neighbors, I had made a habit of walking to the edge of our backyard and peering through the trees, trying to see the mother and daughter that lived there. I felt a little juvenile (and maybe a little creepy), but I was very careful. Of course I had to be very careful – I was hideous. I couldn't imagine what our neighbors would have thought if they ever got a glimpse of me. I smiled sardonically – that would be one way to get the neighbor to sell.

One evening, I decided to walk through the grass barefoot. I was still getting used to how hot everything was, but after the sun went down the grass was only warm. I walked slowly toward the woods, feeling the pine needles sticking to my feet. My skin was thick, durable, and several times stronger than shoe leather, so I didn't mind walking barefoot. I was listening to how quiet the woods got when I entered it. How every wild animal in the woods seemed to sense something unnatural was near them. I was enjoying the quiet solitude, thinking about nothing but the feel of the pine needles, how the bark felt as I scraped my hands along the gigantic pines.

And that's when I saw Lilly's daughter.

She appeared to be about twenty or so, with medium-length black hair, spiked in the front a little. I couldn't see her eyes well, but they were dark, maybe brown. Her skin had a darker tone, probably tanned from being outdoors. She wasn't very tall, but had an athletic build – not thin, but certainly not overweight.

She was sitting on the edge of the woods on a stump, skimming through a book, whispering to herself. It was almost dark, but I could tell she was wearing jeans and a sweatshirt. She was still shivering, though. Of course, being the ice cube I was I didn't know how the air was supposed to feel – I was wearing jeans, too, but had a t-shirt on. I rarely wore long sleeves.

I could hear a tone coming from somewhere, something musical, then she started searching for something. Aha, a cell phone.

"Hey Val," she said, answering the phone. She laughed and said, "No, studying up on English lit. 'Middlemarch'. Yuck. Can't wait 'til I'm done with that class." She was quiet again, then said, "Yeah, we can get together for that. I need to study and besides, it would be good to get out of the house and into the real world. I'll meet you at Coffee Café? Great – see you in a few!"

She piled up her books and papers, then stopped suddenly. She spun around and looked into the woods, turning her head and moving slightly side to side, as if searching for something, like she sensed something. Like she was being watched.

Caught.

I moved behind the tree a little more to hide, hoping she wouldn't come searching and see me. *Then again, I thought, exactly why did you come out here? Did you want to get caught?*

I pushed away those thoughts, ludicrous as they were: me, interested in another human. Scratch that; me, a pseudo-humanoid being, interested in a human.

But still, I wondered about her…

Who was Val and why was she meeting her? What classes was she taking besides English lit? What was she studying for?

All of those questions were intriguing, but even more intriguing were the personal questions of which I was thinking. Would she be interested in me? Could I enroll in college (realizing that the choice would be to spend time watching her, not to gain a higher education)? Would she find me as intriguing as I find her? And was I turning into a stalker? I have never spoken to her, I've seen her for about five minutes, and I was planning to schedule my life around her.

Spooked by how much I was interested, I retreated to our backyard again. Wondering what was wrong with me. I'd never shown that much interest in anyone outside of Devin. And all of a sudden, I see a pretty girl and...

...something was coming back, powerful emotions that seemed to block out all thought. My memory was shot, but I thought I remembered this feeling from sometime before my transformation. It had to be my imagination, but I could swear I felt warmth spreading inside me...

And it hit me: I was in love with her.

Her

Love at first sight. I had read and remembered enough to know that was one of life's cruelest jokes, not to mention one of the worst (and oldest) clichés around. But that's the only thing that could explain my sudden – and continued – interest in my young neighbor. (Yes, sadly, I had become possessive enough to refer to her as "my neighbor".)

I spent more and more time in the woods, trying to convince myself that it wasn't just her I was interested in. As if looking at the carpet of pine needles and the endless pines in the woods were more important than what I saw on the other side of them.

Every time I saw her was a reminder that I was missing out on pieces of life, pieces that others wasted or neglected. Pieces of life that were carelessly thrown away by degenerates, traded for the next hit or the satisfying of some other depraved craving. I tried to push those thoughts away, clearly aware of the anger and rage to follow.

She was taking classes, which I didn't think I ever could. I was a little jealous of that, but I didn't know how I'd ever get into a college, let alone find one that would allow me to attend anything but night courses – by myself, with a videotaped instructor. I also wondered about her friends and if I could be one of them. And in one of life's sadistic ironies, I couldn't think of her without thinking of what I couldn't have, what the limitations were on my happiness. So every time I thought about how happy I *might* be, I was constantly reminded of what my existence really was and how happy I *wouldn't* be.

I tried to push those negative thoughts away and lead them back to my young neighbor. I thought about what could be while at the same time pushing away the thoughts of what couldn't. But of course, lately, it seemed that everything I thought about involved her.

It became even more obvious to me that she was a college student, judging by the Alamance Community College sweatshirts she wore and the textbooks she almost always had with her. I probably wouldn't have picked up on that (she looked young enough to be in high school), except that I started seeing her more and more on my walks – and she was always wearing a sweatshirt. I don't think Devin was fooled by my sudden interest in the backyard and the woods, but he was kind enough not to say anything.

It seemed that every day she wore something with the community college logo, making me wonder if she had paid as much for tuition as she paid for her clothing. I smiled when I saw them, thinking the college should probably pay her, since she appeared to be a walking billboard for them most of the time. The cell conversations I could hear frequently involved a discussion about a class or a professor, with some pretty colorful names and aliases for those professors thrown in: Professor Pain in the Ass, Dr. Doom and Gloom. She was very animated at times, always full of energy and – again, ironically – lively. Call it comic or cosmic, it was definitely irony.

And I realized how badly I was trying to take walks around the times that she was most likely to be outside. I could no longer kid myself about the "solitude" of walking in the woods. It was who I saw on the other side that drew me back time and again to walk through those dark, primeval woods; it was the young woman that guided my bare feet through the darkened woods, like a beacon leading me out of the darkness. Interesting. Alarming, even.

On one particular day, she was carrying a huge stack of textbooks. And no novels this time. The other times that I had watched her (OK, yes, that's a little creepy...maybe more than a little), she usually only carried one book, but on this day it was a stack. She brushed away her short, dark hair on the top of her head and I could see she had it nearly shaved to the skull on the back and sides. Must have gotten a haircut, I thought to myself, somewhat chagrinned that I noticed. She was wearing another baggy community college sweatshirt and purple, nylon mesh shorts with a pair of sneakers.

She was talking to herself – again. She talked to herself quite often. Sometimes I could hear her working out a problem in one of her textbooks or talking through a tough concept she struggled with.

One day, it was bones. "Tibia, fibula, femur. Ulna, radius, and...what's it called...what's it called..." She looked at her book. "Humerus! Crap, why can't I remember that! I can remember the freaking sphenopetrosal fissure for extra credit, but not the stupid humerus! And what's with the names anyway? Why can't they be easier than lacrimomaxillary, temporozygomatic, and palatoethmoidal? They sound like a third grader made them up!"

Sometimes she would have an imagined conversation with a friend, rehearsing lines she planned to say to them. If it sounded like a conversation with a male friend, I'd try to make up lines and say them in my head as if she were talking to me. Pathetic, I know.

On this particular night, she was quietly turning page after page of a book. She didn't appear to be studying, just looking at the pages. I moved a little closer, standing behind a large pine, staying in the darker shadows of the fading daylight. I peered around the edge of the tree and I saw her, flipping pages with one hand and twirling the front of her hair with her other. She stopped and looked up suddenly.

I pulled myself back behind the tree and held still, hoping she hadn't seen me. Had she? Was she building herself up to a scream? I knew this was going to happen. I had pushed my luck too often not to get caught eventually.

"Hello?" she called out timidly, her voice quavering. I heard her as she gathered her books and stuffed them quickly in her bag. "Is someone out there?" I heard her zip the bag shut. I could hear her brushing herself off.

Her footsteps moved away, moving a little bit faster with each successive step. When I was sure she had turned to run, I looked out around the tree and saw her running back to her house. Smooth move, Casanova. She was actually running, not walking. I was expecting her to trip on any one of the hundred roots or branches, but she was like a rabbit – sure-footed and fast.

Frowning, I walked back home. What did I expect? Stalking her in the woods like that, of course she was going to get spooked. Why wouldn't she, especially if saw a gray-skinned, pale-eyed monster staring at her through the woods, hiding behind trees. One who spoke with a rasping growl and looked like he belonged in a B-movie. No makeup required. Maybe that could be my vocation: low-budget horror films. What was I thinking? Stupid.

Devin was on the back porch waiting for me. "Lilly called," he said, an amused expression on his face. "She wanted to know if I had given anyone permission to walk through the woods because her daughter saw someone."

"Sorry," I said in my normal growl. I instantly felt like molding the nearby patio furniture into my own image – something twisted and ugly. "I was just walking through the woods; I do that a lot. I see Lilly's daughter from time to time and I saw her again today. I try to stay out of sight and I stopped to watch for a while today. I should have known that was going to cause problems. And I know it seems a little creepy, but she's…I don't know…interesting."

"Your speech is improving!" His face lit up with joy as his amused expression became a wide grin. "Have you been practicing like I suggested?"

"Not with recorded voices. The CD voices sound like demented actors from children's shows. I picked it up from entertainment," I said. "Music. Movies."

"Whatever works is fine with me. It's simply amazing! You can converse very well, compared to where we were not too long ago!" He shook his head and his wide grin seemed to grow. I had ordered some music and had it delivered to the house, but I doubted Devin would approve of it. Slipknot could hardly be said to help with formation of perfect speech, but it did help with expanding my spoken vocabulary. Admittedly, I wouldn't use *all* of the language I heard on the CDs, though…

"More careful," I mumbled. Walking toward the house, I lowered my head, slumped my shoulders. I liked my walks and the occasional view of my "friend". I knew it was delusional and probably a little unbalanced, but I thought of her as a friend. During my walks and time in the woods, I would imagine that she was very accepting of differences. But I really had no idea if she were or not.

"Wait," Devin said, putting his hand lightly on my arm. "I told her I hadn't given anyone permission, but there was someone who probably was walking in the woods. I told her it was my…my adopted son. I told her that you had been injured in an accident and your injuries had left you scarred. I also told her that you had suffered massive head trauma, which has affected your speech and your memory. I assured her that you were harmless and trustworthy, but that your appearance could be—"

"Frightening? Repulsive?"

"Admirable display of your growing word knowledge, but I was going to say 'intimidating'. At any rate, it gives you an opportunity to speak to her daughter, Therese." He raised his eyes and tilted his head.

"Therese".

"Her mother calls her Tessie."

"Thanks," I said, smiling a little sheepishly. Now I had a name and, odd as I sounds, I felt closer to her, somehow. I also felt slightly more pathetic.

"I told her your name was Theodore. I hope you don't mind. I should have consulted you first before giving you a name, but she put me on the spot and—"

"Theodore." I laughed. It sounded so odd coming from me. It was a deep bass rumble that sounded like it emanated from my feet, but it wasn't anywhere nearly as raspy as my voice. A little, but not much.

"That laugh. My boy, your laugh will light her up, I assure you. Maybe tomorrow during the afternoon you could arrange another walk? I did say you'd be out again tomorrow and you might even stop to say hello." He smiled and put his arm around my shoulders as we walked toward the house. He suddenly stopped and frowned. "I'll need to do measurements tomorrow. I think you've grown. I don't remember needing to reach up so high or so far around to get my arm around your shoulders."

I shrugged my shoulders and continued into the house, up to my room. I sat on my bed, then laid back to look up at the ceiling, thinking through the possibilities.

Tessie.

I smiled.

Measurements

I wandered around the house the next morning, not thinking about much. I tried to block out my impending meeting with Tessie, knowing I would probably blow it anyway without even opening my mouth. Trip and take down a tree. Stumble and fall on her, crushing her and sending her to the hospital. Something like that. I eventually made my way to the lab, though, where Devin was already up. I frowned. He didn't seem to be sleeping much. He motioned me over and started his measurements, motioning for me to put my back against the wall.

"OK, let me see. You were five feet eleven inches last week and – wow – six feet one inch this week." He frowned. "Two inches in one week, hmm."

"I grew two inches?" I asked. "What does that mean?"

"I'm not sure. The compound I gave you was for healing, but it appears as though it's also boosting your growth a little. I'll need to keep a close eye on that. It's an interesting side effect, but not a critical one. I may have to consider how to slow your growth if it continues. Step up on the scale, please."

I stepped up on the scale, which had been left at 215 from the last time Devin weighed me. The balance slammed up against the top of the guide. Devin frowned, pushing the weights further down the arm.

"Two hundred twenty-five pounds. That's up ten pounds from last week and it can't be fat," he said, scratching his head and looking at his chart. He sat on his rolling stool and pushed himself over to his computer, mumbling as he tapped the keys and looked at complex molecular diagrams and growth charts, occasionally typing on the keyboard and watching the lines and graphs change.

"I need to alter your injections, because they are accelerating your growth. The height is one thing. But the increase in weight also indicates that you're adding mass as well – muscle, bone, and who knows what else. I'll need to start taking benchmark measurements of your thighs, your biceps, probably your cranium and chest as well."

"Is there a problem adding to my weight?"

"Well," Devin said, frowning a little, "not that I can think of off hand. As long as you don't grow too quickly."

"Meaning…"

"The human body is designed to support a certain size. There have been cases where the human body grows out of control because of pituitary problems. In those cases, sometimes their bodies aren't able to support the uncontrolled growth. But I don't think that will be an issue here. Have a seat."

He motioned for me to sit in the chair as he felt under my chin and along the sides of my neck. He chuckled a little and dropped his hands, shaking his head. "Sorry, I know your glands no longer function – just checking out of habit, I suppose."

He felt neck muscles, then he put his hands on my shoulders and squeezed firmly. "Have you been exercising at all?"

"No. Why?"

"Your musculature is becoming more defined and toned. I'll need to review the injections more closely, especially for the growth components. I meant them to replace the food that you're not getting, but I think it's the equivalent of steroids to you. It's boosting growth, not just maintaining your health."

He rolled back to his laptop and clicked the keys a few more times. He cupped his chin in his right hand and "hmm"-ed a few times at the screen.

"And?"

He looked up and smiled. "Sorry, almost forgot I left you hanging there. I'm just reviewing some of my notations and doses. I don't want to take you off it completely because I think your body still needs a boost. But I think I'd better back the boost down a bit. How do you feel?"

I wasn't sure how to answer. Physically? Mentally? Emotionally?

"I mean physically," he said, as if reading my mind.

"Fine. I don't feel tired, I'm not in pain."

"How about mentally and emotionally?" He set aside his laptop and leaned forward, putting a hand on my knee. "I'm concerned about that as well."

"Mentally, I'm still confused. Can't think right. I still have problems putting sentences together."

"Emotionally?"

I sat quietly, trying to think about how I felt. I was still very confused over Tessie. The uncertainty of my future was also a thorny problem for me. I felt I'd never be a part of mainstream society; I'd always live on the fringe. And how could I ask Tessie to take part in that?

And there was the anger at people taking what they had that I didn't have for granted. People who wasted the chances they were given and hedonistically broke laws. Addicts, whatever the form; pedophiles, abusers, pushers and dealers, thieves, murders, and on and on goes the list.

But there was something else, something I couldn't quite get my mind around. The images were little more than feelings, like something in the edge of your vision that you can't see or something at the end of a dark field, hiding in shadows. I could see or feel someone being hurt, someone doing the hurting, someone watching...

"Take your time," he said.

"I feel...a lot," I started. "A lot of different feelings."

"Like what?"

"Isolation, anger, sadness," I said. "And there's more. Like I don't belong...anywhere. I don't have a future. I don't know what I'm going to do."

"But that's not true," Devin said. "You do have a future. You're...here." I'm pretty sure he was going to say 'alive', but refrained.

"But I can't work," I said. "I'll never get a job. I can't go to college. Yes, I can learn and I can probably help you around here, but I don't have any...independence."

"What's the worst thing you're feeling? What's the strongest emotion you have?" Devin asked carefully.

"Rage," I said, frowning.

"All the time?"

"No, sometimes. Usually when I think of...normal people," I said. "And not just the ones who are criminals or degenerates. Not just the lawbreakers, but people who are lazy or waste opportunities that I'll never have." My voice is rising, becoming more gravelly and deepening.

"You're angry at everyone?" Devin asked quietly.

"Yes," I exploded. "People waste what they're given! They break the law. They abuse drugs and alcohol. It's as if most people don't think about being—" I stopped, shrugging my shoulders. "But there's more to it than that. Most people know where they came from or who their family is. They plan, even if it's only a little bit. They go to school or learn a trade or go to a job. They go to picnics and movies and ball games. There's no uncertainty in their lives. Their paths are defined. And they take it all for granted. They never think about—"

"Being alive," Devin suggested, looking pained.

"I was going to say being *human*," I said quietly, croaking out the word in my horrible voice. I clenched my hands into tight fists and I could hear my joints creaking.

"But you are human," Devin said, sensing my stress as he spoke to me quietly.

I shook my head violently, standing up abruptly. "I'm not."

"Why not?"

"Because I don't have...some...human things that others do," I said, struggling with the words.

Devin put a hand lightly on my shoulder as he stood up. "Many people have artificial hearts. Even more have prosthetic limbs. There are people who live only because someone else gave them a kidney or a liver or a heart. Millions of people rely on pacemakers to help their hearts beat or medications to regulate their blood sugar levels," he said.

"But *my* body temperature changes with whatever room I'm in," I said, realizing the volume of my voice was rising again with every word I spoke, my anger building in tandem. "*My* pump—not my heart, my *pump*—thuds and moves fluid, but it's not blood. *I* breathe, but not because I need oxygen. My organs are only taking up space in my body. They aren't functioning! My body doesn't work!"

I finished my tirade, spinning away from Devin and viciously kicking a rolling metal cabinet. The doors buckled inward as the hinges sprung. The cabinet lifted a little off the ground and came crashing down, rolling across the floor. The shelves inside collapsed, spilling their contents out onto the floor as the cabinet spun around in a lazy circle, distributing pills, paper, and other supplies as it went. I stepped on broken glass with my bare feet and didn't get one cut.

I picked up a broken bottle and squeezed it in my hand, dropping the shattered remains on the floor. "I'm not even bleeding," I said, holding my hand up for him to see. "My heart rate didn't increase. I don't feel any pain. I'm not breathing hard. And there was no release from my outburst. Just more rage to replace it."

"But you still feel," Devin said. "You feel frustration and anger. You feel lost. And you do feel pain, just not physical pain."

"A feeling corpse," I said. I could see the pain in Devin's eyes as he winced, shaking his head. I slumped my shoulders. "I'm sorry."

"No need to be," Devin said. "It's important that you tell me how you feel. Physically, I must admit you are unique. So different that I don't think the modern medical community could possibly define your state of being. But you are a thinking, feeling being. Don't forget that."

"I can feel," I said hollowly.

"That is what defines us as humans," Devin said. "Not organs or body temperature or bodily processes. How we think and feel. I'd make the argument that some of those criminals and wastrels you spoke about aren't human, in the truest sense of the word. The most rudimentary mammals have hearts that pump warm blood, but they can't think as you do or feel the wide range of emotions that you do. In my opinion, people ruled only by their desires are closer to animals than humans."

"Animals feel," I said.

"Only the most basic of emotions, not the existential pain you feel – it's not the same," Devin said, shaking his head in disagreement. "You are struggling with why you are so different. You are trying to find your place in this world and define who you are because you've lost that. I've taken that from you. You struggle with what you perceive as the wasting of potential in so many people's lives. A struggle I happen to share, by the way; the difference, however, is that you feel isolated because of your differences. My struggles aren't as difficult because I'm not as...unique as you are. All of these types of philosophic questions and problems never cross the mind of an animal."

"Lucky them," I said, bending over to clean up the mess I made.

"Never mind that," Devin said. "I'll have the cleaning crew get it. I'm more worried about you right now. I'm sorry I can't be of more help. Maybe I can find a therapist who would be willing to talk to you—"

"No," I said flatly. "Hard enough to talk to you. Not talking to a...*stranger.*" My anger was starting to affect my speech, slow the process of my thoughts getting to my mouth.

"OK," Devin said. "But I do want you to talk to me. I want to hear these things. It's not healthy to keep them to yourself."

I nodded and turned to go. He gently pulled at my arm.

"You are a remarkable young man," Devin said, the admiration shining in his eyes. "Never forget that. I may have helped you along the way, patched you up and gotten you going again, but it is your will and your desire that keeps you going. Your *humanity.* Your human *spirit.* That is what drives you forward out of the darkness, why you're not giving up. You may not agree with me, but it's true."

I merely looked at him in the awkward silence. He patted my shoulder.

"Enough for one day," he said quietly. "And now, I think you'll need some rest for tomorrow, right?" He smiled at me as I nodded.

Great. As if I didn't have enough on my mind, Tessie was expecting a visit. Social interaction.

And all of my frustrations began coming back at the thought of tomorrow...

Tessie

On a normal night, I sleep very little, if at all. One, maybe two hours is all I need, but I do use the night to rest even if I'm not sleeping. Last night, however, I couldn't sleep at all. And I surely couldn't rest. I tried to plan what I would do when I met her. Tessie. Where would I walk to? What would I say, if anything? When would I go outside?

I got up hours before I normally get out of bed. I showered and dressed, making my way to the kitchen to start coffee for Devin. I don't drink it myself (of course – animated corpses don't need coffee, only blue compounds) and I don't need breakfast, but helping Devin makes me feel better.

As I walked into the kitchen, I saw through the glass doors leading to the lab that the overhead lights were on. I walked over to shut it off, thinking Devin had left it on overnight. When I pushed open the door to turn off the light, I saw Devin at his desk, his head in his hands.

"Devin," I tried to whisper. My voice still sounded like I had gargled with a mixture of ammonia and concrete.

He looked up at me and took off his glasses, rubbing his eyes as he did. "Sorry, I was looking over your medication and lost track of time. I fell asleep at my desk."

"I made coffee. Or do you want to sleep?"

"I'll stay up," he said, sighing softly. "Your speech is getting better every day."

"Sounds awful."

"Not to me. It's the sound of life."

I frowned and turned away, my anger spiking, making me ball up my fists. The strength of my reaction surprised me, but it didn't check my anger. Our conversation the previous day came back to me. I wasn't *alive*, no matter what definition you used. Why couldn't he *see* that?

"I'm sorry," he said quickly, pulling on my shoulder. "I'm tired and I'm not thinking clearly, I'm sorry. That was an awful thing to say and I've hurt you."

"Don't feel bad. My fault."

"Yours?"

I nodded. "I should accept what I am. *Who* I am. Stop brooding."

Devin looked at me as the seconds spun out. I could tell he was thinking and I could see emotions playing across his face: shock, sadness, guilt. He sighed wearily.

"As should we all," Devin whispered, squeezing my arm lightly. He looked out the kitchen window, lost in thought. "As should we all."

It occurred to me that maybe Devin was carrying around more guilt and baggage than I knew. I knew he felt a huge sense of responsibility for my well-being and an even bigger guilt that he carried knowing that he caused my suffering. And in a flash of inspiration, I realized that I was being very selfish and short-sighted.

Wasn't it possible that there may be other things in Devin's life causing him pain? Was I so arrogant to think that I was the only cause of his suffering, the only thing he regretted in his life? Knowing Devin's breadth of experience and the stunning height of his success, it's possible that he's had equally stunning failures. I paused at the stove, thinking about those things for a few seconds. And I mean a few seconds – I was able to process a myriad of thoughts in that one second. Before most people could have even made one decision, I had weighed dozens, maybe hundreds, of considerations.

As Devin lumbered around the kitchen, I pulled out eggs, a Vidalia onion, and a red Bell pepper. While he yawned and tried to boost himself to a more wakeful state with a giant mug of coffee, I cooked some egg whites and onions and peppers. He grimaced at the whites.

"I miss my yolks," he said jokingly.

I grunted. A fitting noise for me. "Your cholesterol levels don't miss your yolks."

"True. So…going for a walk today?"

"Planning on it." I smiled and glanced up at him.

"Good for you. Leave this stuff, I can clean up. Why don't you take a stroll now. Lilly tells me Tessie is an early riser, too."

"Are you sure?" I asked.

"Well," Devin said slyly, "I sure didn't save you so I'd have an extra servant on hand."

I stared at him, shocked. Then I burst out laughing as I saw him chuckling. I walked over and put my hand on his shoulder.

"OK," I said, "I'll see you later."

"Good luck, my boy," he said, raising his coffee mug as a salute.

———

I was nervous. I laced up my black boots and decided to walk around the yard. Normally, I'd walk barefoot, but I thought I'd try to look as normal as possible. Plus, covering up as much gray skin as possible was probably a good idea. I kept walking toward the back of the yard, looking for Tessie. I saw her peek out of the sliding glass door in the back of their house. I even saw her venture onto the deck, looking out into the woods, standing on her tiptoes as if to see further into the woods.

I took a deep breath (at least mimicked taking a deep breath) and stepped into the woods. I made no attempt to hide this time. Then she appeared and I froze.

She saw me in the woods, but she must have been having a hard time seeing me clearly. I was standing in the shadows (intentionally, of course). She was shading her eyes from the glare of the sun, squinting to see through the trees.

"Theodore?" She smiled tentatively and walked down the steps toward the woods.

"Yes." My voice was a whisper. I winced at the grinding sound coming from my throat as I tried to speak more loudly. "Yes."

She stopped and asked, with real concern, "Are you OK? Are you sick?"

"No," I said, frustrated with my voice. To her, it probably sounded like I had had bronchitis and laryngitis for the past year and a half.

"Oh. Sorry, my mom mentioned that she had spoken to Devin, I just thought..."

"That's OK," I said. "My voice was affected in the accident, too."

"So, um, are you going to come out of the woods?"

I chuckled a little and was amazed that it almost sounded normal. "I'm not sure."

"Why not," she giggled.

"I'm afraid you'll go running the other way," I admitted. Why not be honest?

"Oh really," she said, smiling and tilting her head up. "What if I promise not to?"

"I'd still rather talk to you through the trees. Cowardice, I know."

"Not really," she said gently, still smiling. "But I would like to see you. I'd like you to come out of the woods so I could talk to you face to face."

"OK. But be careful what you ask for," I said as I walked forward slowly. "Speak of the devil, and he shall appear."

"Ugh, not another English reference! OK, I'll even meet you half way. Well, not really, but you known what I mean." She walked into the woods toward the sound of my voice, peering around trees as she did. "I'm sorry about the comment I made about your voice. I was just concerned that you might be sick—"

"—and you didn't want to risk your finals," I finished.

"Hey, how do you know about those?" She stopped and looked in my direction, puzzled.

I was caught.

"Walking in the woods," I answered vaguely. I moved closer to her, moving around behind trees, more apprehensive as I moved closer to her. Would she scream when she saw me? "I have to apologize; I've been watching you."

"Spying?" She mimicked a shocked look, mouth in a perfect 'O', and folded her arms in mock indignation.

"No, I was just walking in the woods and saw you—" I was right, she did think I was watching her. I started to panic and stopped walking, but she interrupted me.

"Easy," Tessie said, laughing lightly. "I was only joking. Stalker."

"I also have to warn you. My accident..."

"Devin mentioned that. I'm sorry to hear you were hurt." She continued to look for me, still shading her eyes again against the sun filtering through the trees.

"Thanks. I'm healed, but scarred." And I moved into her sightline. I stood to the side of a tree as she approached, half hiding behind it in the shadows. I was hoping to stay in the darkness a bit more, trying to hide my hideous appearance a little longer and enjoy what little interaction I've had with Tessie so far. I can imagine how I looked – like a villain opposite a superhero, face half hidden, lurking in the shadows. "Well, maybe I'm not totally healed yet."

"Are you going to come out from behind that tree, or are we going to talk through it?"

I sighed. "I'd prefer to talk through it, but I suppose I should show my face. So to speak." I walked out from behind the tree, into a bright patch of sunlight shining through the woods.

And I saw a face up close that I'll never forget, even if I did last 50 decades. I've read writers' accounts of those moments in life or even in history when an event occurs that people point to as a "defining moment". I couldn't remember any from my previous life, but I was certain I would never forget the day I saw Tessie.

As I got closer, I could see that her eyes were bright with excitement and she was flushed, her cheeks a light pink. She was smiling and it might have been my imagination, but she seemed to be trembling a little.

"You're so tall!" She genuinely didn't seem to notice the color of my skin or the scars, the ugliness. Just my towering height (at least compared to her). And she looked directly into my eyes (well, up at them); she wasn't staring at my scars or my off-color skin. She was looking into my eyes – and didn't seem bothered that I had nearly clear irises.

"Just a little over six feet," I said, shrugging my shoulders.

"Well, maybe not NBA material, but you make my five-four look puny."

I chuckled and folded my arms in front of me. "You make up for it with self-deprecating humor and a great smile." Big words. Uh-oh.

She blushed a little and pulled her hair out of her eyes, blowing a puff of air straight up to get it out of her eyes again. "Sorry, the mop is getting a little long and needs to be cut."

"It looks fine," I said, not sure what to say. "I noticed you got it cut shorter than usual a little while ago. It's a good look for you."

"Oh, jeez," she said, swatting lightly at me. "You really are stalking me! Most of the people I hang out with every day didn't notice I'd changed my hair!"

"I don't see how they missed it," I said, realizing how corny I sounded. Like a cheap, dime-store romance novel. Tessie had the good grace not to notice.

"Do you want to sit down? Mom was making more brownies for Devin. We could sit on the deck and talk."

I felt like a king among men. All I could do was nod and follow her.

"My name is Therese, but everyone calls me Tessie," she said, sticking out her hand.

I knew this was coming. I was apprehensive – she would notice my cold skin, the texture of my palms.

"Theodore," I said, grasping her hand firmly – apparently a little too firmly.

"Yikes, easy Hercules!" She looked at my hands and seemed impressed. "Quite a grip! You have to be easy on me, I'm just a girl."

"No you're not," I said immediately, shaking my head, releasing her burning hot hand.

"Not what?" She raised her eyebrows at me.

"Not just a girl. First of all, you're a young woman. Second, there's no 'just' anything about you."

She blushed again and smiled, sighing softly. She looked at me awkwardly.

"Sorry. I don't get out much. I don't really remember how to act in social situations. I embarrassed you."

"Yes you did, but that's OK. You're sweet. Ted," she said, smiling broadly at me.

"Ted?"

"Theodore is much too stuffy. Doesn't anyone call you Ted?"

"Devin always calls me 'my boy' or 'son' or 'lad'. He just started calling me Theodore last week."

She laughed out loud as we headed toward the deck. "Just last week. That's a good one."

"Good one?"

"Yeah," she said, smiling. "A good joke?"

"Not a joke. It's true," I insisted.

"He just started calling you Ted last week?"

"Yes. When he talked to your mother. He hadn't picked out a name for me yet."

"Really?" She apparently hadn't gotten that part of the story. She looked utterly dumbfounded.

"Honestly – I think you found out about my name before I did," I explained.

"What about other people? What did they call you?"

"What other people?" I asked.

"Well, you know, classmates, teachers, other family, friends. Those other people." She frowned a little as she walked up the steps. She picked one of the lounge chairs and curled up into a ball. I picked an Adirondack chair and sat down, wincing as the wood creaked under me. Tessie chuckled a little. "Easy, big guy."

"I'll try to take it easy on the chair. As to your question, there are only two other people. One calls me Ted. And I haven't met your mother yet, so I don't what she calls me."

Tessie's mouth was open a fraction of a second, then she closed it with a snap. "Oh. Sorry, I just assumed...sorry."

Trying to cover up her embarrassment, I used my freakishly fast thinking to come with a quip. "Does your mom call me the scary kid next door?" I asked quietly, then leaned forward a little and whispered. "You can tell me."

Tessie laughed again. "No, it's Theodore. So, don't you go to college?"

"I guess you'd call it home school," I replied, trying not to lie outright. "I've been trying to relearn speaking, but it's coming back better than I thought. At least when I'm relaxed and not angry. I haven't ventured into too many subjects other than speech lately. Devin talks to me about other things – history, music, math, science – but it's not a class. And because of my medical condition – or conditions, since I have more than one – I don't get out much. Literally."

"That's too bad. If you like the woods, you'd love the park. We could take a walk through it someday."

"And have people run screaming in the opposite direction when they see me coming? I'd scare little children and drive family pets into frenzies. Maybe even have the police show up to save you from the hideous, ugly beast."

Her smile faltered. "Do you think you're hideous?"

Trying to recover, I chuckled a little. "Well, I'm not quite abominable, since I'm not big enough. Give that time, though. Maybe hideous is a little too dramatic. But I'm not exactly runway material."

She huffed and said, "You're not runway material because you have both a pulse and a working brain."

I laughed, a good hearty laugh. "I like that one. Funny."

"Well, it sounds like you two are getting along," Lilly said as she stepped out onto the deck, smiling at me. I could see concern in her face as she looked at me. Not pity, though. "How are you feeling today, Theodore? Devin told me your recovery has been a bit difficult."

"I'm doing much better, Mrs.—"

"It's Ms., but please call me Lilly."

"OK. Much better, Lilly, thank you for your concern."

"I hope you don't mind, but I was asking Devin about you—"

"Mom! Don't go prying into his life!" Tessie looked ashamed and maybe even a little mortified.

"It's OK, Tessie, really," I said leaning forward, resting my arms on my knees. "I don't mind talking about it and please, ask away if you have questions. I don't get to talk to too many people. In fact, I usually only talk to one person."

"I didn't mean to pry, Tessie," Lilly said, patting her daughter's hand. "I'm just concerned about him. Devin has done so much for us and I feel like I've known him all my life. I'd like to get to that same point with Theodore."

"Ted," her daughter corrected. "He looks more like a Ted than a Theodore."

I laughed and shook my head. "Please feel free to ask me anything."

"Are you in much...pain?" Lilly's look of concern was very moving. I smiled the best I could and thought about my answer.

"Yes and no. The physical pain is almost gone. Once in a while a twinge will surprise me, but they're very few and it doesn't even feel like pain anymore. The...medication...that Devin is giving me is amazing. It's been healing me quickly, making me stronger. The mental and emotional pain..." I trailed off and didn't know how to pick it up, so I just shrugged my shoulders.

"Bad?" Tessie had pulled her hands inside her sleeves and pulled the bottom of her gray sweatshirt over her bare legs. She must have been a little chilly in the morning air – of course, I felt a little warm.

"Sometimes." I could barely speak. I could feel the frustration mounting, but I tried to hold it back so I could speak clearly. "I'm sure Devin told you of the amnesia, which is only part of the frustration. I don't know who I am or who my parents were or if I have any other relatives. I don't even know how old I am or where I'm from. Although, I guess I should look at the amnesia as a sort of gift, because I don't remember anything bad, either."

"That must be awful," Tessie said. "Not remembering your past."

"That's pretty bad," I admitted. "But then there's the anger. Just last night, Devin and I had a discussion about that. I get angry and frustrated with people who don't have challenges in their lives or obstacles to overcome. So many of them waste what they have. Criminals, drug users. Even just the average, run-of-the mill slacker who doesn't live up to his or her potential. It's frustrating, infuriating. I know I shouldn't focus on what they do because I can't control it. But to see someone waste such potential..."

I stood up and walked to the edge of the deck, turning to look at them both. They were wearing nearly identical looks of concern and sadness.

"It's like watching a talented athlete or gifted musician fall into a downward spiral of drug abuse or self-destruction. To watch so much talent go to waste is a horrible feeling, especially when you know you don't have those talents or if you have some talent, but not as much as they do."

I stopped to collect my thoughts, then added the kicker.

"I feel that way about nearly everyone. But that's not the worst of it."

I turned my back on them for the next part. I didn't want them to think I was rude, but I couldn't face them while I said what I wanted to say next. I hadn't talked to Devin about this, but felt I needed to say it. Needed Tessie to hear it. I don't know what pushed me to share so much after just meeting her, but I wanted her to know. To have her eyes wide open when she saw me and spoke to me.

"And there's more, something I haven't told Devin because…well, he's got enough to worry about. And I know he's carrying around enough guilt as it is," I sighed and struggled to control my voice, but didn't do very well. My speech began to break down and betray me. "But the real pain. Is the solitude. The *aloneness* of being me. It seems. Strange. Since I've lost my memory. You'd think I wouldn't. Feel alone. Since I wouldn't remember relationships. But I know something is off. It just feels wrong."

I stopped and breathed, tried to calm myself before starting again.

"I know I probably make too much about my appearance. And my voice than most people would. But if I'm self-conscious enough about it. Helps protect me. When someone does get scared. Or shocked. When they see me. I see people walking in a crowd. And they all fit in."

I laughed nervously and shook my head, my back still to Tessie and Lilly.

"Stupid speech. Gets this way. When I'm angry.

"Other people. They don't have scars. On their faces. Off-color skin. Colorless eyes. They *blend*. Even people called 'different'. Aren't as different as me. Knowing I'm different…knowing that I shock people…helps when they react negatively to my appearance."

I breathed a deep (unnecessary) breath and looked up at the tops of the trees, smiling at how the sunlight lit them and formed patterns against each other. I waited, calming myself again so I could speak better.

"Sorry for the long pause, but I can speak better when I'm calm. I know I've painted a bleak picture, but that's how I feel." Silence greeted this, so I decided to push on.

"Still," I said, turning around, "I've made two new friends today who haven't gone screaming and shrieking in the other direction."

Tears were rolling down Lilly's cheeks and Tessie's were wet-looking. She was blushing, staring at the floor. My smile faltered a little and I looked at them sadly.

"Sorry," I said, trying to chuckle, "a little too much information on such short acquaintance, I know. I told Tessie I'm still working on my social skills. And I'll also have to work on the brooding invalid mindset a little!"

"No, not at all," Lilly said, rushing forward and putting her arms around me. "Devin has told me so much that I feel that I know you. If ever you need a place to get away from your treatments or recovery, please feel free to knock. At the back door *or* the front door." She pulled back to look me in the face, putting her warm, pink right hand against my cold, gray cheek. "You shouldn't be ashamed of your appearance."

"Thanks," I said, awkwardly hugging her back.

"OK, OK, enough Mom. I'd like the guy to come back, but if you're going to go into mother hen mode every time you see him, you're going to scare him off. Hungry?"

"No, I actually...uhh...I don't eat regular food. Or that much or that often."

"Oh, OK. Thirsty?" Tessie bounced up and was at the back door in one leap. She wiped her eyes with the cuff of her sweatshirt and smiled.

"Nope, I'm OK."

"Well, come in and I'll give you the grand tour. And you can fill in some of the gaps that my mother seems to be so familiar with." She frowned at her mother.

"No problem."

She opened the door and looked thoughtful. "OK. What do you like to do most?"

"Read. And listen to music. Or watch movies."

"How about sports or TV?" She opened the fridge and took out a plastic bottle of water. "By the way, this is the kitchen, in case you couldn't tell by the fridge and the oven."

"Got it. As to your questions, no and no. I mean, I watch some sports on TV and I sometimes watch movies on TV. But normal TV is...not as interesting to me."

She looked at my face and glanced down at my hands. I could tell she wanted to ask something. She bit her lip and then exhaled, blowing her bangs upward off her forehead. Lilly came inside and headed toward the front of the house, wiping her eyes and sniffing.

"Make yourself at home, Theodore—"

"—Ted—" Tessie called to her back.

"—I'll be around." Which I bet meant that she'd be out of earshot so Tessie and I could talk.

"Kitchen. End of tour for now, let's go back outside." She was eyeing the room her mother just went into. "Away from prying ears, just in case."

"I know you have other questions, so please ask them. Really, I don't mind," I said as quietly as I could.

"I know, but some of it seems so...personal...for someone I just met," she said, resting her hand on the sliding glass door. "It's usually not polite to ask those types of personal questions after you just meet someone."

"Well, since I have very limited social experience and no personal context, don't let it bother you," I said. She still looked skeptical. "And keep in mind that I can't remember what 'polite' conversation is supposed to be, anyway."

"OK. What happened?" She took a drink of water and headed out to the deck again. "The night you were hurt, I mean."

I followed her out shrugging my shoulders a little. "I don't remember. The first thing I remember was waking up in Devin's lab. I was a mess. You can see the results of some of the injuries. I had massive head trauma and I've had to learn to talk again. I still don't get all the words right and mess up with grammar."

"Grammar. Ugh. That makes two of us," Tessie grumbled as she curled up on the lounge chair again. "Well, how about physically? I think Devin and my mom must have been talking a lot, because when she mentioned your recovery...well, I didn't think you'd been injured that badly."

"I was. I had extensive injuries. It's a good thing Devin is a gifted surgeon as well as a scientific genius. He had to reattach my left arm and practically rebuild both of my legs. He had to use plates and screws to keep my bones together and he removed parts of some of my organs. Some he had to remove totally. Like my heart."

Her eyes grew wide. "You had a heart transplant?"

"Not exactly. It's an artificial heart, a pump he was designing at the time of the accident. I was the first recipient." I couldn't tell her the rest. Not so soon. I felt a twinge of guilt holding back the crucial difference between me and every other human. Between me and *being* human. "It's a little loud sometimes and doesn't sound like a normal heart, but it keeps me going."

"What does it sound like?" she asked, blushing a little.

I stood up and smiled. "Do you want to listen? You don't really have to get that close. I'm surprised you can't hear it now."

"No, I'm sorry, that's so rude of me, I—"

"Don't worry," I said, laughing. "On a few of my excursions into the big wide world, there have been some places where people could hear it standing a few feet away."

I was thinking of one instance in particular: Devin had taken me to the local library one day and the librarian kept looking for whoever was making the thudding noise. She was standing about six feet away, staring at me as I pointed to my chest and mouthed the words, "my heart". She covered her mouth, blushing furiously, and mouthed "sorry" as she bowed her head and went back to her desk.

Lilly stood up and walked toward me slowly, still blushing and smiling. "God, how embarrassing. How do I..."

"Just lean in and put your head close to my chest. Like I said, you don't even need to get close because..." And her head was on my chest, her hands lightly holding onto my shoulders for balance. If I were still alive, I'm sure my real heart would have been galloping away.

"Wow," she whispered, giggling. "It's so loud."

I chuckled, talking quietly, almost in a whisper. "On a quiet morning in the backyard, I can hear it over every other small sound. It's a bit unnerving sometimes. Annoying at others. But it's better than the alternative of not being."

She sighed, shaking her head. "Unbelievable," she said quietly. "So that's all you remember, the first day after your accident?"

"Well, it wasn't the first day after my accident. I was in a coma for about a month."

"A *month*?"

"Yes. I was out for a month. But all I remember is that first waking day. I don't have memories of anything before, like the accident or any points along the recovery process. Just glimpses, but I don't know if they're real or not."

"Not even in dreams? I've read stories about people with memory blocks who sometimes dream about the situations they've been blocking." She asked me the question, still standing close to me and looking up at me. I was glad I didn't have blood – my face would have looked ten times redder than hers did. Standing so close was a little…intoxicating. Her brown eyes seemed to be growing, taking all the focus of my attention and vision, drowning out everything else around me.

"I don't dream. One of the benefits of the…procedures…is that I don't require a lot of rest."

"No flashbacks?"

"None."

"So how much do you sleep?" she asked, backing away and sitting in her chair.

"About an hour, two at the most," I said, sitting back down in the Adirondack, feeling a little tinge of disappointment that we weren't so close any more. "But I usually rest for about three or four a day, depending on what I do during the day."

"What I could get done with that much time. And to think, you don't have embarrassing memories of tripping in front of the whole class at the school recital or other childhood disasters."

"But I don't get the benefits of memories, either," I said a little too quickly, maybe too bitterly. She looked at me, confused. "I don't remember parents or siblings. First crushes, birthdays, graduations, triumphs, failures, anything. My life is a blank."

"I never thought of it that way," she said quietly. Her blush was receding, making her paler.

"And can I share something else with you? I'm sorry I just blurted all that out and I sound so angry, but I feel…cheated of so much."

"Please," she said, putting her hand on my upper arm. "Wow, you must work out! Your biceps and triceps are huge! And they feel like steel under your skin."

"Another benefit of the treatments Devin gave me," I said, smiling. "Some of the drugs he's been developing are still in trials, but I'm one of his first beneficiaries."

"Sorry, I interrupted you. What were you going to say?"

"I'm sure Devin told Lilly and that she told you, but I have no identity. Devin didn't find any ID or personal effects near me. He reported the incident to local police, but, given his extensive medical background, I think they were happy to have the problem taken care of with private money instead of me becoming a ward of the state. There were no missing person reports fitting my description. So I have no way of knowing who I am or even finding out."

Restless, with the subject open again, I stood and walked to the edge of the deck, gripping the railing. I knew I was probably talking too much, divulging too much information, but there were some things I couldn't say to Devin. Things I didn't want to hurt him or to burden him with.

"DNA tests were inconclusive because of the complications of...some of the procedures. Photos obviously won't work because my face is now a wreck. Devin has had ads run and pictures posted, but no results. And since we don't know where I'm from, we don't even know where to begin to widen the search. We can't canvas the whole country or even the whole state.

"It's maddening," I said, gripping the railing even harder, hearing the wood creak, "I don't know if I dropped out of high school or if I was valedictorian of my class. I don't know if I was attending college or technical school or a clerk at a grocery store. I don't know if anyone cared about me or loved me. I don't know if anyone misses me or if I ever meant anything to anyone."

The anger was building again. I could feel it slipping out as I gripped the railing tighter and tighter, getting closer to the final point of my rant.

"I'm nobody."

And with that, my tightening grip took its toll on the two-by-four railing. I snapped it into pieces with a loud crack. Looking dumbly at my fists, which were filled with sawdust and compressed wood splinters, I tried to think of something to say, but my speech was blocked. Tessie rushed over and her eyes widened in shock as I opened my fists, spilling the pieces of ruined wood onto the deck.

"What was that!" I heard Lilly running out onto the deck. "It sounded like a gunshot out in the—" She stopped in her tracks when she saw the railing. I opened my mouth to speak but nothing came out.

"Sorry, Mom! I was making fun of Ted's gigantic stature and goaded him into breaking the railing!"

"Sorry, Lilly. The maintenance crew will come over tomorrow," I said quickly, wincing at my gravelly voice. Trying to piece together sentences again and finding it impossible. "Sorry. I'll go now."

"Don't be silly," Tessie said, grabbing my arm and trying to pull back. I realized I was dragging her along and stopped walking. "My mom's not going to banish you from the house just because you broke the railing!"

"Of course not," Lilly said, relaxing. "I thought it was a hunter in the woods shooting too close to the house. Of course you can stay, there's no harm done. Wow, you must be quite the athlete if you broke the railing into that many pieces. Just try to be careful with the rest of the deck – I know Devin won't mind having it repaired, but I'm a little partial to the benches in the corner." She winked and went back into the house.

I looked at Tessie, who had a mixture of emotions playing across her face. Concern, amusement, and – the worst – fear. "Are you OK? Did you hurt your hands?" She raised them up to look at the palms and, of course, saw no injuries.

"Sorry. Lost my temper." I grimaced at the simple sentences and tried to explain, again. "It's hard to speak. When I get angry."

"Trust, me, I've had a few of those episodes," Tessie said, rubbing my forearm. "Like I could spit tacks more easily than I could speak English."

I laughed and the tension started to ease a little. I waited a few more moments for my head to clear, then spoke again. "I have to be careful. My strength and my temper are a dangerous combination."

"I'd say so," she murmured, looking at the pile of splinters on the deck. "Although, I could think of some guys that I'd like to introduce you to. Maybe you could help me with some of the grief I'm getting at school."

"Someone is bothering you? Who is it? Why are they—"

"Easy, Hercules," she said, laughing. "It's nothing I can't handle. Besides, I wouldn't want you getting into trouble over something like that over me."

"It would be worth twice the price," I said fervently, realizing how that sounded only *after* I had said it.

She looked embarrassed and cleared her throat, her cheeks blooming pink again.

"Sorry, I barely know you and I'm sounding like the lead actor in a romantic comedy."

"It's OK," she said, smiling. "I don't mind. But you're wrong, you know."

I thought about what I had just said, frowning.

"You're not a nobody."

"Oh. That." I grunted again, again realizing how well that sound fit me.

"I think you might be looking at this all wrong. I'm glad you shared your feelings with me and I'm not saying you're wrong to feel that way," she said quickly, probably sensing the irritation building in me. "But you're right, you have a blank slate. You can reinvent yourself, be anything or anyone you want to be. For most people, that's a liberating feeling."

"Huh," was my only reply.

"Yes?" She looked at me, raising her eyebrows.

"A new perspective helps. Liberation. Freedom. I'll have to think about that," I said, smiling a little.

Measurements 2

The following week, I had another measurement day. But before that, I had to talk to the ground crew foreman and beg him to fix Lilly's deck for me. He was an older man whose first name was all I knew: Louie. I waited outside until the crew showed up. Louie was always first on site, so I waited for the familiar sound of his truck – a '73 Chevy Stepside pickup. He had restored it to pristine condition, painting it a metallic forest green starting at the top and fading into a black metallic at the bottom.

As he pulled into the driveway, sunlight flashed off the chrome rims and threw sparks of sunlight onto the driveway. The chrome side-pipes, which gave the truck its throaty rumble, were almost blindingly bright. The tires glistened like they were made of black glass. He gunned the engine before shutting it off, making it sound like a growling beast. He stepped out of his truck, groaning and straightening his back.

"Too damn old," Louie muttered as he tried to straighten himself.

"Only as old as you feel," I said from the shadows of the porch. I tried not to sneak up on people.

He laughed loudly, throwing his head back and pulling off his Boston Red Sox baseball cap, exposing tight curls of steely gray hair sprouting from his dark scalp. "That's true, Ted! Very true!"

I stepped out from the shadows, smiling at Louie. "Any new members this morning?"

"No, not this morning. Julio decided to stay, even after you scared him, so I didn't need to hire a replacement."

"I'm glad. Sorry I created problems for you," I said.

"No problem," Louie said gently, holding his hand out, shaking mine. He cocked his head a little to the left and looked at me through narrowed eyes. "Boy, I believe you're growing. Last week, I don't remember needing to look up at you. Bet Devin finds out you've grown again."

"Maybe," I nodded, smiling. "I wanted to catch you before your crew got started this morning. I was hoping you could do me a favor."

"A favor," Louie said, rubbing his black gnarled hands. He might be a foreman (and owner), but he still worked for a living. His eyes lit up with greed as he leaned toward me and put a hand on my shoulder, motioning me to stoop in closer. "I love favors. Means I might get to call one in! What do you need?"

"I was at our neighbor's house," I started and he chuckled. "What?"

"Hope you were talking to Tessie," he said, his eyes clearly showing his delight. A few asides from him in the past were enough to tell me that he would be delighted, without even looking at his eyes.

I nodded. "But I lost my temper and broke a railing on their porch."

He held up his hand and smiled. "Say no more. I'll have the boys go over before they get started. I'll have them drive around to the front, though, instead of walking through the woods." His eyes had a mischievous look in them as he leaned in toward me.

"Devin has been talking to you," I said, smiling.

"Maybe. Anyway, I'll have them out there this morning. Shouldn't take long."

"Thanks Louie," I said, holding my hand out again.

He shook it readily, not even flinching back from the grip or my appearance. He laughed a little and said, "I know you sneak in through the woods 'cause you don't want to be seen. And I know you hide from my crew, but you shouldn't. You've got nothing to be ashamed of. They do."

He looked at me hard, harder than I would have expected from him. He held my hand, held it tight and put his left on top of my right, clasping my right hand in both of his. When he spoke, his voice was sharp and had the cutting edge of years of experience.

"You can't let people decide how you live your life because of their prejudices. That's something I learned the hard way. Don't let 'em do it to you, Ted. Don't let 'em. This is your place – don't hide yourself away because people don't know how to act or be polite." He nodded as if that ended the discussion, releasing my hand and patting me on the shoulder.

I nodded back at him and turned to walk into the house.

"Hey Ted," Louie called, his smile lighting up his face once again. "Next time, take Lilly some flowers."

"Why?" I asked.

"A peace offering. Plus, it helps to be nice to the mother of the girl you're sweet on," he winked and laughed his loud laugh again.

I filed that away for future reference, and then turned to go in for measurements.

———

"Six feet four inches this week." Devin frowned. "Three inches more. And your weight is 240 pounds. That's not possible."

"Must be. Measurements don't lie." I chuckled a little, sitting down on one of the stools.

"No, I mean it's impossible because I've taken all of the growth hormone out of your medications. I thought it might actually cause some problems for you, but your growth is still continuing. And your weight – just like last time, it doesn't appear to be fat. If anything, you've lost fat."

"Well..." I started to say.

"I know, I've seen you exercising, doing pushups and sit-ups. But a few days' exercise wouldn't do this. No doubt our neighbor has sparked some vanity, perhaps?"

I grunted. "She sees past the scars. That's not it. It's more... activity, the need to feel like normal living humans."

"Son," he said, putting his hand on my shoulder. "You are human. I know you don't agree, but you are, even if you might not fit the technical medical mold. I'm sorry for what I've brought on you. This is a huge burden for you—"

"I talked to Tessie about that," I said, cutting him off and putting my hand on top of his. "She's given me a new perspective."

He grinned at me, sitting on a stool beside me. "And?"

"She suggested that I have the freedom to remake myself into anything I want."

"*Tabula rasa.* A blank slate upon which you can write anything you wish," he whispered, nodding his approval. "She's a very insightful young woman."

I nodded.

"And I noticed the maintenance crew was doing some repairs at Lilly's house this morning. Anything you'd like to talk about?"

"I was frustrated, angry. I let my temper get the best of me. I'm sorry, it won't happen again."

Devin nodded, standing again. "I'm sure it won't. All the same, perhaps I should get some gym equipment for you to work out some of that frustration and anger. You know, I used to be a boxer in college – maybe a heavy bag and some gloves."

"Maybe," I said, smiling ruefully. "It wouldn't do for me to wreck the neighbor's house every time I got angry."

Damage

I continually walked in the woods, hoping to spot Tessie each time. Sometimes it was only brief conversations – she was in the middle of finals and only had time for quick visits. A couple of times I narrowly avoided detection by friends she'd invited to her house. We had agreed that I should be her "little" secret for a while.

I told Devin all of this when we were sitting in the lab one day; he looked troubled.

"I don't want you to be a shadow in a corner all of your life," he said, clearly upset.

"But this is for the best, wouldn't you agree? I mean, a non-living being isn't something you see every day and I doubt there's any college-aged adult who could keep that secret."

"Except Tessie." A smile played at the corner of his lips. "OK, you're right. You should avoid others for a while, at least until we figure out how we introduce you to the world. Because it's imperative, you know – you need to become part of the outside world."

"Not from what I've seen in the papers," I muttered.

"Beg your pardon?"

"Nothing…" I trailed off and walked out the door, eager for my walk in the woods.

It was late afternoon and I realized I had been standing in the woods for nearly half an hour, waiting for Tessie when she finally appeared on the deck. I quickly moved out of sight in case she had a friend over.

"It's OK Ted, just me," she said laughing. "You might want to work on your stealth. You're about as quiet as a grizzly."

I came out of the woods, growling as best I could with my arms straight out in front of me. Tessie shrieked with laughter.

"Nice try, big guy, but I think you're more apt to laugh your prey to death!"

I jogged up the path to her house that I'd worn in the woods and jumped up onto the deck. Of course, I was trying to be quick, light, and nimbly but I was as graceful as an elephant, shaking the deck as I landed.

"Is that Ted?" I heard Lilly's voice.

"Sorry Lilly, I'll try not to break anything!"

"If you must break something," she said, appearing in the doorway, "break the shed. The roof is starting to give way a bit."

"I'll have the crew stop over tomorrow—"

"You'll do no such thing, Theodore Burroughs! I already owe Devin income from the next 50 years for the stuff he's had done already!"

"It's nothing," I assured her. "The crew doesn't have much to do around our house and we're keeping them gainfully employed. If left to their own devices, they'd play poker in our maintenance garage all day."

"OK, but no new shed. I'd probably wind up with air conditioning and marble floors."

"Is that what you'd prefer?"

"Ted, I mean it," she said, shooting me what was supposed to be a withering look. But Lilly couldn't pull off mean. She walked back into the house, shaking her head.

"Hey," Tessie said, leaning against the newly installed railings. The crew replaced all of them so they'd match.

"How were finals?" I sat in my favorite Adirondack chair and tried to look small.

"OK – they're done. Hey, have you grown? You look, I don't know, bigger."

"A little," I admitted. Honesty was better, or at least that's what Devin and I discussed. "Some of the medications act like growth hormones and steroids to help my body continue to repair. As a result, I'm bulking up a bit."

"No kidding," she said, appraising my biceps and shoulders. "You were big before, but you're getting into the massive category now."

"It will slow, eventually. So how were they?"

"Finals? Boring. Tedious. But thoroughly non-challenging, so I think I'll make Dean's list."

"That's great," I said, standing and holding up my hand for a high-five. She smacked my hand, then started rubbing her palm.

"Ouch. Your hand is like hitting an anvil." She continued to smile as I grinned guiltily and sat back down.

"What are you smiling at? You look like you're up to something."

"I was just thinking that since finals are over and classes are done, I'd have more free time. Time that I could talk to you."

"Me? Are you sure that's what you want?"

Her face had no expression. "Yes, why?"

"Don't get me wrong, I'd like nothing more than to talk to you as much as I can."

"Great, then what's the problem?"

"I thought maybe you'd want to spend time with your other friends. You know, get out and do stuff." I shifted uneasily in the chair, aware that my extra 15 pounds might be stretching its limits a bit. "I'm not exactly a social, public kind of guy."

"Well, you could come with us. Why are you shaking your head?" she asked with a smile that contained a hint of frustration.

"I'm sorry, but I still can't go out yet. I know it seems like I'm using recovery as a crutch, but I shouldn't go out much. You probably think that I'm too ashamed of my appearance and that I want to avoid all the stares, but—"

"That's *not* what I think," she said a little hotly. After taking a deep breath, she went on. "I'm sorry I snapped like that, but I don't think of you as an invalid. That poor defenseless railing that Louie's crew replaced this morning was enough to prove that." She smiled again, winking at me.

"You're right, but I'd rather not push it just yet. Maybe next month we can…go to a movie or something."

"You're on. Next month, you and I are going to a movie. In public. With other people," she said, walking toward me with her hand out. "Deal? Don't squeeze so hard this time."

"Deal," I said, sighing tragically. I barely grasped her hand and saw her wince a little. "Sorry, I barely squeezed that time, honest!"

"I know, I was faking," she said, punching me lightly on the shoulder. "Oww. Stop working out or I'm going to start breaking bones when I poke you."

"So what's on tap today?"

"I thought we'd hang out on the deck – I know, really original, but my exams are over and I want to just sit and not think."

"OK," I said, settling into the chair and slouching a little. More ominous creaking. "I think I might be getting a little heavy for this chair."

"Don't sweat it, it's an old one my mom doesn't even like." She looked at me a little shyly, uncharacteristically quiet for a few minutes. "So..." She was fidgety, a little embarrassed about something.

"...and?" I looked at her expectantly.

"I was hoping I could ask you a few more questions. But if you'd rather not, I'd understand," she said quickly.

"Oh. Well, I was hoping I could ask some of my own questions," I said, smiling at her.

"Really? Like what?"

"Like what's college like?"

"But that's so boring. That's just everyday life," she said, leaning back and resting her head against the back of the chair next to me.

"I know, but...well...I don't know what everyday life is like," I replied, uncomfortable. "I know my story is interesting to you because it's different from yours. But yours is interesting to me because it's different from mine."

"OK, deal. Shoot."

"Well, what do you do all day? I mean, I know you go to classes, but what are they like? What happens in between?"

"Classes can be boring sometimes, especially if the prof is boring," she said, closing her eyes and wincing a little. "Imagine sitting in a huge room with about 50 people watching paint dry. That's what my last history class was like. Labs aren't too bad, though, because we're working with slides or dissections or something like that. They're more fun. Classes are boring because usually we're being lectured to, so we're taking notes. Sometimes we get into discussions about the material, which can be interesting. Unless some nerd hogs the conversation.

"In between there's lunch or studying or library research. Sometimes my friends and I will get together in the student center at the coffee bar or we'll sit outside to talk about our day or plans for the night or weekend. You know, just stuff." She shrugged her shoulders.

"Maybe you should keep a journal some day so you can describe it to me," I said, smiling. "What do you normally do on nights or weekends?"

"Weeknights I'm usually home, studying away my boring, pathetic existence," she said. She snorted laughter and went on. "Friday nights and weekends I'm trying to avoid over-eager guys."

I sat very still, feeling a coldness take over. I tried to calm myself before speaking, trying not to tip her off to my emotions with my voice. I cleared my throat a little before talking. "What do you mean, 'over-eager'?"

Was that jealousy? A cruel voice in my head started to point out the obvious reasons why jealousy was a ridiculous emotion, but I squashed it before it could turn into anger. She was energetic, full of motion and life. I could have been a rock she was sitting next to.

She looked at me carefully, as if she were afraid to answer. She bit her lip and sighed, answering in a resigned-sounding voice. "You know, shallow guys who only see my physical assets, so to speak."

I must have still had a blank look on my face because she fidgeted a little, then sighed, exasperated.

"Guys whose only interest in me is my body."

"What?" I kept my voice down, but even I could hear the anger in it. I tried to calm down, but it was a struggle. "What do you mean by that?"

"Well," she started, clearly uncomfortable. She squeezed her hands together, not quite wringing them, but getting very close. I was torn between the somewhat amusing image of her blushing and fidgeting and the anger that was chilling me to the core. "There are some guys who are interested in only one thing – getting a girl into bed. Especially at college. I swear that seems to be the only reason some people go to college. I can't tell you the number of one-night stands that have happened among some of my friends. Acquaintances, I should say. Or the parties that wind up with late-night hookups."

"Sounds like most guys are jerks."

"With only one exception," she said, looking at me slyly. "But he demolishes our house on occasion. Can't take him anywhere."

"Ha ha," I said, folding my arms.

She shivered a little. The sun had moved lower in the tree line and the shade moved across us.

"Here," I said, taking off my sweatshirt. "Take this, you look cold."

"I can get one inside," she said, getting ready to get up.

"But then you'll start asking me questions and I'm not done yet," I said, tossing my gray hooded Megadeth sweatshirt at her and smoothing out my Black Sabbath t-shirt. I was a little self-conscious because I was starting to outgrow some of my t-shirts – and this was one of them.

"Do you wear anything besides shirts with bands on them?"

"On occasion," I answered, "but only if I haven't done wash in a while."

"You have no body heat," she said as she pulled it over her head. "I swear this thing feels like it just came out of the fridge. And look at the size of those guns! Put the weights away once in a while! And look at your pecs! Cripes, you look like a professional bodybuilder!"

"I've been exercising a little."

"How, by bench pressing small cars?" she asked, raising her eyebrows to match her mocking tone. "What, are you trying to look like the Terminator?"

"That's a horrible Arnold accent, by the way. He's Austrian, not Australian. Back on point, though. No, it helps me...work out some frustration. And it makes me feel a little more...normal...doing things that normal people do," I said, shifting a little in the Adirondack. It had started groaning now, instead of just squeaking and creaking.

"Oh. Sorry." She smiled meekly at me.

"Nice try, but back to the subject at hand. So you were saying most guys are jerks," I prompted her.

"Well, the ones that hit on me and my friends are. And persistent! This one guy always has his arm around me. I keep shrugging it off, but he's a creep and keeps it up. He tried to grope one of my friends, Kristie. She managed to get away from him, but she was scared."

I swallowed hard and tried to keep my voice even. "Hasn't anyone done something about it? You have security on campus, right?"

"Well, it happened at night and it would have been 'she said, he said' since there were no witnesses. Kristie just makes sure she's not alone with him at all."

"You're right, he's a creep," I muttered, looking at the deck and frowning. The anger was building and building. I could feel my self-control start to slip, little by little. I continued to stare at the deck floor, trying to regain my composure, all the while imagining the scene Tessie had described, only putting Tessie in place of her friend...

"Yikes," she said softly. I glanced up at her and she flinched. "If I saw you looking at me like you were looking just a few moments ago, I'd probably die of a heart attack. You OK?"

"Yeah, just...angry," I sighed and stood up. I clenched my fists tightly, hearing the joints crack.

"OK, I can hear your knuckles cracking, which means your clenching your hands. Hey, you aren't going to break anything, are you?" she asked, jokingly. "Just forget about it, he's harmless, really."

"He's not," I said, keeping my voice even, but I could hear the coldness in my voice as I kept talking. "He's a predator. The stuff he does may seem small, but it's not. He exerts his will and diminishes the person he's fixed on."

"Look, he tried to feel her up, it wasn't a big deal. He tried it on me too, you know, brushing his hand against my butt—"

"What did he do?" I spun around and looked at her. A thousand violent images crashed in on me. My self-control disappeared, as if it never really existed. I was seething with rage.

"Nothing, it was nothing, really," she said getting up and coming over to me. She put a hand lightly on my arm. "Relax, OK?"

"He touched you. And you didn't want him to. He's using his power to try to get something from you and your friends. Something you won't willingly give him. So he takes it by force, grabbing you and...groping. That's not 'nothing'," I said through my teeth, clenched so tightly I could hear my teeth grinding, moving in my gums, nearly cracking.

She laced her fingers into mine to hold my hand and my thoughts cleared immediately. The cold fury melting away under her warm touch. I looked at her hand in mine and heard her mutter, "sorry" as she tried to pull her hand away.

"Don't," I whispered. I lightly closed my fingers around hers. "I feel better."

She smiled at me and laughed. "Beauty calms the savage beast."

"Beast?" I laughed, still a little shaken at how quickly my control disappeared. "You shouldn't be so hard on yourself."

"Oh, you are going to get it," she said, pulling her hand away and putting up her fists. "Defend yourself for true, Theodore."

"Shaking in my size 14s."

"Oh my lord, you wear a 14?" Her mouth gaped. "Devin is going to go broke if you don't stop growing!"

"Nice try, but what about this guy?"

"It wasn't that big of a deal. He tried a few times, but I didn't—"

"A *few* times," I said, my voice rising, the anger and rage back in full force all at once, erasing the calm that Tessie's handholding efforts had created.

"Yeah, but it was—"

"Is everything OK? I thought I heard Theodore yelling." I could see concern as Lilly opened the sliding door and stepped onto the deck. She looked at me and walked toward me. "You haven't been upsetting him, have you Tessie?"

"Mom, it's OK, I was just telling him about Chad. You know, the persistent guy I told you about."

"Hmm," Lilly said. "Then I understand why you yelled, Theodore. And you have my permission to do whatever you want to that jerk. Honestly, Roman hands—"

"MOM!" Tessie looked mortified and I could see her blushing, even in the fading sunlight. "I told him about Chad. I told him he tried to...you know, touch me and stuff."

I paced a little, feeling the colder anger spreading like frost across a lawn in late November. "I'm sorry, it's just...I have a hard time controlling my temper."

Lilly came over and patted my shoulder. "I understand, Ted. I felt the same way you do. If I could get that guy alone..."

"I'll hold him, you beat him?"

"Deal," she said. "Sit – I'll get you guys a snack or something."

"A few times," I said quietly, leaning a little on the table in front of me.

"I still think you should tell security that he tried to do more than that and how you had to literally fight him off," Lilly began. "Honestly, it was physical assault, pure and simple. You even had light bruises where he grabbed your arm. Theodore, I swear if he ever tries that again I'll—"

She didn't have time to finish. Letting out an angry growl, I brought both my fists down on the table in front of me, smashing the table top into several pieces and driving the legs of the table right through the deck floor.

Lilly didn't even flinch. She shrugged her shoulders and said, "Oh well. I never really liked that table anyway. Besides, I guess I brought that one on myself. I was asking Tessie to be so careful, too." She sighed and looked at me. My question was probably written all over my face. "Don't worry, Theodore. Devin explained your temper and strength. Besides, I saw the proof of it when you broke the railing."

"But—"

"You didn't honestly think I believed Tessie's story about daring you to break the railing, did you?" Lilly asked, smiling. "A mother knows, Ted."

"10 AM on Monday?" I asked, looking up from the splintered wreck.

"Beg your pardon?" Lilly looked confused.

"The crew starts late on Mondays – 10 AM OK?"

Lilly laughed and nodded as she went back into the house. I picked up the pieces that I could gather and tried to stack them neatly by the steps. Sighing, I walked back to my chair, shaking my head. I turned and looked at Tessie, getting ready to say, "sorry" yet again, but the look on her face stopped me.

She was staring at the pile of kindling I'd left behind with something like amusement on her face. "Sorry," she said. "I know it's hard for you to control your temper. But some day, I want you to show me just how strong you really are. You weren't even trying to do that!"

"OK, when it's your turn, we'll do some experiments," I agreed, sitting back down in my favorite Adirondack…and smashing it to hell as I sat down. "That doesn't count."

Tessie roared laughter, tears forming in her eyes as she laughed. Lilly came out, saw me sitting on the deck floor amidst the pieces that used to be the chair and she started to chuckle. Then she laughed outright.

I shook my head and stood up. "9 AM. I'll call Louie and let him know. They've got a lot of work to do." Lilly nodded and walked back in the house.

"Oh, by the way, Ted, I want you to stop by tomorrow around noon. I'm having some friends over that I'd like you to meet," Tessie said, smiling, wiping her eyes.

"Are you sure that's a good idea? You don't have much furniture left." I looked at the various piles of kindling lying around the deck.

"Well, I'd like them to get to know you. And if we're going on a date, I'd like them to meet you."

"A date?"

"That's what I thought I'd call our little movie excursion, if that's OK," she looked at me tentatively.

"A date. Wow."

"I mean, I don't think we need to start picking out china patterns or anything," she said, blushing slightly and tossing her hands up in exasperation.

"Right. It's just a...date," I said, looking at her carefully.

"Scared?" She was still blushing a little, but she also looked like she was having fun. I knew she was light years ahead of me in this game, but I wasn't about to let her see that.

"No," I said, lying through my teeth. "Just trying to decide which band is date-appropriate for the t-shirt I'll wear."

"Ugh. Anything but that freaky Six Feet Under shirt with the skull," she said, wrinkling her nose.

"I think I just decided which one," I said, smiling as I back away from her playful swat.

———

Panicked, I literally ran back home after saying good night to Tessie. Not exactly light on my feet, I probably sounded like a herd of elephants stomping their way through the woods.

"Devin," I yelled as I walked into the house. "DEVIN!" Where was he? All I could think of was the one word sure to find him – I'd never called him that before, but my scrambled brain figured it would probably work.

"DAD!"

"What's wrong," he said, rushing back into the lab from the kitchen, practically running.

"I…uh…I…"

"Are you hurt? Are you sick?" He grabbed my shoulders and sat me in one of the chairs in the lab, pulling over a rolling stool and a lamp.

"No, I'm not hurt, it's just…"

"But you called me 'Dad'," he said, clearly a little pleased, but still concerned. "You've never called me that before. Not that I mind, but I thought you were in real trouble."

"No, it's just…it's Tessie. She…she invited friends over tomorrow."

"Can't say I'm surprised," Devin smiled, relaxing a little but still looking a little concerned. "I'm only surprised it's taken this long. Lilly has said she's quite taken with you."

"Why?" I was sure I'd be shaking – if I had any adrenal glands to produce adrenaline, that is.

"Part of it is because you actually listen when she talks. And you're interested in her, not just her appearance," he said, switching off the lamp and relaxing a little. "Did she say who was coming over?"

"I'm guessing Kristie and Val, two friends she's mentioned before, but I don't know who else. What am I going to do? They're bound to notice I'm not normal!"

"Tessie will have already told them that," Devin said. "Relax, my boy, relax. She's your friend. She'll have already eased your introduction and warned her friends not to upset you or stare. And if they're friends of Tessie that

Lilly approves of, they'll be polite enough not to do any of that anyway."

"What if they ask questions? I don't mind talking to Tessie but total strangers?"

"That's your call," he said shrugging. "I doubt they'd ask anything, but if they do you have every right not to answer.   Chances are, Tessie has probably already answered most of their questions and warned them not to ask others. Relax. Try to enjoy yourself."

"Relax. Right."

Introductions

If I were a breathing being, I would have been hyperventilating and if I had a heart, it would have been pounding out of my chest. I was walking the path toward Tessie's, self-conscious about everything: my shirt and jeans, my shoes, how I fixed my hair (basically wash and wear). I got halfway there when I heard someone moving up ahead.

"Hi," I heard Tessie's voice calling out to me. "I thought you might be a little nervous, so I figured I'd meet you half way. Plus, I didn't want you chickening out and running away."

"Thanks. I am a bit nervous," I admitted gratefully.

"Relax, they'll like you. And I've already told them a lot about you. Kristie can't wait to meet you. And Sharon and Val—"

I stopped. "How many friends did you invite?" I was almost panicking again. Then she laced her fingers into mine again, calming me instantly.

"OK, that always seems to work," I said, looking at her hand in mine and almost forgetting about the crowd waiting for me on her deck.

"Yeah, well," she said, turning pink, "you look like you could use some support."

"I can. But be careful," I advised, smiling at her.

"About what?"

"I could get used to this," I said, holding up our intertwined hands.

"Good," she said shyly. "So could I."

We stood looking at each other quietly, my huge, gray, cold hand clasped in her small, pink, warm hand. I cleared my throat, scaring away several small birds as I did.

"So how many friends?" I asked again – but not as panicky as before.

"Only three. Kristie, Sharon, and Val. I've told you about them before, so they're not really strangers."

"But I've never met them. Knowing who they are and talking to them face-to-face are two completely—"

"Relax. They won't bite," she said, punching me lightly. "Hey, you should have Devin measure you again. You look bigger."

"I am. Six feet six inches, 250 pounds, and practically a size 16 shoe now. And no signs of slowing yet."

"Wow." She looked at me in awe. "I'm going to have to start wearing platform shoes."

She started to walk back to her house. "Come on. I told them you were painfully shy and that I'd have to meet you halfway to convince you to come over."

"That predictable, huh?"

"You've no idea," she smiled. She pulled me toward her house and I could hear three voices: two high-pitched, higher than Tessie's, and one husky, low-toned voice.

"Tess, is that you? Do you have the mystery man in tow?" The girl with the husky voice was leaning over the railing. The other two were seated at the new table the maintenance crew built this morning. I could see a fresh new Adirondack, more sturdy-looking with reinforced wood bracing practically everywhere, sitting nearby.

"Yes, and his name is Ted," she called back. The other two girls stopped talking as we entered the clearing. I could hear all three of them gasp.

"You were right, he is a giant!" One of the high-pitched voices.

"You must be Kristie," I said, smiling. My shattered voice compared to hers was like comparing a vulture to a swan.

"Hi Ted. How did you know?" She looked slightly pleased.

"Tessie has told me a little about you, too," I replied. "And you're Val?"

"Yes," said the girl with the husky voice. "Hi, Ted. She talk about me, too?"

"She said you were athletic – I noticed you were wearing running shoes, not just sneakers. And that physique certainly didn't come from sitting on the couch watching TV. Which makes you Sharon," I said, looking at the blond who was easily shorter than Tessie and barely five feet tall (if that).

"Hi Ted. Nice to meet you."

"Nice to meet all of you as well. I know Tessie has probably explained to you already, but I'm horrible at social situations. So if I sink into the background, don't feel bad."

"Oh, we won't let you do that, sugar," said Valerie in her sultry voice. "We're dying to talk to you to see what man actually got Tessie's attention. All those semesters of college and no man to show for it."

Tessie blushed and hissed between her teeth, "Shut up, Val."

"Not too hard to see why empirically, though," said Sharon in an almost squeaky voice. "Research has proven that males with broader shoulders—"

"Enough, we're done with classes," moaned Kristie. "No more, Pipsqueak. Come have a seat, Ted. Looks like the sturdy Adirondack is yours." I could see a smile playing at her lips.

I stopped in my tracks and looked at Tessie accusingly. "You told them."

"Of course, they're my friends. Besides, they thought it was funny." She shrugged her shoulders nonchalantly.

"Hysterical," Sharon said.

Tessie nonchalantly disengaged her hand as I walked up the steps and sat in the chair – it didn't so much as creak.

"I saw that," Val said.

"Me too," Kristie said.

Tessie turned and stuck out her tongue at both of them while they chorused "aaawwwww" after her.

"So how tall are you?" Sharon asked.

"About six feet six inches. How about you?"

"Yikes, over a foot shorter."

"Don't you mean two feet, Shorty?" Val asked. Sharon chucked a plastic spoon at her.

"Well, since we all know why we're here, I'll start the inquisition. Tell us everything. How did you two meet?" Kristie asked.

"I saw Ted in the woods one night and almost freaked. I knew Devin lived in the house behind us, but I didn't know about anyone else. I saw this gigantic shape moving in the shadows. I thought he was...a hunter or something." I smiled a little at her trailing off – I'd bet she was going to say 'Sasquatch'.

"Actually," I said, ignoring the flinches my voice caused in the other three. "I saw her first. And I have an admission to make."

"Uh-oh, out with it," Tessie said, raising one eyebrow.

"I was watching you before then. I used to take walks and venture into the woods to watch you."

"You mentioned that before and now you're admitting it in the presence of witnesses. Stalker," she said, getting up and walking over to me, crossing her arms as she stood in front of me. "And I never asked: what did you see?"

"You studying, mostly. And that thing you do with your bangs when you're thinking."

The other girls laughed. "I know what you mean," Val said. "She twirls her hair when she's concentrating."

Tessie laughed, too, and sat on the arm of the chair I was sitting in, putting her arm around my shoulders. "My stalker. My giant."

"Do you have a brother in my size?" Sharon asked, blushing a little. I laughed and shook my head. "Oh well, it was worth asking."

"Yeah, I'm on the lookout, too. Chad's been getting too chummy," Val said, looking suddenly angry. "That guy better keep his distance or he'll wind up—"

"*Val*," Kristie said, poking her.

"Oops, sorry Shug," Val said to me. "Tessie told us you do a little...redecorating when you get mad. I should have known his name might get you a little angry."

"That's OK," I said, hiding my anger. So he wasn't just after Tessie. He was after Tessie's friends, too. Anyone that he perceived to be weak, anyone he could push and control. Hearing it from them directly made it a little more real, hearing their concern. "I think I'm done redecorating. But just for the record, the chair was an accident – all I did was sit in it."

While the girls were laughing, Lilly came out carrying a snack tray of sandwiches. "Here you go, girls," she said, setting the tray down.

"I feel guilty eating in front of you, Ted," Sharon said, picking up a sandwich. "Tessie told us you don't eat regular food – did you bring anything with you?"

"No, but that's OK. I really don't get hungry," I explained. "One of the side effects of my injuries. I don't really have an appetite and meal supplements that Devin created are all I really need."

"Any chance I could get a hold of some of them?" Val asked, shaking her head as she munched on chips Lilly had just set down. "Thanks, Lil. Maybe if I took what you're taking, I wouldn't have to spend two hours a day running to keep my thighs and butt from exploding."

Kristie shrieked with laughter and tossed a napkin at her. "Not while I'm eating! I'll spray food all over the place and Ted will think I'm an ignorant boor."

"He's going to think that anyway, because you are," Val said, chucking the napkin back and winking at her.

"So what do you do to work out?" Kristie asked, "and don't tell me you don't. You look you're in training for Mr. Universe."

"I do some weight training—" I began.

"—with a VW bug," Tessie finished.

"Nice," I said as the girls laughed. "As I was saying before I was rudely interrupted, I do some weight training and Devin is working on getting some boxing equipment. He thought it might be better than me smashing Lilly's house."

"Wait, didn't Devin box in college or something like that? I thought Mom might have mentioned it," Tessie said, reaching for her water glass. She took a sip and shook her head. "I can't imagine nice, polite Devin beating the crap out of someone."

"You haven't seen him angry," I said. "He did box in college and probably would have kept it up, but he was concerned about the long-term damage he might get if he got any concussions. He never went on to the professional level, but he was very good in the amateur ranks."

"Just what you need," Kristie said dryly, "more violent outlets."

"I'm just hoping he has the bags anchored very well," I said.

"Do they even make gloves that fit hands your size?" Tessie asked, popping the rest of her sandwich in her mouth and winking at me.

"No, I just tie pillows around my fists," I said sarcastically, rolling my eyes.

"And did you just roll your eyes?" she asked, raising her eyebrows.

"Couldn't you hear them? I did it hard enough you should have."

"Ooooh," Val said, "I smell a fight."

"I'd win," said Tessie. "Hands down, no contest."

"How do you figure that?" I asked, folding my arms in front of me, knowing full well how that made my arms look.

"Holy crow, look at those massive arms," Sharon squealed. "I wish you were there for anatomy instead of the stupid plastic model we—wait, that sounded bad, I mean, you know, because of your muscles, you know, not—"

Val laughed raucously and almost fell out of her chair. "Don't worry, Hon, we know *exactly* what you meant."

"Please Sharon," I said in my most innocent voice. "Could you explain? I'm not sure I know what you meant."

Sharon blushed and threw a piece of ice at me. "No fair picking on the short person."

"So, what movie are we going to see?" Kristie asked. She had a mischievous look in her eye.

"Oh no," I groaned, "you told them *that*, too?"

"Of course," Tessie said, smiling. "Whom did you think I was talking about when I said we were going with other people?"

"And you invited them along? I thought you meant there would be other people in the theater," I said. I looked around at the other three and they were looking at each other knowingly. "Those looks...wait, you think...no, hold on, I didn't mean I wanted Tessie alone or anything—"

Then I saw Tessie's face and knew I'd just stuck my big foot in my mammoth mouth. "Not that I don't, it's just that—"

Then I saw the girls' faces. I held up my hands. "I quit. I'm done, no more talking."

Tessie laughed. "It's so easy to trip you up."

"Sure, make fun of the invalid," I said sarcastically.

"Right, an invalid who can bench press a truck," she said.

"Don't let the Herculean body deceive you," I said quietly, flexing my arms in an Atlas pose and stretching the seams of my t-shirt.

The other girls hooted while Tessie laughed and said, "That's enough, that's enough!"

"Well, I guess if we have chaperones, it might as well be them," I said, waving my hand dismissively at them.

"You'd prefer no chaperone?" Tessie asked.

"OK, like I said, I quit," I said, chuckling. "You're not going to trap me."

"Looks like it's already too late, Shug," Val said in her deep voice, eyeing Tessie knowingly.

Date

"Nervous?" Devin was looking at me with his eyebrows raised.

"Maybe a little," I said as I smoothed out my black polo shirt and picked pieces of lint off my khaki pants.

"You look fine. Besides, I doubt Tessie would care if you wore cutoff jeans and a dirty t-shirt."

"Maybe," I admitted. "I know she doesn't care about my appearance. I was hoping that by dressing this way, I'd be less conspicuous. But what do I do if people are staring? I don't want to start any trouble or get Tessie into trouble."

"Then don't," Devin said softly. "There are people out there who will stare at you because you're different. They're the same people who stare at a quadriplegic in a wheelchair or an amputee on crutches or a blind person with a cane. Don't let it bother you. You could always make yourself feel better by knowing they have no idea just how different you are."

I laughed, nodding my head. "True."

"Have fun – try not to worry too much," Devin said, putting a hand on my shoulder gently. But he looked worried, too.

"There's something you're not telling me," I accused him.

"No, no," Devin said, smiling and smoothing out the creases in his forehead. "Just a...father's concern, I guess you'd call it. This is a big step for you and I won't be there for you. I'm anxious."

"Not as anxious as me," I assured him.

"You're probably right," he said chuckling. "Just be yourself. That's who Tessie likes, you know."

Tessie was driving because I hadn't gotten around to getting a license yet. Having no history made things like that difficult. Devin thought he could pull some strings to get one, but I was in no rush. Besides, I wasn't sure if I could remember how to drive, if I ever did decide to get one. And what would happen if I lost my temper in the middle of a busy street? Talk about road rage.

I was meeting everyone at her house, since it would mean driving about a mile around our property for her to pick me up at our front door. I smiled at Devin and headed out the back door, across our lawn, and into the woods. I could see the deck light was on and Tessie was anxiously looking into the woods. Sharon and Kristie were sitting on one of the benches, chatting.

"Relax, Tess," Kristie said. "He'll be here."

"Yeah, even if he were to show up now, he'd be about half an hour early," Sharon agreed.

"Thirty-five minutes, by my watch," I said as I walked into her backyard, smiling. She was wearing a pair of black jeans and a red short-sleeved shirt. "You look great."

"You're not too bad on the eyes, either," Tessie said.

"Oh, these old rags?"

Sharon and Kristie giggled, sticking their fingers in their mouths and making gagging noises. Tessie turned to give them the evil eye.

"OK, guys, quit it. If this is the way it's going to be, I'm walking," Sharon said, tossing a seat cushion at Tessie's back.

"Well, let's go – we can walk around downtown while we wait for the show," Tessie said. "Val said she might drop by later and there are some other friends of ours that might be there."

"I feel like a show dog," I said, walking up the steps to her. I looked down at her and smiled.

"More like a show horse," she said, looking up at me. "You can't stand that close if you want me to look you in the eye – I'm going to get a muscle cramp in my neck."

"How romantic," Kristie said, rolling her eyes.

Sharon looped her arm through Kristie's and said, "Shall we" in a voice that was obviously supposed to be a parody of mine.

"Stop that, Pipsqueak," Tessie said, blushing. "Don't make fun of his voice!"

"That's OK, I really don't mind," I said, laughing. "Besides, she can do anything she wants as long as she doesn't stop making those delicious cookies with the rest of the elves in the trees. So is Keebler like a family name, or is that just a marketing gimmick you and the other elves thought up?"

While Kristie and Tessie were busy laughing, Sharon shrieked in mock indignation and punched me in the gut. Then she started howling in pain. "OWWW! What do you have under there, a sheet of metal?" She reached out poked my stomach, then started rubbing it with her hand. "Holy six pack!"

"OK, OK, yes, he has great muscle definition," Tessie said, pulling Sharon away from me and pulling me forward. We walked through Tessie's house to the front door and she called out, "Bye, Mom!" She no sooner opened the door than her mother appeared.

"Wait," she said. "I want to get a picture!"

"Mom!" Tessie blushed furiously. "What for? It's just a movie!"

"Yes, but this is a pretty big event. Sharon and Kristie know what I'm talking about."

"Yeah, you actually going out somewhere with a guy," Sharon said, putting her arm around my waist and her head against my arm. "Wow. And *what* a guy! Eat any more Wheaties and we're going to have to put you in the circus." She squeezed my arms. "Flex for a second."

"That's probably not a good idea. The polo doesn't quite fit; it's a little tight around the arms."

"And?"

"I could rip it," I said honestly.

Everyone laughed, but Tessie seemed to be laughing a little less than everyone else, probably knowing how true it was.

"OK, but I want to see you flex at some point tonight," she said.

"I did on the deck. The day we first met, remember?"

"I know, but I swear your arms look bigger – they're like tree trunks! It would be worth buying you a new shirt to see you tear the sleeves apart!"

"Picture," Tessie said shortly, moving in on my other side and putting her arm around my waist, joining Sharon's.

"Great, where do I go?" Kristie asked, hands on her hips.

"Here," I said, holding out my arms.

"I don't get it," she said, eyeing me suspiciously.

I leaned forward and scooped her up and off her feet, cradling her in my arms.

"Oh!" she squealed.

"Don't get too comfortable," Tessie said. "I'm not the jealous type, but take it easy."

"Sharon, you were wrong about his arms. They feel like chunks of steel encased in a thin layer of cotton!" I was thankful she didn't comment about how cold I must feel.

"Quick, take the picture, Mom, before Kristie gets too comfortable," Tessie grumbled, smiling daggers at her friend.

Her mother snapped a couple of pictures, then wanted one of just me and Tessie. Tessie kept her arm around my waist, lifting my arm to place it on her shoulders. "That's better," Tessie murmured so only I could hear her as her mom took a few more pictures.

"There, that should make Devin happy," she said, meeting my eyes and smiling. I smiled back, thinking how much the man worried about me.

"OK," Tessie said, "everyone in the car! Ted has shotgun."

"Wait a second, why does he get shotgun over your best friend?" Kristie asked.

"Best friend?" Sharon asked, raising her eyebrows.

"Look how long his legs are. Do you really think he'd fit in the backseat of my Civic? He'll probably have to pry himself into the front seat as it is."

"Actually, I was thinking of taking out the front seat and sitting in the back to give me more leg room, but I'll manage," I said. "Devin has taken me out in his Lamborghini a few times and I don't get much—"

"Wait, did you say Lamborghini?" Sharon asked, her eyes suddenly glowing with interest. "What kind?"

"A Murcielago," I answered.

"Coupe or Roadster?"

"Can we stop the car conversation?" Tessie asked, laughing.

"Roadster," I whispered. "Get Tessie to bring you over some day and Devin will probably let you take it for a spin."

Sharon moaned with longing. "Oh, is Devin married?"

"If you two keep drooling over cars all night we'll never make it to the movie theater. Car! Now!"

We all piled into Tessie's Civic and she was right, I had to wedge myself in. But it was no worse than Devin's toy.

"Can you turn off the airbag," I groaned as I folded myself in.

"No, why?" Tessie looked concerned.

"If it goes off, I think it will blow off my kneecaps." Sharon and Kristie laughed in unison in the backseat.

"Fine, we'll take the Murceleggo next time and Sharon and Kristie can ride on the roof. Or stay home."

"Murcielago," I corrected. "No offense guys, but I think she's got a deal."

"OOOoooo," Sharon and Kristie cooed together. "Ted and Tessie sittin' in a tree..."

Tessie cranked the radio to drown them out. Some type of sugar-coated, inane drivel was blaring through the speakers: typical pounding bass, whiny vocals, and lyrics about as meaningful as the ingredient list on a box of Twinkies. I made a face.

"What?" she asked, glancing over at me.

I shrugged. "Our tastes in music are a lot different."

"How about this?" She changed the station to rap.

"That's an old one – Beastie Boys. Not bad guitar work, decent vocals. But rap in general, ugh. Definitely not."

"Oh, I've got it." Classical this time.

"Gustav Holst. 'The Planets' isn't bad – this is Mars, by the way, the bringer of war. Still a little painful, but better than the first two at least."

"This?" Blues.

"B.B. King is one of my favorite blues singers – this one is 'Blues Man'. Not bad for an early Sunday morning, but not even close to what I really like. How about this," I said, spinning the dial to the metal station I usually listen to.

"Yuck, can he scream any louder?" Tessie turned the volume down.

"You actually listen to this?" Kristie asked.

"Yes I do listen to this. And yes, *she* can scream louder. It's a woman."

"No way," Tessie said, looking incredulous and disgusted at the same time.

"Yes. That's Arch Enemy and trust me, Angela has a set of lungs on her."

"You listen to metal?" Sharon sounded incredulous.

"Well, metal is a very broad category, but yes, I listen to speed, thrash, death metal, doom metal—"

"Whoa," Sharon said as Tessie and Kristie laughed. "I didn't know there were *sub*categories!"

"Sure there are. And they're all a little bit different, but it probably takes a bit of listening before you can tell the difference."

"Huh," Sharon said.

"OK, what does 'huh' mean?"

"Well, I never pegged you for the type."

"Does that surprise you that I listen to it?" I asked, struggling to turn around to look at her. I quit after I heard the seat creak and the dashboard crack a little. "Sorry, I'll sit still." I grinned at Tessie and she laughed again.

"Well," Sharon began, carefully, "I don't know, you struck me as..."

"More intelligent? More sophisticated? More normal?" Tessie was filling in the blanks, poking me with each one.

"I was going to say more mainstream."

I laughed. The way I looked, with the gray skin, colorless eyes, and gigantic size, and she thought I'd be more mainstream. "Actually, I prefer jeans and a black t-shirt or any one of the band shirts I own. And I usually walk around barefoot all day."

"Yikes," Kristie said. "Think you know someone. But how did you know the other songs? You knew the musician or composer in only a few notes."

"I've got a good memory – short-term, of course. Plus, I can pick out songs really well. Just one of the freaky little quirks I have," I said.

I didn't go into the treatments Devin had given me and the benefits I reaped from them. Obviously, that helped me to quickly remember – and scan through – entire songs and albums in my head before most people could identify the few seconds of music they had just heard. For the music I had just listed off, I was able to think through all of the works each band did. In chronological order.

Angela had stopped her screaming and now it was Chris Barnes up. I smiled, since his voice sounded only slightly more guttural and growling than mine when he sang. "This is a great song. One of my personal favorites. 'Decomposition of the Human Race' by Six Feet Under."

"Hmm," Tessie said. "Clearly you are someone with anger management issues if you listen to that."

"Possibly," I said quietly, low enough for only her to hear.

"OK," Tessie said, switching back to a rock station. "Compromise. Hard rock?"

"Ahh, AC/DC, 'Back in Black' from the album of the same name. Not bad. Deal," I said. "Anything but that manufactured, pre-packaged, soulless garbage that gets mass-marketed as Top 40 music these days."

We rode on to the theater, laughing and joking. I shared more of my music preferences, much to the others' dismay; they weren't very impressed with Lamb of God or Meshuggah. They talked about college and summer plans as we rode on through the city. I enjoyed the friendly banter, the imagined feeling that I was being included. I say "imagined" because maybe it was my own morose disposition, but I knew that I could never be part of the lives they led. Maybe I relished the role of outsider; maybe I liked being alone. I knew Tessie and her friends would include me and defend me against narrow-minded "villagers", but I'd never be part of what they had.

While Sharon and Kristie lapsed into a conversation about some of their male classmates (and their various redeeming qualities and flaws), Tessie smiled slyly and quietly asked, "What are you thinking?"

"How great this is," I said, equally as quietly.

"Really?"

"Yes," I said. "I didn't know what I was missing by confining myself to home. This is fun."

"I'm glad," she said. "I'd like to do this more." She took a hand off the wheel and rubbed my shoulder.

"Ooh, physical contact," Kristie chirped.

"Yeah, don't think we didn't see that," Sharon joined in.

"Hang on to the oh-my-God handle above the door," Tessie said. "I'm going to shake them up a bit in the back."

"I'm packed in so tightly, I don't think I'll move," I admitted, grasping the handle, only to have it snap off in my hand. "Sorry!"

Tessie laughed as she pulled sharply into the parking lot of the theater, shifting Kristie and Sharon around in the back. They squealed with laughter, hollering in protest.

"On the way home, we get the giant in the back," Kristie said. "That way, he'll wedge us against the side so we won't move."

I managed to extricate myself from the car. I looked down at the tiny Civic and wondered how I ever fit into it in the first place. I held out my hand to help Sharon out of the backseat – she pretended that I yanked her out of the back of the car, making Kristie howl with laughter. We realized we were ridiculously early, so we decided to take a walk toward downtown Burlington.

"You guys want to get a shake or a cone? My treat," I said. I tried to ignore the stares and looks as well as the whispered comments. Looking at Tessie, knowing this was a pseudo-date, helped me keep my anger in check. Barely.

"Sounds good to me," Sharon said, linking her arm in mine, looking up at me and positively beaming.

"Sorry, may I cut in," Tessie said, wedging herself between Sharon and me. Sharon rolled her eyes theatrically.

"Soo territorial," she said, shaking her head.

"Very. So jealous and sad," Kristie said, linking her arm in my other.

"Ladies, please," I said, laughing.

Tessie laughed, too. "I think we're embarrassing him."

"If not for my natural color, I'd be blushing. Gray has its benefits. There are times where my…ah…differences, we'll say, are a good thing." I looked over her shoulder at a few people who were staring at me. I stopped walking. They didn't drop their eyes or look away, which irritated me.

"What is it?" Tessie asked, looking around.

I didn't say anything as I stared back at the two guys and girl that were staring at me. I let go of Tessie's arm and turned around, crossing my arms, fully aware how my forearms must look. I frowned at them and tried to look furious – not too hard, considering my anger was starting to grow.

"Something wrong?" I asked, raising the volume and intensity of my voice slightly, dropping the pitch.

They quickly dropped their gazes and hurried away in the opposite direction, looking over their shoulders – presumably to make sure I wasn't going to follow them.

"Ted?" Tessie tugged at my arm.

I turned and smiled at her. "Just giving the villagers something to talk about. You know, so they can go home and grab their torches and pitchforks." I tried an impression of Mike Meyers in Shrek as best I could, but failed miserably. "'Grab your torches and pitchforks everybody, let's go get the scary ogre!'" They laughed at that as we crossed the street to the local Cold Stone Creamery. Tessie stopped short as we reached the other side of the street.

"You know what, I changed my mind. I don't think I want anything," Tessie said, steering me away from the Cold Stone. I saw her shoot a look to Kristie and Sharon.

"Are you sure?" I asked, wondering about the sudden change as I turned to walk with her.

"OK, Sharon and I will grab something and be right back out," Kristie said, pulling on Sharon's arm.

"Here," I said, handing over a 20. "A promise is a promise – my treat."

They laughed nervously as they turned to go back. Something was definitely going on. The two of them looked like they didn't want to go in, either, but were obviously trying not to arouse my suspicions. They weren't very good at it. Tessie continued to pull me down the street, away from the Cold Stone.

"OK, so why do you not want me near a Cold Stone all of a sudden?" I asked, amused. My anger over the villagers was fading a little.

"No special reason," she said innocently enough.

"Nice try," I replied. "I saw the look you gave Sharon and Kristie. And they looked like they were even less interested in going inside. What was that about?"

"Nothing, it's just—"

I stopped short. I could tell she was afraid of something. I took her chin in my hand and gently lifted it, fully aware that this was a different kind of first contact. I'd never touched her face before and I wondered how my hand felt. Her face felt warm and soft.

"What are you afraid of?" I whispered.

"You. I mean, how you'll react if I tell you what I'm afraid of. What you'll do." She was whispering, trembling. She looked at her hands as she interlaced her fingers and flexed them back and forth.

"What do you mean? You don't have to be afraid of me," I said, dropping my hand. She was upset, scared. Because of me. She pulled both my hands into hers.

"I know, but your temper…well, it's bad. I know you don't mean to be violent and for most people, the way they explode isn't a big deal. But when *you* explode…"

"Deck furniture gets destroyed." I sighed.

She laughed quietly. "It is kind of funny, but I do worry. Especially if you got as violent with people as you do with deck furniture." She finished the last sentence in a little more than a whisper, looking up at me with eyes that were a little wetter than usual.

"I'd never hurt you. Or Lilly or your friends. You know that, right?"

"Of course I do," she said urgently, squeezing my hands. "I never feel safer than I do when you're around."

"Then don't worry," I said. She smiled and started to pull me down the street again.

And that's when I heard Sharon and Kristie yelling. And cursing. I frowned – that language was out of place for them. And they sounded furious, which was also out of place. I tried to turn but Tessie pulled back with all of her might, holding onto one of my arms with both of hers.

"Please – remember your temper."

"Get OFF me you jerk," I heard Sharon saying.

"Aw, come on, you don't mean that," I heard a male voice say.

"Maybe you should leave her alone," another male voice said. "Come on, please don't start any trouble."

"And maybe you should mind your own business unless you want to get hurt," the first yelled back.

"Come on, Chad, let her go," I heard Kristie's voice.

I spun around, dragging Tessie with me as I turned, literally lifting her off the ground. I could see Kristie, red-faced from yelling, pounding her fists on some guy's chest. No, it wasn't just "some guy" – I knew who it was. She was pounding her fists on *Chad's* chest while he was pushing her away. Shoving her almost as hard as he could.

He was standing behind Sharon and had his other arm hooked around her waist, holding her close to him. Laughing about it as if it were some kind of joke.

I dropped Tessie's hands and walked quickly back to Kristie and Sharon, covering the ground with amazing speed. People who had turned to watch quickly moved aside as I neared them, some of them gasping, most of them making a comment to their friends as I passed.

"Holy—"

"Did you see the size of that guy?"

"He's frickin' huge!"

A couple of patrons came out of the shop to intercede, asking Chad to let Sharon go.

"Come on, let her go," an older man said, his wife trying to pull him back into the shop.

"Just let her go," a young woman said, her friends nodding in agreement.

"Mind your own business," Chad snapped at them. "Pops, I'll shut you up good. And you, little ladies, maybe I'll set my sites on you." He leered at the young women as they backed away, shooting glares at him.

"She said no, creep," Kristie said, getting close enough to grab Sharon's arm. "Let her go."

And he put his hand over her face and shoved her again. To the ground. Her feet got tangled and she landed on her side. Hard. I could hear the huff of air when she hit the ground and the sound of her hands scraping the sidewalk.

And that did it. Something clicked, something flashed in my head...

...a woman being shoved to the ground by a man...

...who was yelling and screaming and cursing...

...she was crying, cowering on the floor, shielding her bloody face with her hands...

...he was yelling screaming shouting...

"HEY," I shouted in my inhuman voice, well-fitted to my equally inhuman rage. And *everyone* looked, not just Chad. The patrons all took a few steps back as I approached. Even Kristie and Sharon looked scared. That concerned me – I didn't want to scare them. It also hurt a little, because I wanted them to feel safe, like Tessie. To know that I'd never hurt them. It only made me angrier that

Chad was causing this – causing them to look at me like that. And even though I was hurt and regretted scaring Tessie's friends, all those emotions were well behind my first emotion: rage.

Everyone else was scared. But Chad wasn't scared. Of course not. He looked supremely confident, arrogant, like he had an ace up his sleeve.

"LET HER GO!" I didn't bother lowering my voice, even though I was only a few feet away. I was hoping for attention, hoping that would make him drop it, hoping he wouldn't want a scene. But not Chad.

"Why should I? And what's it to you, freak?"

"That's Mr. Freak to you," I said quietly as I helped Kristie off the ground. "Are you OK?"

She nodded, tears starting to run down her cheeks. I brushed them away with my huge thumbs and squeezed her shoulders lightly. I moved in front of her to stand between her and Chad, pushing her lightly behind me. Then I turned to Sharon.

"How about you?" She nodded, looking a little calmer even though Chad's hands were still all over her.

"I'm OK," she said a little breathlessly, her voice quavering.

"Buzz off, pal, I'm busy," Chad said, pulling Sharon closer to him. "Why don't you go find a preschooler to scare?"

"Let go of my friend and I'll go away," I said. "I won't even hurt you."

Chad laughed derisively. "You think I'm afraid of you? Freak?"

"Shut up, you moron," Kristie said, stepping forward and backhanding him across the face.

I saw Chad raising his hand and heard him say, "You hit me, you bi—"

...that word, making her cower every time it was shouted at her, every time it was spat at her...

...a voice screaming it at the woman on the floor...

Everything after that happened in an icy blue haze. My anger was cold, freezing. And I was seeing everything very clearly. It didn't look like slow motion, with everyone moving slower than me. Rather, it looked like everyone was moving regular speed, but I was moving much faster.

As Chad swung his hand forward to slap Kristie, I shot my hand up and grabbed his wrist, smiling at the flat smacking sound that filled the night air and the wince it elicited from Chad. I shook my head slowly and squeezed his wrist, gently grinding his bones against each other. He never got the rest of the word out.

"Don't you dare raise a hand to my friend," I said with anger that was lethal, my voice cold as an arctic blast. I could see the pain in his face, but there was rage, too. Anger at being thwarted and denied something he wanted. He looked like a petulant child. "And let my other friend go."

"No," he yelled back. I put my other hand on his shoulder, pressing my thumb into his clavicle.

"If you don't let her go, I'll break your wrist," I said, squeezing harder on his hand and twisting it as I did, "and your collar bone."

I pressed my thumb harder and squeezed his shoulder more. I could feel his clavicle start to give as he groaned involuntarily, his knees buckling a little. As his arm weakened from the pressure, Sharon was able to wriggle free.

He tried to move to get her, but I quickly moved my hands to the front of his jacket, making them into fists as I grabbed double handfuls of leather and picked him up off the ground. I shook him like a doll a few times, and then threw him against the plate glass window of Cold Stone Creamery. The gigantic glass sheet cracked, sending patrons inside scurrying away from the window. Chad was pinned helplessly between the cracked glass and both of my fists. Good thing my fists were filled with his jacket – otherwise, they'd be busy pounding his face.

He looked down at me, loathing me. He relaxed. "Fine."

"Good. Now apologize," I said, letting him go and crossing my arms in front of my chest, realizing how large it made me look. But of course it didn't matter to Chad. Not Chad.

He spit in my face. And the blue haze darkened to near black as I shot my left arm out and grabbed the front of his jacket, lifting him off the ground again—with one arm this time—so I could see him eye to eye. There were gasps in the small crowd. I ripped off a small part of his t-shirt and wiped the spit off my face.

"Ted," I heard Tessie's voice say quietly through the haze.

"I should put you out of our misery now," I growled. "But I'll settle for a truce." I continued to hold him off the ground.

"Put me down first," he said in a small voice.

"Fine," I said, dropping him to his feet. He stumbled and fell to the ground. So I picked him up and set him on his feet. Not very gently. "Now, I want you to stay away from these three young women and Val as well. I'm sure you know who she is."

"Yeah, she's that n—"

I shot my hand out and covered his mouth with my hand, feeling his lips mash against his teeth as I pinned his head between the window and my hand. My hand was large enough that I could have covered his whole face.

"You watch your mouth," I said, sticking the index finger of my other hand in his face. "Finish that sentence and I rip your face off, got it?"

He shook his head angrily, humiliated.

"I want you to stay away from these young women. In fact, I want you to stay away from any young woman who isn't welcoming your advances. Which would be *all* women, in my book. Got it?" I removed my hand from his face so he could talk. Blood was trickling down his face from his split lips.

"And what if I don't?" His voice was shaking, but I could see the defiance. And it made me furious.

"Then imagine this is you," I shouted in his face as he cowered back.

I turned on my heel, walked toward a parking meter, and punched it as hard as I could. It exploded in a shower of change as the housing cracked open and the pole supporting it bent. Change was still spilling into the street as I walked over to a park bench that was bolted to the sidewalk. I kicked the shattered remains of the parking meter as I went, embedding its shattered remains in the trunk of a large nearby tree.

I stood behind the park bench, lifted my foot, and stomped it first through the back, then through the seat, dead center, all in one motion. The bench cracked into two pieces, the wood burst into splinters. There were some shrieks from the small crowd this time and some people quickly walked away. I grabbed one of the metal side supports and pulled it out of the sidewalk, snapping off the anchors that bolted it to the concrete. I held it in my hand, turning back to Chad, then slammed it down into the sidewalk, splitting the slab of concrete I was standing on and embedding the support in the slab. I brushed off my hands and walked up to him as close as I could without touching him, towering over him. I could see the concern in his eyes now, but it wasn't quite fear.

"Like I said, what if I don't?"

It came out as a whisper and I knew it was false bravery. But my rage finally broke, like a wave over a small iceberg in the North Atlantic. I threw my arm out and hammered him in the chest with the heel of my hand. He flew straight back into the plate glass, leaving his feet and creating more spider web cracks in the glass. I pulled my fist back, grabbed his jacket again, and yanked him forward as I drove my fist forward.

And I stopped my fist an inch from his face.

"OK, OK, you win, you win!" He was cowering now, flinching away from me. "I'll leave them alone! I won't bother them."

"And others?"

"OK, OK, I said you win, all right, what do you want?"

"Fine," I said, letting go. I watched him crumple and cower. Disgusted, I walked into the store and up to the counter. "Can I speak to the manager?"

A scared-looking kid came to the counter and said, "Um, I guess that's me. Look, I don't want any more trouble." His voice was shaking and he was obviously thinking that tonight, he wasn't being paid enough to be shift manager.

I nodded, grabbing a napkin from the dispenser and a pen off the counter. "I'm sorry about the damage. Have the owner call me at this number and I'll arrange for the window to be replaced."

"Oh, OK," the guy said. "Sure, no problem."

"Any idea who I'd contact about the parking meter and the bench?"

"P-probably the city," the guy stammered. "There's a parks and rec office, try there."

"Thanks. Sorry for the altercation. I lost my temper," I muttered, walking away. I could see patrons shrinking away, some using the side exit to get out of the building, away from me. Crap.

I walked out the door and heard Kristie yell, "Ted, look out!" just as something hard and metal hit me in the face. I turned, confused, I knew who it was, but had no idea what had been used. Not that it hurt – but it was harder than a fist. Then I saw what it was: Chad had sucker-punched me with a trashcan lid.

"Idiot," I said, tearing the lid out of his hand and folding it in half again and again, crushing it into a small metal ball. As I did it, he stared, stupefied, but then his senses returned. He turned to run but I grabbed the back of his jacket and pulled him back to me. "So I guess we'll do this the hard way."

I pushed him away and said, "Hit me."

He raised his fists and stared at me.

"HIT ME, YOU COWARD! YOU CAN RAISE YOUR HAND TO A DEFENSELESS WOMAN HALF YOUR SIZE, BUT NOT ME?" I screamed at him, my voice tearing at my already broken throat. I sounded like an inhuman beast trying to imitate human speech. "HIT ME!" I roared so loudly that I could hear the eerie quiet in the street immediately afterward.

Chad pulled his fist back and rammed it forward, punching me in the face. I barely moved. He shook his hand and looked like he was in pain.

"Again," I said, stepping toward him. He hit me again, with the same result, except that he was shaking his hand even more.

"OK, stop," he said. "You win again."

"No. You wanted this. Remember? You wanted to hit me. Hit me." I glanced over at Sharon and Kristie; they were holding each other, frightened, crying a little. Tessie was standing a few feet away, paralyzed. She was in shock, staring at me with her mouth open. Her eyes had a glassy, disconnected look that I didn't like.

I didn't want them to see this. I didn't *want* this. But he caused it; he set it in motion. Chad. He placed the order, I was just delivering. I tore my eyes away from them and focused my attention – and rage – on Chad.

"HIT ME!" I screamed again, even louder than before, shaking with the effort.

Chad launched his fist forward and I moved into his fist, driving my forehead into his fist. He shrieked as I heard the bones in his hand crack.

"That looked like it hurt," I said, chuckling a little.

I felt a little demented, like my thoughts were spiraling out of my control. Violent images flashed through my head, showing dozens of ways for Chad to die. And some part of me took great satisfaction in those images, enjoying them with maniacal glee. I tried to calm myself a little, because I could see numerous ways that this night could end badly for Chad – and put me in a prison cell.

So I squared my shoulders and set my jaw. "My turn now," I growled through clenched teeth.

I punched him in the face and he started to fall to the ground. Before he could, I caught him and hit him in the jaw with my forearm, spinning his head around. I caught him before he could fall again, driving my fist into his gut. He sputtered for air as he collapsed to the ground.

"Done?" I asked. Dazed and in obvious pain, he nodded, looking beat, covered in blood. I felt sick, debasing him like that. But he…

…shouting that word at her over and over…

…the woman screaming and bleeding…

…the child in the corner…

…scared and crying…

Those images again, sparking my anger, feeding it. I wanted to hit him again. And again. Until his face was no longer recognizable, until it was a bloody mess of pulp.

And I wondered what was happening to me. The anger felt comforting and so…right. Like I should always feel angry, like it was what I *was*. Fighting against it sometimes felt like fighting against my very nature. Fighting it only made me more angry, whereas letting the anger have full reign made me feel…not happy, but maybe satisfied. Fulfilled.

I tried to clear my head and forget what I wanted to do to Chad. "Good," I said, walking away, "I'm done, too."

I walked toward Kristie and Sharon. I made an effort to lower my voice, to soften it a little. "I'm sorry. I lost my temper. Are you OK?"

They nodded, Sharon crying quietly. I put my hand on her shoulder and said, "It's over. You don't have to be afraid of me."

"I'm not," she said, looking at me with surprise. She smiled a little and laughed weakly. "I'm only cuh-crying because you didn't break his f-f-face."

I chuckled softly and shook my head. "You're wrong. I think I may have fractured his cheekbone and his jaw. Maybe a few ribs."

"He still got off easy. He's lucky I'm not your size," she said. "Thanks."

I only nodded, not trusting myself to answer.

I looked at Tessie, who was staring at me. I couldn't read her face, but I could see that she wasn't just scared; she was terrified. Just like I thought she'd be. She wasn't disgusted by me, which was very surprising. I would have thought the gratuitous show of violence and anger would have been enough to sicken her. Apparently, she was stronger than I gave her credit. But she did look as if she'd never seen me—or anything like me—before in her life.

"If you want to go home, I'll understand," I said quietly, knowing that I'd probably blown any chance I'd have with her. "I can walk; it's not that far. I can—"

She shook her head. "No way, you're not getting off that easily. You promised me a chick flick," she said, her voice shaking slightly, a little higher pitched than usual. She slid her hand into mine. I could feel her trembling, but her grasp wasn't tentative at all. She squeezed my hand and held on tightly, as if she never meant to let go. Or as though she could keep my hand from wreaking any more havoc that night. "And that's what we're going to see."

I looked around for Chad, but all I could see was his back as he brokenly trotted back to his car. "Think we should wait for the police?" I was looking around at the dispersing crowd, who seemed to be eyeing me warily.

"No sweat," the Cold Stone manager said, standing in the open doorway and sounding a little more composed. He watched as Chad ran off, hooking his thumb. "Chad is a regular and he's a pain. He's usually doing that at least once a weekend. When the cops show up, I'll tell them he finally got what's coming to him. And I'll tell him the damages are being paid for, so there's no need to file a report. I'd watch your back, though. Chad is sneaky and he doesn't know when to quit. Plus, do you know who his uncle is?"

I shook my head. "Should I?" I asked. I could see Kristie and Tessie getting a little anxious, exchanging uncomfortable glances.

"I'd be really careful. His uncle is Donnie Lawson," the guy said, dropping his voice a little and stepping a little closer. "You don't want a visit from Uncle Donnie."

Sharon gasped. "Donnie is Chad's uncle?"

The manager nodded, but seemed to shrug it off, looking me up and down. "Although, what am I saying? I think you can handle yourself."

Chick Flick

We walked to the movie theater in awkward silence. Tessie was holding onto my hand, nearly dragging me as quickly as she could toward the theater. Kristie and Sharon walked close to me, too, glancing at me anxiously.

"Guys," I said quietly. "I'm not going to explode."

Sharon and Kristie smiled a little, but still looked frightened. I stopped walking and Tessie nearly panicked, trying to yank me forward. "Relax," I said, pulling her back. "I'm not going to do anything. I'm sorry I upset all of you. You don't have to be afraid, I'm not going to hurt you. I got it out of my system and I promise I'll be on my best behavior from now on."

Kristie laughed nervously and Sharon covered her mouth to hide her smile. "It's not you," Kristie said. "Chad's behavior was getting worse and worse as we got closer to the end of the school year. But the guy at Cold Stone Creamery is right – Chad isn't going away."

"And I'm not afraid of you," Sharon said quietly, dropping her hand from her mouth to expose a light smile. "You just scared me a little, that's all. I've never seen *anyone* so angry. It's like you were coming unglued right in front of us."

Her fading smile disappeared as her forehead creased as she frowned. She started to walk slowly again, but stared at the concrete as if she were in deep thought. Her frown never left her face as she continued talking.

"It was like you were going insane, really losing your mind. I thought you were going to literally kill him, right in front of us…" Her voice faltered a little and she hitched in a breath.

I reached my free hand over and put it on her shoulder. She looked up and put her hand on top of mine. I could feel her trembling.

"It's OK," I said quietly, pulling her closer as she started to cry. She buried her head in my midsection and cried quietly.

"It's OK, Sharon," Tessie said, dropping my hand and putting her arm around Sharon's shoulders. Kristie rubbed Sharon's back softly, moving in closer. I put my now free hand gently on the back of Sharon's neck and I could feel her muscles relax.

"Your hand is like a cool compress," she said as she chuckled weakly.

"Is this a free love-in, or are you charging a fee?" I heard a husky voice calling across the street.

"Hey Val," I called back, smiling at her with as much normalcy as I could muster.

"What's up, Gigantor? I could see you—" She slowed a little when she saw Sharon standing in the middle of our little group, trying to collect herself. "What's wrong with Sharon?" she asked as she started running across the street, her boots clicking loudly on the pavement.

Sharon laughed a little, her voice shaking. "I'm fine, I'm fine," she said, sniffing. "Look, I got your shirt all wet!"

"Don't worry about it. If we really have to go see a chick flick, I'll probably be crying on it anyway," I said.

"You're a sap for them too?"

"No, I'd be crying because I have to watch it," I said in a croaky whisper.

"All right, what happened? And don't tell me 'nothing', because Sharon's crying, the two of you look white as ghosts, and Gigantor looks like he wants to break a whole *warehouse* full of deck furniture," Val said, pulling Sharon toward her and into a hug.

"We ran into Chad," I said, clenching my fists tightly. I heard my knuckles popping. Apparently, everyone else could, too, because they jumped a little and looked down at my fists. All except Val.

"What did that piece of trash do to you, Honey?" Val said quietly, holding Sharon at arm's length to look at her. "Did he hurt you?" Val glanced over at me with a critical eye. I couldn't tell if she was trying to read my emotions or trying to judge how little she should believe Sharon's explanation.

"He didn't get the chance," Kristie said. "We went into Cold Stone Creamery and he started in on us. We turned to leave and he grabbed Sharon and wouldn't let go. Thankfully, Ted was with us."

"You should have seen him, Val," Sharon said quietly, peeking at me from under her bangs with something like reverence. "It was a little scary. I think he broke Chad's hand."

"And the window in front of Cold Stone Creamery, a trashcan lid, a parking meter, and a bench," Tessie said, punching me in the shoulder. "It will probably cost Devin about two grand to pay for all the damage."

"How did you break a parking meter?" Val asked, a confused look on her face.

"He *punched* it," Kristie said.

"You *punched* it?" Val shook her head a little and chuckled. "For real?"

"No, you should have seen him Val," Kristie said. "He was…I don't know…"

"Demented? Insane? Unhinged?" I suggested each adjective, trying to make light of the situation.

"I think unhinged does it," Kristie said honestly.

"Wish I would have been there," she growled. "Ted would have had to hold me back from that piece of filth. You're going to have to put me on speed dial, Tedster, 'cause I don't want to miss the next time."

"Deal," I said.

"OK, enough excitement for one night – you promised me a chick flick," Tessie said, wrapping her hands around one of mine and pulling it. The trembling was almost gone. Almost.

"Getting awfully cozy, are we?" Val raised her eyebrows at our hand-holding. "Miss one itty bitty get-together and look what happens – I fall eons behind in relationship news."

"Shut up, Val," Tessie said, blushing and giggling.

"Look at you, acting like a little schoolgirl," Val said, bumping Tessie with her hip and shaking her head. "So what are we going to see?"

"Tessie said a chick flick," I answered, wincing.

"Ouch," Val said. "Well, I wanted to see the HorrorFest feature, but it doesn't sound like I'll have any company."

"Oh, fine," Tessie said. "I don't feel like splitting up the group again. Do you girls think you could stand a horror show?"

"Yeah, we'll just talk through the whole thing," Sharon said, laughing shakily. "Besides, the special effects are usually hilarious. I mean, how many different ways can people to be butchered with a chainsaw?"

I tried to pay for Tessie's ticket, but she firmly refused, buying mine instead. So I settled for buying popcorn and sodas. I was standing in line, ignoring the stares from the counter servers and the people waiting in line. I was also wondering how many of them might have seen my little performance earlier. I sighed and Val showed up.

"What are you folks staring at? Haven't you seen a giant before?"

"Val," I said, laughing. "Stop."

"He's big, he's gray, and he's got a bunch of scars. Big deal. Didn't your mothers ever tell you staring isn't polite?"

"You're a piece of work, you know that?" I smiled at her and patted her gently on the shoulder, thankful she said something before I did.

Val batted her eyelashes and rested her chin in her hands in a coquettish way. "You say the cutest things. Shame Tessie snatched you up when she did." She tried to bump my hip with her hip, but since she was quite a bit shorter, she got me in the thigh instead and was immediately sorry. "You are made of steel! That hurt! What do you do, live on a Stairmaster?"

I snickered and shook my head. "No, but I do lift a little."

"And by 'a little', do you mean thousand pound squat thrusts?"

"Close," I said.

"Uh-huh," she said, then lowered her voice a little. "Tessie told me Devin has you on some sort of super health cocktail. Any chance I could get in on the trial? My thighs and buns are killing me. I mean, if they get any bigger, they'll need their own zip code!"

"No chance," I said, smiling. "It's only in an experimental phase. Besides, why mess with perfection?"

"Aw," she said, batting her eyelashes again. "Don't you say the sweetest thangs?"

We sat near the back so we wouldn't disturb anyone, but there weren't many in the theater – almost everyone there seemed more interested in talking than watching the movie, anyway.

I could hear Sharon and Kristie whispering behind us – Tessie, Val and I sat in front of them, picking apart the movie and the effects. It was pretty awful. Thankfully, it was a short one and no one felt like staying for the next one.

"I have to admit, I'm disappointed," Val said. "The body count was way lower in the sequel. Nothing beats the original."

"Yuck, I don't know how you watch that stuff," Tessie said. "It's disgusting."

"I don't know," I said. "It's better than the one you wanted to see. Sitting through a soppy, messy tear fest would probably have me retching in the aisles." She aimed a slap at me and I dodged it. She aimed another and I sidestepped.

"OK, it's on," she said, lunging after me. I backed away and quickly ducked out the side door, trying to run while laughing. She easily caught me, since I'm not that light on my feet – and she runs almost every day. "Say uncle," she said, trying to twist my arm.

"Oh please, the pain," I said, laughing again. She let me go and started to walk away, but I quickly – and easily – scooped her off the ground and into my arms.

"Oh," she squeaked. "Hey. Hi." She was a little breathless.

"Aw, look what we walked in on," Kristie said as she came out of the theater.

"Yikes. Ain't puppy love grand," Sharon said, smiling.

"Hmm," Val mused. "Except it's more like cub love: he's more bear than dog."

Ride Home

Val got a ride with us, so we dropped her off first. Then Kristie, then Sharon. I walked all of them to the door, though, feeling a little protective of them. Val couldn't stop laughing, even when her five-year-old niece opened the door and shrieked when she saw me. Val called her out to the porch so she could see me better in the light, then told her to apologize to me. I picked her up so she could touch the porch ceiling and she giggled.

"Your hands are cold," she squealed as I set her down.

"Cold hands, warm heart, isn't that what they say, Ted?" Val asked, smiling as I nodded in agreement.

Kristie climbed onto my back, insisting on a piggy-back ride to her doorstep. She then insisted on me proving that I could rip the arms on my shirt. So I held up my arms and flexed my biceps. The stitching on the sleeves of my shirt didn't stand a chance. The stitching slowly started to tear, then finally let go, shredding the fabric as they gave way. She felt my biceps, then fanned herself melodramatically and pretended to swoon.

"Goodnight, Mr. Universe," she called out as she walked through her front door.

Sharon, though, was a lot more subdued. "Thanks," she said. "For helping me tonight, I mean."

"Hey, what are friends for?" I smiled and shrugged.

"Bend down for a second," she said, smiling. Puzzled, I did as she said and she put her hands lightly on my shoulders and kissed my cheek. "Tell Tessie I said she has to do one better than me," she said, winking at me.

As I wedged myself back into Tessie's car, she asked, "OK, what was that all about?"

"Sharon said you have to do one better than she did," I said, laughing. "Not sure what she meant."

"I know you're big and strong, and that you're supposed to be a tough guy. But even for the big guy stereotype, you're really thick," she said, shaking her head, pulling into traffic and making her way slowly through the city streets.

"Only when I want to be," I said quietly.

She started laughing and I joined in. She took her eyes off the road, reached over, and pulled my hand over to her. "I like being near you," she said, looking back at the road. "God, I sound like a middle schooler."

"I think it's cute," I said.

She drove us to her house, then walked me to the back of the house to 'our deck'. "We'll have to try something different," she said. "The night was kind of a bust."

"It wasn't that bad," I said. "I had fun with you guys." I looked out into the dark woods, hands in my pockets, remembering the fight with Chad. I was still angry and now I was getting angrier because Chad was intruding on my time with Tessie. And I couldn't shake the images I saw, which was why I had my hands in my pockets. I didn't want Tessie to see my clenched fists.

Remembering the images, I couldn't shake the woman I had seen, or the degradation she was suffering at the hands of the pathetic tyrant I kept seeing, standing over her. Was that part of my past? I tried to remember the images, tried to capture them so I wouldn't forget what they looked like. They were already fading, blurring at the edges. But the anger remained.

"Something wrong?" Tessie asked. "You look a bit preoccupied."

"I was just thinking about the fight."

"I'm sorry," she said. "I'm glad you helped Kristie and Sharon, though."

"It's not that – I was glad I could help them, too. It was something else. I was seeing…images."

"Images," Tessie repeated.

"Yes…I don't know…memories. It felt like I had seen something like what Chad was doing before," I said, squeezing my head between my hands and bending over to rest my elbows on the deck handrails. "It was so strong, that it was feeding my anger. I was plenty angry to begin with, but those images just fed my rage."

"Are you OK?" Tessie asked, concerned. She put her arm around my shoulder as best as she could, resting her head against my side. Thankful for the human touch, I clumsily lifted my arm and put it on her shoulders, pulling her in closer. I wanted her closer, but at the same time was very conscious of the steps I was taking, conscious I was getting closer to her.

I nodded, then shook my head. "It's so frustrating. It's like there is something right there, so close, but I can't…"

"You think it's a memory," she said quietly, more of a statement than a question.

"I don't know." I sighed, shaking my head. "Oh well, maybe it will come back."

I wasn't sure if I wanted it to. Would I want to know more, based on what little I'd seen? Who would?

"You know, you were a little frightening tonight," she said.

I nodded my head, but couldn't say anything. This was it – she was going to tell me to leave. Get out. Don't come back.

"Ted," she said, pulling my free hand into hers. I looked at her. "Is that the anger you keep talking about? Do you feel like that...a lot?"

I hesitated. Should I tell her the truth, or hedge? I didn't want to push her away, but I couldn't lie to her. By lying, even lying by omission, would put her in danger. It would subject to her to a life of violence. I couldn't do that.

The truth, then, and consequences be damned.

"Yes," I whispered. "Almost every day I feel it. It never goes away. And sometimes the smallest, most insignificant thing will set it off. Like a news story or a magazine article. Criminals—*animals*—hurting and taking away everything that's good. Chad is a prime example."

I paused, focusing on her small, fragile hand encased in my large, nearly-indestructible vice of a hand.

"But sometimes, it's just normal people with normal faults. They may be a little lazy because they're not realizing their full potential. Or I might overhear someone complaining about some everyday, ordinary annoyance. And I'll become enraged because I don't have those things – the things that people complain about day to day won't be a part of my life. I can't control it, the anger. The cold rage."

"What complaints bother you?" she asked, frowning.

"Little things, like a job. Or paying taxes. Juggling a work schedule with a home life."

"Or complaining about finals or homework," Tessie said, smiling guiltily.

I laughed and shook my head. "None of your complaints have bothered me, no."

"Good," she said. "But do you feel like that all the time?"

"Not like you saw me tonight," I said. "That happens more often than I want to admit, but those outbursts only happen once in a while. However, it does seem that every time Devin and I go out into public, something happens that sparks my anger. And I can't control it or predict when it will happen or what will light my fuse. I never know who will be my next target."

I could see her swallowing hard, preparing herself for the next question. "Have you…"

"—hurt anyone else?" I finished her thought. She nodded, looking anxious. "No. Not before Chad. But I trashed a guy's car at a stoplight when I was with Devin once. For staring at me. It was broad daylight and I did thousands of dollars worth of damage to his car."

"But that was a while ago, right?"

"Yes," I said, getting angry again at the memory. "But it happens more often than is convenient. Like tonight at the movies. If Val hadn't said anything to the people staring at me in line, I probably would have said something – or done something."

"I'm sorry," she said. "It's my fault. I put you in that position. We can do other things—"

"No, it's OK," I said. "Like Devin says, I need to get out in the world. I need to be in public. Anyway, enough brooding. I did have a good time tonight."

"Hmm," she said, eyeing me strangely.

"What?"

"Don't you remember?" she said, blushing enough that I could see it in the porch light from the deck.

"Remember what?"

"Come here," she said, turning to face me, beckoning me coyly with her index finger.

Intrigued, I turned and faced her. She raised both of her arms and tried to lock her hands behind my neck. "Little help?"

I smiled, put both hands on her waist, and lifted her gently off the ground so she could lock her hands behind my neck.

"Better," she whispered as she moved her face forward. I pulled her up closer, wrapping my arms around her. "Much better," she said, smiling and kissing me on the lips.

It lasted only a few seconds, but I swear my heart pump stopped. And for a brief couple of moments, I forgot my anger. I forgot about the scars, my voice, the gray skin. The fact that I was still an animated corpse. Fear of the future and what lies ahead. I felt carefree and...alive. For the first time since the accident. And Tessie was responsible for that. She was actually kissing me, ignoring my temperature and the scars on my lips, the leathery feel of my skin.

She broke the kiss and looked at me intently, smiling. She rested her forehead against mine and sighed.

"Wow," I said, putting her back down.

"Was that better than Sharon's?"

"No contest. A peck on the cheek compared to that? I'll have to thank Sharon for upping the ante."

"Dog," Tessie said, swatting me and turning a deeper shade of deep red.

"Seriously, though," I said, taking her hand this time. "I had a good time. No, scratch that – a *great* time."

She smiled back and said, "Me, too."

We looked at each other, not feeling awkward at the silence.

"Well," I said, "I'd better go. Devin will want to hear about my first...date. Maybe I'll edit it a bit."

"Right, like you've never been on a date before."

"I haven't. Well, at least not that I can remember."

Tessie looked at me, understanding lighting up her face. "So, I'm your first date?"

"I know you'll find it shocking, but I don't have a very full social calendar," I said, smiling.

Tessie grinned from ear to ear. "Wow, now I do feel honored."

"And I'll tell you something else," I said, lowering my voice a little, stepping closer to her and putting my hands on her shoulders. "For a few moments tonight, I forgot all of my problems and worries. And just now, when you were one-upping Sharon?"

"Once again, you are a dog," she said, stepping closer and reaching up to rest her hands on my shoulders. "You were saying?"

"Just now, I felt…normal," I said, smiling.

"You *are* normal," she said quietly, stepping even closer and resting her head on my chest, laughing. "Your heart is just a little louder than most people's."

I laughed and pulled back. She stifled a yawn and said, "I better get inside. My mother will be wondering where I am."

"Good night," I said and started walking toward the path, into the dark woods, then stopped. I turned around to look at her, standing under the bright white deck lights, and said, "You want to have dinner some night? Just the two of us? I won't eat, but you can get something expensive, plus desert. And it would give the girls something to talk about."

"It's a date," she said, turning to go inside. She looked over her shoulder and said, "Goodnight, Ted."

I couldn't stop smiling, even after I went to bed.

Rundown and Measurements

"Six feet, seven inches. And 260 pounds. So the height is starting to taper off, but the weight continues," Devin said, shaking his head.

"Maybe I'm growing into my height," I said.

"Hmm."

"Devin," I said tentatively, as he continued with his measurements, frowning. "I asked Tessie to dinner."

He abruptly stopped what he was doing and looked up in shock. His face immediately broke into a smile as he put down his pad and pen. He sat on the stool and motioned for me to sit in a chair. "And?"

"I was surprised she said yes. Even after my little…display with Chad," I said, a little chagrinned.

Devin frowned a little. The bill didn't concern him (it was, as Tessie suspected, a little over two grand); but my actions did. He seemed to think that it might be his miracle cure that was causing the anger and the violent outbursts. He pleaded with me to exercise a little more self control. But I didn't promise anything.

"So you asked her to dinner," Devin prodded, interrupting my thoughts as his face quickly switched from a frown back to a smile again.

"Well, I don't know what to do," I said, flopping into the chair—Devin made sure to buy really sturdy furniture, so when I flopped I wouldn't break anything. "I don't know where to take her, what to wear, how to act, what to order—"

"Slow down, my dear boy, slow down," Devin said, chuckling. He rolled the stool closer to me and put a hand on my knee. "One thing at a time! Don't worry about what to order – she'll figure that out on her own and order it herself! As to what to wear, that depends on where you pick, but I'd go with a green shirt. I think Tessie favors that color on you." He winked.

"And where to go?"

"That's a tough one, I'll admit," Devin said, sitting and folding his arms. He looked up at the ceiling in the lab. "Let me see, let me see. Are you planning to make it the end of a day-long activity, or just a quick bite to eat?"

"Ahh. I hadn't thought about it," I admitted.

"OK, well decide if you want to spend the day with her and cap it off with dinner, or if you want it to be a dinner-only event."

"Well, there are some shops and museums in the city or we could go to Raleigh," I admitted. "But I hate crowds. And they're not particularly fond of me, either. I guess we could go to the shore—Kure Beach isn't that crowded. Make it a late afternoon stroll on the pier and stop for dinner somewhere nearby. Something informal."

"Good choice," Devin said, nodding. "Tessie doesn't strike me as the type to enjoy fancy dress and fine dining."

"You have no idea," I said, shaking my head.

"So go with that – you know her tastes much better than I do. Trust your instincts," he said, winking.

"I know, it's just…a little stressful. I don't remember if I've ever done this before. It's tough to anticipate what will happen or what will make her happiest," I admitted.

"Son," Devin said, chuckling softly, "men have been struggling with that for years. And most of us haven't quite figured it all out. That's part of the dance, by the way. But I'm sure Tessie will love whatever you plan – especially since she'll be with you. That's all she really wants, by the way."

"You and Lilly have been plotting again," I accused, raising an eyebrow and looking at him critically.

"I haven't the slightest idea what you're talking about," Devin said, going back to his notes with a smile on his face.

"Right," I retorted, standing back up. "Are we done?"

"With measurements, yes. With your development," Devin began, shrugging. "I must admit, I'm at a loss for theories at this point. I thought taking you off the medication would correct the issue, but it hasn't. Which means there must be some other reason or latency that's being picked up just now due to your change in...ah...aspect, we'll call it."

"So I might continue growing?" I looked at myself in the mirror and shrugged my massive shoulders. "Well, at least I don't have to worry about protecting myself."

"Speaking of which, do you feel OK? I know you're nearly invincible, but it doesn't mean you won't ever get hurt or sick."

"No," I said. "No injuries and I'm not feeling sick. I know it might seem a little incredible, even to you. But nothing that happened the night I was out even remotely hurt me. But there was something else."

"Yes?"

Before I answered, I thought carefully. I could still remember what I saw, but they were only fleeting images. I walked over to the sliding door and looked out into the back yard.

"I saw some...things...before and during the fight. They were images flashing in my head."

"Do you remember what they were?" Devin asked, walking over next to me.

"Yes. There was a woman. She was cowering on the floor. Covered in blood, crying. A man had hit her and knocked her to the ground and he was cursing at her. He was screaming and yelling."

"Do you think it's a part of your life? Memories, perhaps?"

"I can't tell," I said. "I think so. It seemed too real to be a TV show or a movie that I might have seen. But I can't be sure. And..."

"Yes?"

"There was a child, too. It might have been me. It's just so frustrating."

"Ted." Devin put his hand on my shoulder, turning me toward him. His eyes were sad, concerned. "The woman."

"Do I think it was my mother? I can't tell. The man yelling could have been my father, but I don't know. I just don't know."

Devin nodded and opened his mouth to speak. He closed it, looking very uncomfortable. "You know I think of you as a son." He was barely whispering.

"I know," I said. "I'm grateful for what you've done for me."

"If I can help in any way, I will. Even if it means...losing you," Devin said, trailing off, his eyes looking moist all of a sudden.

I frowned. "How would you lose me?"

"If you found your family. I know you'd want to—"

"Stay with you," I finished.

Devin looked shocked. "But surely you'd want to see them, to stay with them?"

"See them, maybe," I said. "Stay with them, no. You said I'm like a son to you. You're like a father to me. You've given me my life and you know me, how I am now, better than anyone. The person I was before the accident is dead. *You* gave me my life, the life I have now. Besides, if my family is like what I saw in these images..."

"But you should be with your biological family. It's only natural—"

"Nothing is natural about that family," I growled harshly. "If that's what you could even call it. The boy and the woman looked like prisoners held captive by a sadist. Besides, like I said, this is my life now. Leaving you would be like starting all over again. And I can't do it. Once is enough."

Devin nodded sadly, then looked at me for a long time, as if he were going to say something.

"Come on," I said, smiling a little. "I know you want to say something."

"You know, the man may have a mental illness. He may not be able to control his actions, depending on what type of disease he may have."

"That doesn't matter," I said sharply and a little too loudly. "He's a predator. He..." I trailed off, having difficulty expressing myself around the ice blue anger again. I shook my head as I turned away from him and walked slowly toward the staircase to my room. I stopped and turned back to him a little, hesitating.

"If my family is like what I saw in those images, then I think the man in those images needs to be taught a lesson," I said quietly. "Just like Chad."

Dinner

I talked to Tessie the next day, stopping over shortly after lunch. She was sitting on the deck, finishing up a couple of chips that were on her plate, reading a well-worn paperback. I walked quietly across the lawn and up the steps to the deck, leaning down to her shoulder before speaking.

"Anything good?"

"Yikes," Tessie yelled, jumping. "You have to warn a person before sneaking up on them like that!"

"Six-seven, 260, and I sneak up on you?" I asked. "Maybe you need to get your hearing checked!"

"Ha ha, the stealthy giant makes a joke," Tessie said, folding her book. "What's up? Besides your height and weight, that is."

"Ha ha, right back. I came to see if you were doing anything tomorrow," I said casually enough, but my voice betrayed me. I tapered off a little as my nerves started to take hold.

"Oh? And if I'm not?" She was having fun, I could tell.

"I thought we could go to the shore, you know, walk the pier, the shops, have dinner afterwards. A leisurely day."

"Ted Burroughs, are you asking me on a date?" She batted her eyes at me and smiled.

"Yes. Yes I am."

"I can handle that," she said, smiling. "What time?"

"I'll stop by around 10? We can stop to have lunch before we begin our excursions on the pier and the beach." Even though my heart pump was always a steady 45 pumps a minute, I felt like it should have been clipping along at twice that rate.

155

"Sounds good," she said. "Do I need a bathing suit?"

"Only if you want to go in the water," I said. "I have to warn you, though, I don't swim. My density makes me sink."

"You sink?"

I nodded. "I tried to swim once, but couldn't. I'm getting heavier, but it seems like I'm getting denser."

She snorted a little and I raised an eyebrow. "I get it. I'm dense. Funny," I said. "So no swimming for me."

"But you might get wet anyway," she said, smiling deviously.

———

I wandered through the woods to Tessie's house the next day. She was sitting on the deck, an eager look on her face. She grinned at me when I emerged, picking up two or three bags as she stood up.

"Were you planning on spending the night?" I laughed at the spectacle of her carrying what looked like luggage for a week-long stay.

"No, silly, a girl needs things. I'm bringing a change of clothes for after the beach," she answered primly, batting her eyelashes.

"Right," I said, looking at my shorts and sandals. "This is what I'm planning on wearing. I did tell you we were going to the Fish Shack, right? Not a fine-dining experience."

"Don't worry," she answered, laughing. "I didn't bring 'the little black dress' and a pair of stiletto heels."

"Good," I shot back, "because we'd look ridiculous if we were both wearing them."

She snorted laughter, blushing. "I just snorted," she said, mortified.

"Yes, but you did it ever so elegantly."

"So, are we taking the Civic or am I driving one of your toys?"

"I thought we'd take one of mine," I said. "Not Devin's Murcielago, though. Too showy. I thought we'd take the Goat."

She groaned. "But the engine is so loud! Remember the day you started it up in the driveway to show off the new exhaust? You revved the engine a couple of times and that was enough to make my ears ring for about half an hour. For a nearly three-hour drive, that's a bit much. How about a compromise?"

"OK," I said. "Maybe you're right. Shouting at each other over the engine could be a bit tough. We'll be hoarse by the end of the drive. Or you will be, anyway. I'll still sound the way I do now. How about the Silverado? It's comfortable, it's got plenty of storage for your hundreds of bags—"

"I only have three," she said with mock indignation, pouting exaggeratedly.

"Are you pouting? What are you, three years old? I meant for *after* you visit all the shops. You'll probably come home with at least that many."

"OK, deal," she said. "Besides, we can take it down on the beach. Devin still has the permit, right?"

"Just got the renewal last week," I confirmed. "OK. Shall we?"

"Bye Mom!" Tessie called as she lightly ran down the deck stairs. "See you tonight!"

"Have a great time," I heard Lilly call out. "Call me if you get hung up or you're going to be late!"

"OK," she said. In a lower voice, she said, "You'd think that by 20 years old I'd get a little slack."

"She's concerned for your safety," I said. "She's not asking for you to call to get permission."

"Sure, take her side" she said, punching my shoulder. "Oww, stop working out, will you, please? Hurts my arm every time you do a pushup or a pull-up!"

"Only when you hit me," I reminded her. "Let me carry those." I grabbed the bags before she could protest and started into the shadows of the woods. When I noticed she wasn't following, I asked, "Are you coming?"

"The woods are a little creepy. Ever since I was a little kid, I've been spooked by them," she said, shivering.

"But you spend most of your study time in the woods," I said, smiling.

"At the edge of the woods. I don't venture in too far."

"But you walk through them to visit me," I pointed out.

"Usually with someone or I'm meeting you in the middle. Or—and don't laugh—I run through them. Scary things hang out in the woods."

"Scarier than me?" I held out my arms and looked myself up and down.

"Good point," she said, smiling and moving close to me. "Would you think I'm a chicken if I asked you to hold my hand? Protect me from the big scary beasts?"

"You could have just held my hand and I wouldn't have known. Besides, I'm the biggest, scariest beast in these woods. Nothing would dare touch you."

"True. But if I didn't tell you the real reason I wanted to hold your hand, that wouldn't be honest," she said, grabbing my hand. "And I want to be honest with you." She smiled and practically skipped next to me.

Her happiness was infectious and I could feel a smile forming. We walked through the woods in silence and into the back lawn. I could see Devin in the lab and I frowned. He looked up from his bench and smiled, waving at us.

"He must love his work, to be inside on a day like today," Tessie said as she waved.

"I'm his work, so I guess you could say that. It makes me feel a little guilty, sometimes, knowing that I'm the reason I wake him up in the lab in the mornings, still dressed in the clothes he wore the day before."

"I'm sure he doesn't see it that way," Tessie said, looking concerned. "He gets to work at a job he loves and he's doing it for someone he truly cares for."

"I suppose," I said, smiling. But I was uneasy. Devin was spending so much time in the lab, I wondered if he were driven by guilt. He worked tirelessly, but I thought part of it might be because if not for him, I wouldn't have been in a coma or become less than human.

"Hey. No sour faces today," Tessie said, shaking my arm and smiling. "Only a happy day today."

"Deal," I said, opening the door to the garage and waiting for her to walk through.

"Such a gentleman," she said, "I'm impressed! You—" And she gasped. "Wow," she said breathlessly. "I've seen some of the cars, but never...wow."

"Nice, huh," I said, flipping on the lights to the garage. It had the same décor as the lab, with its high ceilings, exposed beams, and bright lighting. The floor was painted a light gray with a special non-slip vinyl coating and had giant chrome floor grates for drainage. It was divided into bays separated by thick wooden beams stacked on top of one another, and each bay held a car or truck. There were overhead systems for washing, waxing, lubrication, oil changes, and just about every other automotive need known (and some I swear that are unknown).

My black 1969 GTO Judge was parked in the first stall as we walked in the door, paint shining and black custom rims gleaming. I sighed as I walked past it. Devin's Murcielago was parked across the garage in the second stall. There were other, less jaw-dropping vehicles, like a Chevy HHR and PT Cruiser parked across from each other. Apparently, when Devin went shopping he couldn't decide which one to get so he made the only logical choice – he got both. The Silverado was parked in the stall closest to the huge garage doors and across the aisle was a 1970 Mini.

"So," she said slowly. "How do you drive all of these with no license? Or am I not supposed to ask that question."

"I'm shocked," I said with a false sense of indignity. "Of course I have a license."

"But how? I mean, you said you had no past."

"Devin managed to get one. He has a lot of contacts and he's very well-thought of in high-ranking government circles. Of course, he only got me one after he'd made me take driver's training, the online test, and about a hundred different other tests, including defensive and offensive driving courses that I took with private security firms."

"Wow. So if we're being chased by a terrorist—"

"We'll be fine. And I can parallel park the truck by reversing, locking the parking brake, and spinning 180 degrees into the spot."

She looked back at the cars and said "Wow" again.

"It's a little showy, but you're one of the few people who've seen the garage," I said, walking toward the truck, a little self-conscious about the number of vehicles in the garage. The price tag on the inventory easily ventured into the millions.

"I'm not much of a car person," Tessie began, "but these look awesome."

"Most of them are Devin's and they never leave the garage. He comes out here once in a while and just sits in the seat. Sometimes he'll hook up the exhaust hoses and turn them on, just to feel the engines working."

She stopped in her tracks. "We're taking *that*?"

"I told you we were taking it. Why?" I looked at the Silverado, wondering what she was getting at. "I mean, sure, it's a little big, but it's a crew cab. And you said you wanted to go shopping, so we needed the space. And you mentioned the dunes, so the four-wheel drive is necessary. It has a small lift kit on it, but it's not that much higher than a stock truck."

"I know, but it's huge! I thought it was a normal pickup! You know, just a bench seat for three, not a passenger cabin with seating for 12."

"Six," I corrected.

"Still, it's enormous! I mean, we could fit Val, Kristie, Sharon, and everything they would want to buy in that thing."

"I doubt we could get everything *you* want to buy, let alone everything—"

"OK, OK, let's go," she said, exasperated. She opened the door to get in and looked like she was trying to scale a mountain.

"Excuse me," I said, putting an arm around her waist and hoisting her up into the cab.

She turned to me, a little flushed. "Muscle man. Get in the truck, daylight's wastin'!"

I gave her a mock salute and marched around to the other side of the truck. I opened the driver's side back door and put her bags in the back, then stepped into the driver's seat, while Tessie snickered into the back of her hand.

"What?"

"You actually had to stoop to get into the truck," she laughed outright.

"Well, yeah," I said, a little uncomfortable. "I'm a growing boy."

"I'm glad you brought that up," she said as I pulled out of the spot. The garage door automatically began to rise as she shook her head. "It's like Wayne Manor more and more."

"Oh, that," I said. "Infrared sensors activate the door when you get close to it."

"Right. Anyway, I wanted to ask you about your growth spurts."

I shrugged my shoulders as I drove slowly down the long driveway to the main road. "Devin still hasn't figured it out. As I mentioned before, it's related to the drugs he was giving me while I was healing. He's altered the medication several times, but I still keep growing. He's even tried an anti-growth version, but that didn't work, either."

"So how big do you think you'll get?"

"I don't know," I said quietly, meandering through the trees and landscaped rock gardens. Tessie whistled softly as I drove past a particularly detailed setup that Louie's guys recently put together: a wagon wheel, a fake cow skull, and an old pitcher pump that constantly ran water into an old-fashioned galvanized tub. The water was used to irrigate some of the nearby plants, but some of it got recycled and ran back into the pitcher pump.

"Does Devin think there will be...you know, any problems?" she asked, the worry evident in her voice.

"Devin is working on a larger heart pump. The one I have is good for certain-sized frames. He thinks there's a chance the pump won't be able to keep up with my growth."

"So...so that does that mean you'll need to have another one put in?" she said quietly. Her voice sounded very small.

"Yes," I said, but smiled. "Don't worry, it's perfectly safe."

"Safe! But how, they have to stop your heart and—"

"No," I said. "Not they. He. Devin."

"I don't understand."

I sighed as I pulled out of our driveway and onto the main road. "You know, you shouldn't worry. Everything is going to be fine. Devin will be doing the operation because it's his equipment. He knows the procedure better than anyone; he's a very skilled surgeon. He did the original surgery."

"By himself?" She was incredulous. "But...how did he get all the equipment? And the blood? And everything else he'd need for that kind of surgery?"

"Like I said, he's very skilled. But he didn't need blood – he used the compounds he was developing as a way to slow my bleeding. It helped, because he was able to complete the operation without needing to do a transfusion. But it had other complications."

Tessie frowned, shaking her head as I guided the truck onto the onramp to 40 East towards the Outer Banks. "Other complications?"

Here we go. I knew the time would come, but I didn't want it to be this day. I was looking forward to this as much as Tessie was. A chance to get out and do normal people stuff. To feel normal, almost human. And this line of conversation would definitely change the outlook of the day.

"I don't want to ruin the day for you," I said, merging into traffic and setting the cruise at 70. "Maybe we should talk about this later."

"I'm glad you're so considerate," she said wryly, "but I think I can handle it."

"I'm not so sure. What if you learned something about me that set me apart?" I said. "Made me different."

She reached over slowly and pulled one of my hands off the steering wheel. "I know you should have these at ten and two, but I want one for a few minutes. Trust me, different isn't bad. That guy that you saved Kristen and Sharon from? Chad? He's not different – he's just like most of the other jerks at college, it seems."

"He's still human," I muttered, squeezing the steering wheel with my other hand.

"No, he's not," she said, tugging on my hand gently. "The term 'human' isn't just a term applied to anyone who walks on two legs and has a heart that pumps blood. It applies to how you act and feel, how you treat other people, and—"

"Stop," I said quietly.

"What? What did I say? Ted, you're the most kind, compassionate, protective giant I know! Just because you're huge doesn't mean—"

"It's not that."

"My comment about a heart," she said, instantly apologetic. "I'm sorry, I wasn't thinking!"

"It's not that," I said, barely whispering.

"What, you think you're not human? Of course you're still human. There are people who have artificial pumps who are just as human—"

"I wasn't talking about the pump," I said, shaking my head. "Maybe we should talk later."

"Ted," she said, turning in her seat to face me. "I like you. You're a nice guy, whether you think so or not. You're the most *human* human I know!"

"But I'm not. I'm not human. Not in the strictest sense of the word, at least."

I checked my mirrors and moved back into the slow lane, backing the speed down to 65 and wondering how I should continue the conversation.

"You lost me," she said. "If we're not talking about the pump, what are we talking about?"

Sighing, I said, "You said a human is anyone whose heart pumps blood. And you would say that 'human' would also include people who had pumps instead of hearts."

"Right."

"What about people who don't have blood?" I stared at the road ahead, afraid to look over at her.

Silence filled the truck as we drove on.

"Say that again?" she asked slowly.

"I said, 'what about people who don't have blood.'"

"What do you mean?" she asked, giggling nervously. "Everyone has blood." I glanced over at her nervously. "Don't they?"

"Devin's drugs did something to me. I'm sorry I didn't tell you before, but I could never find the right time. And I was afraid to. The compounds changed my blood to something...else," I said, talking in a rush. "When he performed the operation to replace my heart, he used a synthetic compound to slow the bleeding. His hope was that he wouldn't need to do transfusions and he could only focus on removing my heart and adding the pump. But he wasn't betting on what happened after that."

"Wait, are you saying you don't have blood flowing through your veins?" She looked at me incredulously.

"No. I don't have blood flowing through my veins."

"How is that possible? It's not possible." She blinked, squeezing my hand and pulling it closer to her. "You're joking, right?"

"No, I'm not. The compound Devin used still distributes oxygen, but only to prevent the fluid from coagulating. I don't know how it works – Devin tried to explain it to me, but I got lost in an explanation that sounded to me like a bunch of multi-syllabic nonsense. Basically, I can survive without oxygen, but I still need it to keep things moving and so my fluid doesn't go…stagnant."

"So what is this fluid you keep talking about?" she said, turning sideways a little and putting her hand on my shoulder.

"The compound replaced my blood with…something else. I have to take daily injections to keep the supply at a constant level and to monitor it. Devin thinks I could go as long as a week or more without an injection. Perhaps a couple of months at the longest. But since my body doesn't replace any of what flows through my veins, Devin thinks I need to be careful."

"So, you have something like blood, but not blood?" Tessie asked. She shook her head. "It's a little too complex to understand, but I've never heard of that before."

"Because it never existed until now," I said quietly.

"But what about your organs? I only took basic bio, but even with that I know your blood does a lot of things other than provide oxygen," she said, real concern edging into her voice.

I sighed. "Are you sure you want to have this conversation?" I checked the road signs and saw we were still at least an hour away from the shore.

"Yes, more than anything. If you wanted to stop somewhere right now, that would be fine with me," she said.

I smiled weakly, "I made reservations and I hate to break them."

She laughed a little, then looked seriously at me. "But you're changing the subject."

"OK, here it goes: I'm not really alive."

She laughed, throwing her head back, and I had to smile. Even though it was short-lived, it was good to hear her laugh like that.

"I'm serious," I said, turning a somber look in her direction. "How do you define alive?"

"OK, a pulse," she said. "Which you have."

"OK, so a water pump is alive?"

"Technicality."

"OK," I said, growing a little frustrated. She was willing to overlook my non-human qualities. For some reason, that annoyed me. "What would you say if I told you my body temperature is normally 70 degrees?"

"I'd say you were lying," she said, looking at me as if she were the butt of a joke. It was her turn to start getting frustrated. I knew she had a temper – nowhere near like mine, but based on some of the stories I'd heard from Lilly, it was bad enough.

"And what if I told you my kidneys don't function. Or my pancreas. Or my liver. My stomach, intestines, lungs, none of them. The pump circulates a compound that repairs my body and keeps it from rotting. It keeps my brain active, delivering electrical currents to keep me going. I can see, I can talk, I can move, I can think.

"But my body processes are nowhere near human. I can pull air into my lungs and I appear to breathe, but I don't have to. I don't have any normal, human bodily functions."

I didn't look at her as I continued to drive. I didn't dare. After a few minutes of silence, I glanced over at her and she was staring at me. She yanked her hands back and said, "And I thought you were different."

Stung, I glanced over at her and asked, "What do you mean? I don't know how much more different I could get!"

"You're making up some story about how you're non-human! That this accident turned you into a modern-day Frankenstein's monster. Is that supposed to drive me away? Am I getting too close to you? Smothering you with my neediness?"

"Smothering me with—where did that come from?"

"I've heard that a lot," she said angrily. "I just didn't think I'd ever hear it from you."

"You didn't," I said. "I never said that and I never would. If anything, I'd be concerned the opposite were the case."

"Then why are you lying to me?" she asked, her voice rising with each sentence she said. "*Are* you lying to me?"

"No! Everything I said is true!"

"Fine. Prove it," she said, almost yelling.

"How do you want me to prove it?"

"Take your temperature," she said.

"I don't have a thermometer, how am I supposed to—"

"Get off at the next exit and get one," she snapped, folding her arms.

"Fine," I said, "but promise me you won't run off when I go in?"

"Fine," she answered curtly.

Checking the signs, I took the next exit. Good – I saw a sign for Wal-Mart. I turned right to head toward the store, pulling into the parking lot. I turned off the truck, rolling down the windows before I did. I turned to her and could see she was furious.

"I'm sorry you feel the way you do. But you're wrong – I'm nothing like the other college guys. On any level. I just hope the proof doesn't scare you away," I said, getting out of the truck.

I walked into the store, trying to ignore the stares and whispers. "What do you think is wrong with him?" or "You'd think he'd stay home!" After one group of teen guys followed me around the store, I grabbed a metal travel mug off a shelf and turned abruptly around. I squeezed it as hard as I could, making it a misshapen blob and handing it to one of the guys.

"Keep following me, and I'll twist you into a pretzel," I growled at them. They backed away and scattered.

I wandered through the store, grabbing a thermometer off a shelf. I sat there looking at it. It seemed like a simple test. Too simple. I needed something more. So I grabbed a pack of sewing needles off another shelf as I wandered through the store, staring people down as I went – even employees.

I walked over to the housewares section and grabbed a steak knife. I then walked to the home and garden section. After looking over the pesticides, I tucked a box of rat poison under my arm and looped my pinky through the handle of a bottle of pesticide. Looking at the stuff, I decided to go to the grocery section and buy a container of Drano. Devin wasn't going to be happy later, but I was desperate. I paid for the stuff and walked out the door.

I got back to the truck and Tessie was still fuming, not looking at me. I was starting to get angry. I got into the truck and pulled to the back of the parking lot, past a few trailers, to relative privacy. I ripped open the thermometer.

"Do you want to try it first?" I asked sarcastically. "Or do you trust the calibration?"

"Just take it so we can turn around and go home," she lashed back.

I put the thermometer in my mouth and set my stopwatch. After a full minute, I pulled it out and frowned at it.

"It's high."

"Like what, 98.6," she said curtly.

"No. Like 75." I handed her the thermometer. She stared at it for a few seconds, then looked at me. Confused.

"Do it again," she ordered, handing it back.

So I reset it and took it again. Seventy-two. I must be calming down.

"It's still high, but 70 is about right. During the winter, it can get as low as 50."

She looked at the thermometer and me. "It's a trick. You're doing something to it," she said, tossing it back to me.

"I thought you might say that," I said, pulling the pack of needles out of the back and holding it up. I pulled one out and handed it to her. "Prick my finger."

"What?" she asked, genuinely confused, her anger forgotten.

"Prick my finger," I said, holding out the needle.

"Hey, if you're that masochistic, do it yourself," she said, shoving it back.

"This test only works if you try. I doubt you can," I said quietly, handing the pack back to her. "Please. You wanted me to prove I was different and I'm trying to do that. I won't ask you to do anything else. I'll turn us right around if you want, and never bother you again."

She seemed to soften a bit and took the needle. "This is going to hurt," she said.

"I doubt it."

She looked at me tentatively. I nodded. She shrugged her shoulders and put the point to my finger tip, pressing gently. She tried to push the needle in, but it only pushed against my skin, not breaking it.

"Push harder," I said quietly. She pushed harder until she was nearly gasping. She stopped and looked at me.

"What...how...why aren't you bleeding?"

I took the needle and pushed at my finger. Nothing happened. I pushed harder and harder until the needle bent, then snapped in two. I took out another and did the same thing. And another.

"It takes a lot to break my skin. In fact, I bought something that probably still won't do the job, but it will be a good indicator of how different I am," I said, pulling out the serrated steak knife.

"I'm not stabbing you," she gasped.

I chuckled a little. "I'd never ask you to," I said. "I want to prove to you that I'm not like other people. I won't even be able to puncture my skin with this. It's pretty cheap – I didn't think it was worth spending a lot of money on expensive knives to try. Devin has a few scalpels that will prove the point, but this should suffice."

"What are you going to do?" she said, looking frightened. I put the knife down and reached out to take her hand, very tentatively. She let me.

"I would never hurt you."

"I'm not worried about me," she said, exasperated. "I'm sorry I said those mean things, Ted, please don't—"

"Stop worrying," I said gently. "You know what happened with the needle?" She nodded, still hyperventilating a little. "The same thing will happen with the knife. I promise. But first."

I took the knife and cut through the thermometer box. "Here," I said, handing it handle first to her. "Check and make sure it's real."

"It looks real," she said, backing away and refusing to take it.

"Watch – I promise I won't even break the skin," I said. I pressed the knife into the palm of my hand, hard. I showed her my palm, showing there was no blood, no puncture, not so much as a red mark.

"Now, a little harder." Before she could protest, I pressed the tip of the knife into the palm of my hand until the blade began to bend. Then I bent it over in half until it snapped off. I took the broken piece and sawed it across my arm, then tried to stab my leg with it as hard as I could. I showed what was left of the knife to Tessie.

The serrated teeth of the broken blade were dulled and bent, some broken off. The tip was almost rounded and it was warped in several spots. "Do you want to check it?"

She took the broken pieces and looked at them. "What's going on here?"

"Before I answer, I have one last demonstration, which I think I'll do outside the truck in case I spill," I said. I got out of the truck and walked over to the passenger side.

"What are you going to do?" she asked, her voice shaking.

"Nothing that will hurt me," I said gently. "Before I do this, I want you to know that I'm not going to be hurt, so please don't shout or call anyone."

I opened a bag and showed the package of rat poison. Before she could stop me, I opened the box and swallowed half of it. I opened the container of pesticide and swallowed half of it to wash the rat poison down, as it was clogging my throat. I emptied the rest of the rat poison and finished off the pesticide.

Tessie was gaping in horror. "Oh my god oh my god oh my god you're gonna die you're gonna die," she said in one long sentence. She fumbled with her seatbelt and yanked on the door handle repeatedly to open it, stumbling out of the truck toward me.

"No, I won't. But time for the piece de resistance," I said, upending the small container of Drano and swallowing it all. I knew none of this would have any effect on me. But I would have to have the chemicals removed from my abdomen at some point. Otherwise, they would slosh around annoyingly.

"I should be writhing in pain right now," I said quietly. "Any one of those chemicals would be enough to kill me, were I human. Some of them would burn the skin right off my face while I tried to drink it. But it didn't," I said, moving closer to her, reaching for her hand, even as she backed away. "It's OK, Tessie, I'll be fine. I am fine."

"That's not possible," she said. She was gasping, starting to cry. "You're going to die and it's my fault! All because I said you were joking, right? I'm sorry, I take it back! Please call someone call 911 anyone PLEASE!"

I moved forward rapidly and pulled her to me. "Listen," I said, holding her head against my chest. "Does that sound like I'm dying?"

My heart thudded, totally oblivious to what happened. I continued to function, to be, regardless of having ingested enough poison to kill half a city block.

"It hasn't even accelerated. That's not possible," Tessie said faintly. I gently lifted her into the passenger seat and looked her in the eyes.

"It's OK, Tessie. I'm not hurt." She looked frightened, scared. I wiped my mouth off, frowning at the residue. "I'll have to be careful. I don't know how much residue there might be on me. I don't want to burn you or poison you because of my stupidity."

"My God, what are you?" Tessie was looking at me in awe. But mixed with awe, I could see fear. Even from Tessie. She might accept me, might accept my differences, but there would always be fear lurking in the corner of her mind. She would always be a little afraid of me. It felt like a huge, heavy iron door had just slammed, forever sealing me off from the rest of the world in a dark prison, black as night.

"I'm not human."

"I'm afraid," she said. "I don't know what you are or how you did what you just did. I'm confused. I don't know what to think."

"Do you want to go home?" Tessie thought for a moment and shook her head, still dazed. "Good, because I still have reservations. At the restaurant, I mean." I smiled, but she still looked shell-shocked. I closed her door and walked over to the driver's side, staring at the ground for a moment or two. I sighed and opened the door, getting in as I did.

"Are you sure you don't want to go home?" I asked again.

"I'm sure. Just drive," she said in a small voice.

I headed back to the highway and set the cruise at 70. I kept quiet for a while until I could stand it no longer.

"What are you thinking?"

"That I should be riding with a dead man right now," Tessie said weakly. She laughed a little, looking out her window. But the laughter was too forced, verging on the sound of hysteria. "I honestly thought that you were dead. After you took that stuff…"

"For the record, if I weren't sure I would survive, I never would have done that," I said. "If I thought there was the most remote chance, I wouldn't have done it. I knew that I would be fine."

"But I didn't," Tessie said, her emotions getting the best of her as she sobbed. She started yelling, then hitting me and slapping me. "I thought you were committing suicide, you jerk! You moron, you idiot! I thought you'd had enough of me and you were—"

"Aw crap," I said, pulling onto the shoulder and slowing to a stop. "I didn't mean for that to happen! I never thought you'd…"

I unhooked her seatbelt and slid her to the center seat, re-buckling her, fending off her feeble attempts to hit me. She finally gave up and slumped in her seat a little. I checked for traffic and pulled back in, putting my arm around her and pulling her close. She tensed at first, then relaxed a little.

"It's still me," I said.

"I know," she whispered in a shaky voice. "It's just that…all that stuff you did. The needles and knife couldn't even cut you. And then the poison. I don't know what to think. It's just…it's all too much…I—" She broke off with a strangled sob.

"I'm sorry, Tess," I said. "I never thought of that. I knew it was one hundred percent safe, so I did my little science experiment. Please don't cry."

She quieted a little and seemed to calm down. After a few minutes, she turned toward me and rested her head against my shoulder, slipping one arm behind my back and putting the other across the front of my abdomen.

"Jerk," she said quietly, with a watery chuckle. "You could have clued me in."

"I'm sorry," I said fervently, squeezing her shoulders maybe a little too tightly. "I never thought you'd take it this way."

"OK, for the record, don't EVER do that again, OK?"

"OK. Point taken," I said. We rode along in silence and the suspense was killing me. "So, what do you think about me now."

Moments passed. Finally, she spoke.

"Well, I think I need to redefine what I think a human is," she said, smiling up at me.

"Ugh, not that again," I groaned.

"What?" she asked.

"Devin and I have an ongoing debate about whether I'm human or not."

"You don't think you are?"

"How can I be?" I said, exasperated. Even Tessie, after seeing what I had just done, was still willing to argue with me. "Your question was a good one. Remember, you asked, 'My God, what are you?'"

"I know. And I'm sorry. It's just...I've never met someone like you. But humanity is more than just a list of physical traits," she said softly.

"I know but...never mind," I said.

"No, come on," she said. "What were you going to say?"

"That the reason you and Devin want me to be human is because it helps *you* handle how different I am," I said.

"That's not true," Tessie said, sounding a little frustrated.

"Then let's say for the sake of argument that I'm not human. Would your feelings change about me?"

She was quiet, obviously thinking it through.

"Be honest," I said. "How would you feel about me if I were so different that I weren't even considered human? It would change how you feel, wouldn't it?"

"No," she said immediately.

"I don't believe you."

"Let me finish," she said, smiling a little. "It wouldn't change the way I feel, but it would definitely make my feelings more difficult. I hadn't thought about it quite that way."

"I think the reason Devin argues so strongly is that part of him would believe it unnatural to feel as attached to me if I weren't human," I said.

"Ted, do you really think that's a fair assessment? I mean, I don't think Devin would care how you're categorized. Besides, I thought we'd agreed that it's not just physical traits that make us human?"

"OK," I said, nodding. "You're right. There's more to it than that. But what about my anger? My violence? What I do to people who make me angry?"

"Don't you dare feel sorry for Chad," she said, sitting up a little and jabbing me lightly in the chest with her finger. "If you're not human, then he's even less human than you are."

"I wasn't saying he didn't deserve it and more," I admitted. "All I'm saying is how many humans can do that? How many can perpetrate that kind of violence and want to do more...and...even..."

"Enjoy it?" she asked quietly.

"Yes. There was part of me that enjoyed it." I sighed and shook my head. "What kind of person enjoys that?"

"Don't feel too badly. I can think of several people who would have enjoyed doing what you did much more than they enjoyed watching it," she said. "Val is probably one of them."

We rode along in silence. I was still battling with my emotions, still feeling like even Tessie didn't get it.

"What's wrong?" she asked.

"I just can't explain myself very well, I guess," I said. "I feel so isolated and alone, cut off from every other human on the planet."

"Just because you are different."

"Different enough to be a new species, so yeah, because I'm different."

She laughed a little and hugged me tightly. "Honestly, I think it's your differences that attracted me to you in the first place. But you're not isolated and alone – I'm right here."

She turned her head up to me and kissed my cheek, then rested her head back on my shoulder.

"Then thank goodness I'm different," I said, chuckling.

Dinner, Part 2

After riding along a little more, both of us trying to define the word 'human', we finally reached the beach. I pulled onto the path leading on to the beach, heading toward what I hoped was an isolated part – and having no luck finding one. I sighed internally and just parked near some other trucks, hoping for the best.

"This is going to feel so good," Tessie said, hopping out of the truck.

"Which bag?" I asked, reaching in the back.

"The neon green one," she answered. "It has the beach stuff."

I grabbed the bag and shut the door, locking up the truck with the key fob as I did. I walked around to her side of the truck only to catch her t-shirt and shorts in one hand and flip-flops in the other as I dropped her bag.

"Race you," she yelled as she sprinted across the parking lot and onto the sand. I ran after her, fully aware I had no intention of going into the water. She waved as she ran into the water and dove into the waves crashing on the beach. I watched her swim out, amazingly confident and happy, and found myself gaining a whole new appreciation for just how attractive she was.

She had a very modest one-piece bathing suit, but you could still tell she was athletic. The baggy sweatshirts, t-shirts, and shorts she normally wore hid an unbelievably well-muscled body. I could almost see the definition of her abs.

I spread out a blanket and sat on it, watching her as she swam. I ignored the stares and comments yet again. It was really beginning to grate on my nerves. I was busy looking for Tessie's sunscreen when I heard someone comment "Why doesn't he just go back to the morgue?"

"Shut up, moron," I heard Tessie's voice shout at the guy. She was coming up out of the water, apparently having seen the small crowd near me.

"Oooh," the moron said as he chugged from the beer can he was holding, "are you going to make me?"

"I will," I growled, standing up.

"Are you going to scare me to death?" Moron asked. He was obviously in great shape, more brawn than brains. But he was still the underdog; I was easily six inches taller, 30 pounds heavier, and more muscular. And he clearly must have started to understand that as I got closer, because he suddenly looked unsure of himself.

"Only after I beat you senseless," I said, trudging forward through the sand. Tessie ran up the beach and stepped in front of me putting a hand on my chest.

"Please," she said, "remember your temper."

"Good one! Does he sit up and beg, too?" Moron laughed and high-fived one of his friends. Obviously the alcohol was fueling his confidence.

"If you were the one with her, you would, too," I said, turning my back as his friends razzed him.

"Don't turn your back on me," Moran yelled, grabbing my shoulder.

I turned slightly and shoved him by planting my hand on his chest and thrusting it forward, sending him flying through the air and sprawling in the sand. It looked like the equivalent of a pro football player shoving an adolescent. His friends murmured to each other, clearly concerned.

He got up and took a swing at me, which I blocked by catching his fist in my hand. It felt like a golf ball, it was so small compared to my hand. I shoved his hand away and grabbed both of his arms, squeezing hard, lifting him off the ground so I could look him in the eye.

"You may want to rethink your present course of action if you want to stay out of the hospital today," I said, then dropped him to the sand, where he stumbled and fell back on his butt.

"Come on man, let's just go," one of the other guys said.

"After what he just did?" Moron looked outraged – but he was smart enough to look concerned, too.

"He shoved you across the beach like you were a little kid," the guy said. "You honestly want to go back for more? Go ahead, but I'm getting out of here."

Moron glared at me and stalked off with his friends, berating them for walking away.

Tessie grinned sheepishly at me and said, "For the record, I feel a little guilty doing that. Hiding behind a guy."

"Well, based on our conversation earlier today, I'm not really a 'guy'. More like a 'being'," I said solemnly.

She cracked up and doubled over with laughter.

"Sunscreen," I said, tossing her the bottle. "You'll burn to a crisp out here in a matter of minutes."

"Fine, Mom, but you need to do my back." She sucked in her breath as I started applying some to her back. "Your hands are freezing!"

I didn't think that would be a problem, but I neglected to take into account how much back there was to do with her suit. It was a one piece, but most of the fabric was in the front, completely covering her abdomen and tying up behind her neck. Her entire back was exposed – and I found myself spending a little more time than absolutely necessary applying the lotion. Still, I appraised my job and shook my head.

"You'll be red as a beet, but I did the best I could," I said.

"That's OK, it should be enough. Thanks," she said, pecking me on the cheek.

"That reminds me. I need to rinse out my mouth," I said, heading toward the men's room. "That would cap off a perfect day if I poisoned you because of my dumb stunt. Go have fun. I'll be back."

I found the nearest restroom and went in. I rinsed my mouth well, remembering the stuff I swallowed and that it would burn or possibly kill Tessie if she got too much of what I'd taken in. I finished up and walked outside into the sun. I could easily see Tessie – she was not only the most attractive young woman on the beach, but she was also a brave and daring swimmer, going out far enough to earn a warning whistle from the lifeguard who waved her back in.

We spent a couple of hours on the beach. Tessie would go out in the water for a while and then come back. We had a light lunch on the beach – well, Tessie did.

Finally, she came out of the water and said, "I think I'm ready to shop." I groaned and fell back on the blanket. She jumped on top of my chest, soaking me with ocean water.

"You're getting me all wet," I protested, sitting up and setting her down on the blanket. She was shocked at how easily I did it, but did a good job trying to hide the fact that I noticed.

"I didn't bring a change of clothes!" She crawled back into my lap and put her wet hair against my shoulder, drenching my shirt.

"That's your problem. Besides, it serves you right," she said demurely, rolling off me sitting cross-legged on the blanket.

"OK, I deserved that. I'm sorry," I said.

"Apology accepted. Now, let me go get ready and we'll have fun shopping," she said, pinching my cheek. "That's hard to do, by the way."

"What?"

"Pinching your cheek. Your skin is hard to get a hold of," she said, struggling to get some between her thumb and index finger. She shrugged her shoulders and went off to change.

"Few more weeks and you probably won't be able to at all," I murmured as she walked away.

Dinner, Part 3

After what seemed like hours of shopping, Tessie was finally done. Shoes, clothes, accessories, even books and CDs. Of course, feeling supremely guilty, I offered to provide her with more spending money, but she politely refused.

"That's not a very healthy way to run a relationship, by the way," she commented.

"You're right," I agreed. "But I can't think of any other way to make it up to you."

"Oh, don't worry," she said looking slyly, "I've got a few things in mind."

"As long as it doesn't involve a pop rock or Top 40 concert," I said, groaning.

We walked back to the truck – I was carrying about ten bags of stuff. Eleven, counting the one she didn't see me pick up while she was in line getting a soda at the mall.

"Next time, we'll get the trailer," I said, groaning again as I put the stuff in the back.

"Funny," she said, hopping into the passenger seat. "So, are we really going to The Fish Shack?"

"Yup," I said. "As promised."

"Really," she said, practically beaming, "I've been meaning to go there. I've heard the food is great and the atmosphere is awesome."

"Devin pulled a few strings to get us in on short notice. And just so we're clear," I said, a little awkwardly, "I'm not eating because of the heat. It got to me today and I'm not feeling well."

"Right," she said, smiling.

We got to the restaurant and there was a line. I would have dreaded standing in line, but in true Devin fashion, we were on the quick entry list – and he must have given a good description of me (and a financial incentive to ignore my appearance), because the guy working the front didn't even bat an eye when he showed us to our table.

Of course, I declined to eat anything, and was not surprised to see Tessie order next to nothing. While Tessie ate, we talked back and forth and she really seemed relaxed again. But not quite.

"So, do you forgive me?"

"Of course," she said, quickly taking my hand into both of hers and squeezing. "I can see now that you were doing what you thought was right. You can't help how I interpreted your actions."

"OK," I said. "Good. But what about what you found out about me?"

"Not during dinner," she said, winking. "I think the waiter likes me."

I looked over my shoulder and could see the waiter quickly looking away, the smile leaving his face. I scowled at his back and turned around. "Should I rearrange his body parts?"

"Easy with the angry faces," Tessie said smoothly. "You look like a mass murderer when you do that."

"Sorry," I said, smoothing my face. "Better?"

"Yes. But no, you shouldn't rearrange our waiter," she whispered. "Too messy."

The Ride Back

After dinner, we walked back to the truck, joking about the waiter. And I found it very easy to ignore the rude stares and whispers – with Tessie clutching my arm and laughing, her eyes sparkling in the lights of the parking lot, it was all too easy.

"He was totally clueless," she said. "My father? How could he possibly think you were my father?"

"Wishful thinking," I said, opening her door for her.

"Such a perfect gentleman," Tessie said, reaching up for the handle inside the truck to pull herself up.

"Allow me," I said, putting both hands on her waist and boosting her into the seat. She flushed again, laughing.

"I still can't get over how strong you are."

"And I still can't get over how much you blush when I do that." I smiled, walking around to my side of the truck. I got into the truck, turned, and looked at her seriously.

She frowned. "What's wrong?"

"I have a confession to make," I said, sighing and turning my head to look out the windshield.

"What is it? You can tell me," she said, turning to face me, looking concerned as she slid across the seat to sit next to me.

I reached behind the seat and grabbed the eleventh bag, setting it in her lap. "I bought you something," I said. "I confess."

"Oh no," Tessie said, reaching into the bag. "I told you it was too expensive. I told you—" Her gasp interrupted her sentence as she pulled the small box out of the bag.

When she was shopping, she had seen a bracelet that caught her eye, but she said it was too expensive for a casual purchase, even if she did have the money for it. It was small, but had a gold charm attached to it with an old-fashioned sun face on it, like you'd see on a sundial.

"Oh my God, I saw the price tag, I can't accept this!"

"Too late," I said. "It's engraved with your name. No returns on engraved items."

"You cheater," she said, swatting me, but looking pleased.

"Let me help you," I said, taking out the bracelet and clipping it on her wrist, fumbling with the clasp in my over-sized hands. "It looks good on you."

She blushed again, very embarrassed. "Thank you," she said, leaning over and kissing me. "It's still too expensive."

"Consider it an early Christmas present," I said, starting the truck. "Now I don't have to go through the pressure of trying to find something for you."

She looked at her wrist, clearly admiring the bracelet. She spun it on her wrist, smiling after she saw the engraving on the inside of the charm. "Wait a second, how did you get it engraved so quickly?"

"I bribed the clerk," I said. "It didn't take much, believe me. I have a feeling he would have done it for free just to get me out of his store."

"What's it say? I can't read it," she said, squinting.

I turned the interior light on so she could see it, hesitating a little. I hoped I hadn't stepped over a boundary, hoped I hadn't gone too far. But I'll bet this was *exactly* what Devin meant about getting out and living – take a chance. Tell the truth and shame the devil.

"'Eternal Summer'. And today's date," she said, looking a little confused. "Eternal summer…hmm…that rings a bell."

"It should," I said, smiling and turning off the light so she couldn't see my expression. I was definitely having second thoughts. "Think back to the semester you just finished. When I was in the woods watching you, I even heard you read it out loud. In English you read—"

"Shakespeare's sonnets! Oh my God," she said, her voice shaking a little. "I think I might cry! It's 18, isn't it? The one about him writing her beauty into a sonnet to preserve it forever!"

"That's the idea," I said quietly. "I know it's a little hokey. Definitely cliché. And I've ripped off one of the greatest authors of all time—"

"Shut up," she said softly, pulling one of my hands off the steering wheel. "You're ruining the moment." She leaned her head on my shoulder and put my arm around her shoulders. "It's beautiful. And sweet. Thank you."

"You're not…crying…are you?"

"Maybe a little," she said with a soft chuckle. "But it's a good cry. A happy one."

"OK," I said sighing a little, relaxing. "Then you like it?"

She laughed and lightly slapped my leg. "Of course, you giant buffoon! It's so thoughtful, I can't believe you came up with it that quickly."

"Actually, I've been thinking about it for a while. I was thinking of 'Time in a Bottle'," I said, a little uncomfortably.

"Wait, you mean you listen to Jim Croce?"

"How do you know that song?" I asked.

"Lilly's record collection."

I started laughing and she sat up to look at me. "What?"

"I heard it in Devin's. But it made me think a little about the time I spend with you and how I wish I could spin it out forever. So when I got the bracelet, I wanted to put something on it that would remind you of the time we spend together, but I wanted it to go with the sun and the summer…and today."

She reached up and kissed me again. "My gentle giant," she said quietly. "You really are an amazing man, Ted Burroughs."

She laughed, then looked out the window at the darkening sky. We rode in silence for a few minutes and I turned on the radio, making sure I selected a rock station and not a metal one. Tessie was so absorbed in her thoughts that she didn't even notice.

"Are you OK?" I asked.

She jumped a little, giggling. "Yes, I was just thinking of your exhibition today."

"Sorry," I said wincing. "I should have found a better way."

"Well, probably," she agreed. "One that was a little less stressful and one that didn't involve a couple of hours of Devin's time to clean you up. But it also brought up some other questions."

"Such as…"

"Well, is there anything that can hurt you?"

"I'm pretty sure I'd be somewhat injured if I got hit by a train."

She snorted her signature laugh, covering her mouth at once in embarrassment. "What about a car?"

"I heard that snort, by the way," I said, trying to avoid her swatting me. "I might get injured, but the car would probably be totaled."

"How is that possible? I know you said your body doesn't function like other humans, but don't your bones break?"

"Devin's not sure," I said. "I have the same bones I had before the accident, but they're denser than regular bone. That's part of why I can't swim. The metamorphosis that changed my blood also changed my bones."

"OK, so they're denser, but what do you mean it's 'like' bone." Tessie turned to look at me.

"Devin is still testing, but like all of my other body tissue, it doesn't have the characteristics of living bone. No marrow for one thing; it's been replaced by even more densely compacted material than bone. Not only that, but it also has a different structure, almost a totally different molecular makeup. It's a little too advanced for me to follow closely, but if Devin's amazed by it, it's probably pretty big," I said, slowing the truck down a bit.

"Why are you slowing down?" Tessie asked, looking at the side mirror and behind us. "Cop?"

"No, it gives us more time to chat. Plus, the longer the drive takes, the more time I have you to myself." Tessie beamed at me.

"Next question," I prompted.

"So you weren't kidding, then," she said. "You could get hit by a car and what, just walk away?"

"Probably," I said. "But I'm not anxious to try it. I don't know if my bones will heal if they do break."

"Wow. What about cuts or scrapes?"

"I don't get those," I said, shrugging my shoulders. "You saw what happened with the knife. I've done worse than that and not gotten so much as a scratch." I laughed and shook my head.

"What are you laughing at?"

"On one of my morose days I thought I'd be a little reckless, so I grabbed one of the motorcycles out of the garage," I started.

"Wait, I didn't see any in the garage," Tessie interrupted.

"I'll get to that part. Anyway, I took the motorcycle out and was riding it in our driveway, just doing some figure eights, realizing that I was going to have to try to clean them up at some point. I wasn't having a very good day, so I thought I'd—"

"Try to see if you could maim yourself?"

"No, I was trying to work out some aggression," I said evenly. "But I tipped the motorcycle over."

"Doesn't sound too bad," Tessie said. "Were you hurt at all?"

"Well, I was doing them very fast; you should have seen the tire marks, shredded rubber, and smoke I left all over the place. Anyway, I fell off, slid across the pavement, and cracked my head on the side of the garage."

Tessie sucked in breath between her teeth. "Ouch. What happened?"

"Like I said, not a scratch. But the driveway and garage didn't fare so well. I left two long gouges in the driveway where my hands dug into it. And I knocked a pretty large section of brick off the corner with my head."

"I'll bet Devin was livid," Tessie said, giggling.

"Well, a little. But after he saw the damage I had done and that I had been unharmed, he thought it was hilarious."

"Men. Testosterone. Yet another mystery to me," she said resignedly.

"It's a guy thing," I agreed as she sighed. "His biggest concern is my safety, since it's not like he can get spare parts if I damage something."

"And the reason there are no motorcycles?"

"Ah, yes. Since Devin is so concerned with my safety, he decided to remove temptation by getting rid of the motorcycles," I explained.

"I see. So have you ever had a stubbed toe?"

I laughed right out loud. "I did stub my toe once, but I wound up splitting the side of the dresser."

"OK, how about colds or the flu? Ever have those?"

"No. Since my body isn't technically alive, then organisms can't live in me. I have no immune system, but I don't need one."

"So you've never been sick and you've never been injured?"

"Not since the accident," I amended.

"Wow," she said. We passed a few more exits as she thought.

"What are you thinking?" I glanced at her and she seemed preoccupied.

"I was thinking about how much fun I had today," she said. "How much fun I had with you."

"Really?" I asked. "Huh."

"Your science experiment didn't ruin the day," she explained. "It was a minor setback. I had a great time. And not just because you bought me an expensive gift. That was nice, but the thought behind it and the explanation of the engraving...that was even better. I'm starting to tear up again just thinking about it. But the part I most enjoyed was spending time with you. It was the perfect day, really."

"I'll have to see about raising the bar," I said, winking at her.

Clean Out

I'd seen Devin a little angry before. Frustrated. His tone was usually clipped and he had a "clinical" sort of anger: it felt like he was lecturing. But this was totally different.

He was livid.

Even with my huge size, knowing Devin would never get violent, I was cringing a little. He had his back to me, staring at a computer monitor. Then he suddenly swung around and gave me the full force of his stare.

I flinched.

"Do you happen to know the active ingredient in some rat poisons is brodifacoum, a sort of superwarfarin that thins the blood? I know you don't have blood, but I don't know what that would do to your fluids. Warfarin interferes with the body's ability to make certain proteins used in clotting, so—"

"But my body doesn't make anything. It doesn't have blood to clot, or proteins, or—"

"I know," Devin said, obviously frustrated. "But I haven't fully tested the...compounds...I've been using on you. So I don't know what could happen."

Compounds. He's called the drugs he's given me different things, but I've never found out what they really were. I probably wouldn't understand it, anyway, but I've wondered if Devin was shielding me from something. Something that might be unethical or even outright illegal.

He was busying himself with the machine again. "And did you also know that the active ingredient in the pesticide you used is carbaryl, known as 1-naphthyl methylcarbamate, and kills by interfering with the nervous system? So you've basically taken a poison that would stop clotting and another

193

that would stop your nervous system from functioning. And the caustic—"

"Isn't this a moot point, since we've already established that I don't have blood? And my nervous system really doesn't function like a normal—"

"I don't know how you're nervous system functions, so I have no idea how that chemical would work on you!"

"If at all," I pointed out, cringing a little again.

Devin sighed and busied himself with the equipment again.

"I don't suppose you could have just tried to explain it to her?" Devin asked as he prepared the stomach pump.

"She asked me to prove it," I countered.

"From what you told me, she asked you to prove your temperature. Not that you're nearly indestructible."

"I thought a demonstration would be better," I said, sitting on the stool and watching him as he hooked up hoses and wires.

"I doubt she would agree, based on the reaction you described to me."

I winced. He was right. Of course.

"Besides," he said, finally dropping the tubes and wires. "Did you stop to think—never mind."

He turned around abruptly and stretched out one of the clear tubes to the chair I was sitting in. I could see his hands shaking. He wasn't really doing much, just moving things around, waiting for himself to calm down. Waiting to gain control again.

"What were you going to say?" I asked, dreading his answer.

"I have to drain all of the fluid from your body," Devin said, raising his voice, dropping the things he was holding with a loud clatter. He was beyond any adjective used to describe anger – I'd never seen him like this before. "I have to replace it and I probably have to drain it again at some point to make sure none of the chemicals you ingested leached into your bloodstream."

"I don't have blood," I reminded him.

"I know! It's a figure of speech! And you're changing the subject. I also have to pump your stomach to dispose of the witches' brew you drank. I'm sure I'll get it all since you don't really digest, but if anything goes wrong, I'll have to operate to make sure I clean it all out."

"I'm sorry I created so much extra work for you," I said, standing up. "But I was desperate. I know you spend a lot of time working on my health and I'm sorry to make it worse."

"It's not that. You know I enjoy my work – very much. And I'd do anything for you, without regret or the least feeling of umbrage," Devin said, motioning for me to sit in the chair next to the pump. He sat on the stool and breathed deeply, lifting his glasses slightly so he could rub his eyes with his right hand. "You didn't know what would happen when you ingested those chemicals."

"You're wrong – I knew nothing would happen, or else I wouldn't have done it."

"No, *you're* wrong," Devin said. "We *think* nothing can harm you, but it's not like I want to test every poisonous chemical and concoction known to man. Some safe chemicals when mixed together can become very dangerous. I don't know how the fluid in your veins will react to anything – I've never tested it that way."

"But nothing happened," I argued.

"But it *could* have," Devin said, abruptly standing up and walking away from me to look out into the back yard. "I truly do think of you as a son."

He turned to face me and I could see the stress was taking its toll on him. His usually jovial face was drawn and pale. I could see dark circles under his eyes, most likely from using the lab table top as a pillow.

"What have I done?" he whispered softly to himself.

The sunlight streaming in from outside was casting part of his face in dark shadow, making it difficult to see his full expression. But the sunlight hitting the other side of his face magnified the crows' feet around his eyes and the gray stubble on his cheek. His hair looked tangled and wild, giving half of him the appearance of a slightly deranged man.

The other half, masked in darkness, seemed even more ominous, with hardly any facial features. That side of his face appeared to have no feeling, no warmth, no expression. As if it were a literal, clinical reflection of the way his brilliant mind thought over a problem.

Or how it developed a solution to one. A dark solution to a dark problem.

I pushed those thoughts away as he looked at me, his half-haunted face half-hidden in dark shadows.

"I don't want to lose you," he whispered. "What if it killed you? I've never told you how alone I was before...the accident. I would give up all of this if I could go back and undo that accident, but I can't pretend I'm sorry you're in my life. My life before you was existence, not living."

That hit home. It threw my arguments with Tess about my humanity into new light, as bright and as large as the size of a solar system full of suns. *Existence. Not living.*

"I'm sorry," I said. "Really sorry. I never thought...well, that much is obvious. I wasn't trying to—"

"I know, I know, I'm sorry to react this way," Devin said, chuckling a little and moving into the light. With the smile on his face, no matter how strained, he looked like his old self again. His face fully lit lost its ominous quality. "I know you didn't do this to make more work for me or to hurt yourself."

"But it doesn't change the fact that I hurt you." I walked over to him and put a hand on his shoulder. He seemed smaller, somehow. Vulnerable. "I'm sorry I hurt you. I promise I won't do it again."

"Good," he replied, patting my arm. He walked back to the machine he was working on and said, "Now, which do you want first, the carbide diamond-tipped needle or the tube?"

He held up one of each in his hands, raising his eyebrows.

Chad

The next few days proved uneventful, but I knew it couldn't last...

Tessie called me to invite me to the park. She was meeting Val, Kristie, and Sharon and they were planning to stay until the fireworks late that night. I agreed to go, smiling sadly at the thought of all the little kids that would go screaming in the opposite direction when the fireworks lit up my ruined face. I also thought it might be a bit awkward with Tessie's friends after our last meeting. I was wrong.

After I had parked the Judge and started toward the park, I heard a high-pitched shriek, which meant that I had been spotted. Sharon came bounding across the park and jumped into my arms, literally, giving me a huge hug and a kiss on the cheek. Kristie gave me a strong hug and a peck as well. Val played it up a bit in front of Tessie and pretended to swoon as I hugged her.

"Hands off my giant," Tessie said, stepping up and pulling Val off.

"Easy girl," she said, smiling playfully.

Tessie smiled and jumped up into my arms, lifting her legs up so I could catch and cradle her. She kissed me full on the mouth while the girls hooted and howled in the background. She tried to get back down, but I didn't let go.

"Where are you going?" I smiled and lightly tightened my hold on her.

"I'm getting down," Tessie said, struggling to get free.

"I don't think so," I said, tickling her gently as she began to laugh.

"Stop," she said, laughing uncontrollably. "You're going to make me pee my pants!"

I finally let her down and she almost punched me, but remembered she kept hurting her hand. "Wait until later," she said, shaking a fist at me in mock anger.

"I'm shaking in my 18s," I said.

"Eighteen! Wait, I thought Tessie said you wore a 14," Val said, raising her eyebrows.

"Different style shoe," I said evasively, thankful that I couldn't blush when I lied. I saw Tessie flush a little bit and fidget, feeling like a culprit in the lie. I hated it, but it was better than the alternative. Telling Tessie was one thing. And I liked her friends, but I didn't know if I could be as open with them as I was with her.

We were having a lot of fun, bantering back and forth, chucking popcorn at each other. I even made a show of hefting Val over one shoulder and pretending that I was going to throw her into the pond.

"Don't you dare, big boy," she yelled, laughing harder than she yelled.

"I don't know," I said, "the ducks look lonely. And you look like you need to cool off."

"I don't care how much bigger you are than me," she laughed, "I will tear you down, Jolly Green Giant."

I set her down, laughing. "Actually, I'm gray, but thanks for noticing the difference in my skin tone. Diversity makes the world go 'round."

But I should have known the fun and good times wouldn't last. Especially since I was in public. And of course, things got a little out of hand, as they always do when I'm on display. A few housewives actually cried out in surprise when I walked around a corner, prompting Val to scream out and act as though she were running in slow motion.

"Run! Save yourselves from the Thing With Scars!"

I laughed and shook my head. But this time, it was Kristie's turn to be indignant.

"What is wrong with you?" she yelled. "Tell me you've never seen the victim of a car accident!"

"Sorry," one of the women said lamely. "He just...startled us a little."

Val was still running in slo-mo. "He's catching up – hurry! Save yourselves."

"Val, quit it," Kristie said. "You're not helping."

"Aw, come on K," Val said, chuckling. "I was just having a little fun. At the expense of the village idiots." Thankfully, she said that last bit quietly enough for only our little group to hear.

"Let's just go," Housewife Two said, pulling at sleeve of Housewife One.

"Yeah, make sure you take your kids or he's liable to eat them," Val called to them as they hurried off.

"You're a piece of work," Kristie said, shaking her head.

"I try," Val said. But she wasn't any match for the second run-in we had.

Chad showed up.

With friends.

I saw him circling the park in his car, but ignored him. It was as if he were looking for me. How he knew I'd be at the park, I had no idea. Just another one of those cosmic ironies.

I was hoping he'd fade into the background. But he didn't. Instead, he decided to step up and take center stage. He parked his car near us and I saw four guys get out with him. Five guys in total. I sighed.

"What's wrong, Ted? You look really angry. And sad," Sharon said, taking my hand in the two of her tiny ones.

I looked down at her hands, lightly tanned from the good weather we'd been having. My giant gray hand looked out of place next to her petite one, like a cadaver's hand. And I imagined how the two of us probably looked standing next to each other: a colorful, lively sprite standing next to a gray, giant ogre.

"Nothing I can't handle," I said, forcing a smile. Judging by how the girls gasped a little (except Val, of course), my smile probably looked more predatory than I intended. "But I think the four of you should go somewhere other than here. Maybe back to the pond to feed the ducks."

"What—" Val began but was cut off.

"Hey, Mr. Freak," Chad's voice rang out. On his face, I could see the remnants of the beating I had given him. I felt a little twinge of remorse, but then remembered why I had given him the beating. And the anger started to spread slowly, like frost on a lawn at midnight in late November. "How tough do you feel today?"

I moved in front of Sharon and glowered at Chad and his friends. They were all bigger than him, ranging from the slightly stocky build of a rugby player to the all-out huge, Neanderthal size of a bouncer in a roadhouse. But all of them hesitated as they got closer to me, glancing uneasily at each other, realizing they were still smaller than me. They looked like they weren't sure what they were getting into. But not Chad.

"Ooooh," Val said, stepping forward to my side. Her eyes glinted maliciously as she cracked her knuckles and rolled her head side to side. "They want to dance."

"No," I said, turning my back on them and putting my hands on her shoulders, stepping in front of her so she couldn't see them. I looked her directly in the eyes, shaking my head.

"Excuse me?" Val looked miffed, hand on her hip. She motioned at Chad and his friends moving up behind me. "After what he's done to *my* friends? They've been my friends for *years* longer than they've been yours! Besides, do you think you're going to have all the fun? I've been waiting for this chance for months and now—"

"Trust me," I said quietly. "This won't be a normal fight. It won't even last a minute."

Tessie pulled Val back by an arm. "Do what he says, Val," she whispered. "Stay out of his way."

"Promise me one thing," I said to Tessie.

"What?" Her voice was barely above a whisper.

"Please don't let them run off until I can explain," I said, feeling the anguish in my voice. I knew this had to be done and that I had to be the one to do it. I hated how I knew I'd be, the violence that I knew was coming with the cold winter storm raging in me. The subzero anger I felt taking over that would control every movement I made when it started.

But I also knew that I *wanted* it. The release, the payback, the balancing of the scales – and being the one to do it. The opportunity to let my cold rage loose.

The final confrontation – or so I thought at the time.

"OK, I'll try," she said. "But if things get bad—"

"You'll go. I know. And Tessie?"

"Yes?" she asked as she backed away.

"I'm sorry," I whispered, feeling the true sorrow in my throat, but without the tears. Of course there weren't any tears, yet one more proof of my inhumanity. I could feel something tearing apart inside of me. I knew I was about to cross some invisible barrier, but I was helpless – I couldn't avoid it. I shoved the pain aside, the anguish, the remorse and regret. There was no room, anyway, as the rage spread like a cancer, freezing out any other feelings, blighting and blackening every other emotion, turning every feeling malignant.

I turned back around, straightened my shoulders, and walked forward to meet Chad, who had his arms behind his back.

"Hello, Chad," I said. "Looks like you're almost healed. And I see you brought some playtime pals this time."

"Well," Chad laughed. "I thought it only fair since you were a giant. I mean, I can't win one on one, but five on one ought to even things up."

"Wrong," I said simply. Standing still. Luring them in. I could feel the energy building and building, a nor'easter blizzard that would eventually peak and break itself over the five idiots stalking toward me, burying them in cold fury.

The five of them formed a loose circle around me. One of the guys ventured forward to shove me. He stepped toward me and threw his hands out into my chest, but I didn't budge. He grunted and I grabbed one of his wrists. I hit him on the shoulder with the heel of my hand and sent him to the ground, sprawling and clutching his shoulder with a pained gasp.

"Jesus," he said, rubbing the spot where I'd struck him. I could hear one of the girls suck in a breath, maybe Sharon.

"Leave now or it gets worse. You can see what I did to Chad the last time we met," I said in a low but clear voice.

"Leave now and I won't hurt you. Stay, and I swear I will put each of you in the hospital."

I looked Chad in the eye and let the anger take hold of my face.

"Or maybe you'll wind up in the city morgue," I said. And I could hear Kristie and Sharon murmuring in unison behind me.

"I doubt it," Chad said.

One of his gang shot forward, throwing a roundhouse. It connected with my face, but he was the one left screaming in pain as I heard the bones in his hand crunch. He turned around, doubled over and cradling his mangled hand. I grabbed his shoulder roughly and spun him back to face me, driving my fist forward into his face. He crumpled to his knees, his good hand held to his gushing red geyser of a nose. I stepped forward and shot my elbow into his forehead, snapping his head back and knocking him out cold.

"Damn," I heard Val say in awe.

"That's one," I said, looking at the remaining members of Chad's unlucky group.

"Get him," Chad yelled, pulling his hands from behind his back. He was holding a baseball bat. I heard Tessie scream as two of the guys grabbed my arms and Chad swung his bat, connecting with my head. It was an aluminum bat and I could see the vibration hurt his hands. He looked uncertain as I stood tall, unharmed.

I grabbed the left elbow of the idiot on my right, the right elbow of the idiot on my left, and squeezed. Hard. I could feel the bones of their forearms begin to give as I crushed their elbows. As they started to howl in pain, I yanked the two of them together, relishing the sound of their heads smacking together. They fell to the ground, unconscious.

"Two left, Chad," I said quietly. The other guy charged me. I drove my fist forward into his chest. He fell to the ground, wheezing, then staggered to get up. I took his head in my hands and drove my knee into his face, hearing a sickening pop as I did. Blood leaked from his mouth, nose, and one of his eyes as he fell to the ground. Knockout.

"And then there was one," I said.

"Wrong," he said, smiling a deadly smile.

"Look out Ted!"

I heard Tessie's voice yell and turned to see one of Chad's buddies had a razor. The first guy I thought I knocked out pulled out the razor and was flicking it around. He slashed forward a few times, shredding my shirt. I could feel the blade against my skin, but knew it wasn't penetrating or even so much as scratching my skin.

Tessie and her friends had started screaming as they saw the guy slash again and again. Furious, I reached out, grabbed the guy's hand, and yanked the knife into my chest near my shoulder. The blade tore a hole in my shirt, but snapped off when it contacted my skin. My attacker stood for a few seconds, staring dumbly at the handle he was holding, glancing at the blade that had fallen to the ground: it was a misshapen lump of metal.

"What the—"

But the guy never finished the sentence. I punched him in the jaw with an uppercut, spraying blood and broken teeth in a high arc above his head. I then brought my fist down on his clavicle, like I was trying to drive a nail with my clenched hand. I smiled sadistically at the pops and cracks I heard as he screamed his way to the ground.

"You were saying," I said to Chad as he advanced with the bat.

He tried to hit me, but I continued to block hit after hit with my forearms. He was huffing and puffing, but I didn't feel a thing. At some point, I thought he would begin to see he wasn't doing anything, but he never did. Not Chad.

Finally, I'd had enough. I took the bat from him and hit a nearby tree with it, swinging like I was at Fenway Park aiming for the parking garage across Lansdowne Street (or maybe the Mass pike beyond that). I stepped into the swing like a big-league slugger. The tree was only about six inches in diameter, but I drove the bat right through it. The bat split, sending the head spinning off into the grass. I grabbed him by his shirt and lifted him off the ground.

"Stop," I heard Kristie calling to me, sobbing. "Stop Ted, please." I ignored her, hoping I'd be able to explain.

"I'm going to tell you one more time," I warned, holding the jagged edge of the bat handle against his throat hard enough to draw a little blood. "Leave them alone. If you don't, I'll hunt you down. And what I do then will make what I'm about to do look like play time."

I drove my forehead into his, then shook him to keep him conscious. "Not yet, sweetheart," I growled in his semi-conscious face, "I'm not through with you yet."

I punched him in the ribs, the chest, the face, and the shoulder in rapid succession, hearing snaps and cracks with each hit. By the sound of it, he had fractures in his ribs, face, skull, and arms. He had started screaming after the first punch, moaning after the second, but was motionless after the third. And yet I continued to hit him again…

…the woman screaming again…

…and again…

…the man was hitting her again…

…and again…

…the boy was crying again…

"Ted," I heard a voice yell. But it wasn't very close, or didn't sound like it.

I wanted to take one more swing, but didn't dare. It would probably kill him. So I dropped him on the ground. I had other things to think about anyway.

I was shocked at how clear the images were becoming. They had started fuzzy, out of focus. They were almost clear now, clear enough I could see faces. I might not have been able to pick the faces out of a lineup, but I could definitely feel the pain, the horror and fear, see features. And bruises. Cuts. Swollen lips and swelled eyes. The woman was wearing a light yellow dress with tiny blue flowers on it, three small drops of blood staining the right shoulder.

I shook my head to clear it, to bring me back to what I was doing. What I had done. I looked at Chad and felt slightly saddened, regretting the injuries I'd just given him. Yes, I wanted to give him a beating, but I could have easily disabled him as well. And maybe I had.

And what was I doing to myself? What was I becoming, every time I administered a beating like this? Bloodthirsty? Lawless? Something worse than Chad? Definitely a vigilante.

Of course, if Chad didn't leave Tessie and her friends alone after this, he might not get off so easily next time. The next time may be his last…

"Ted," I heard Tessie's voice quietly calling me. I felt her hand on my arm and I shrugged it off. I couldn't take pity right now. Or any softness or understanding. It was too much after what I'd done.

"I'm sorry," I said, turning around to look at her. I could see her eyes wide and bright. Kristie and Sharon were crying quietly, not looking at Chad and his friends. Even tough Val looked a little shaken, but she shook her head slowly.

"No, Shug, you don't need to apologize for anything," she said crossing her arms and trying to look tough. But her voice was shaking slightly. And her bottom lip was quivering a little. "He got what was coming to him, so don't you dare feel guilty or waste an ounce of regret on him." She sounded angry. But sad, too.

"We should get out of here, though," Tessie said, tugging on my arm. Chad's friends were coming around and one of them started dragging him away from me.

"We're calling the cops, freak," one of them shouted as he held his head, spitting blood onto the grass.

"Are you stupid," the one dragging Chad said. "Chad had a weapon! He had a bat! And Carl had a knife! Do you think we're going to look like Sunday school kids? It was five on one, or did you forget that?"

"We'll be back, freak," the first one called back.

I started to walk toward him, dragging Tessie easily as I went.

"Then I guess I'll just have to take your head off right now," I growled angrily. I shouted at them as they tried to run away, supporting each other and carrying Chad's unconscious body with them. "Come back here, you cowards! Come on, tough guy, I'm not even out of breath! CHAD PREYS ON WOMEN AND YOU'RE HELPING HIM! GET BACK HERE!"

And I felt other hands on me, trying to restrain me, one on my other arm, another set of arms grabbing me around the waist from behind. Tessie then stepped in from of me and I felt Val taking her place at my arm.

"Stop, please," she said, her voice trembling, tears rolling down her face. She wrapped her arms around me and buried her head in my chest. "No more."

"You realize they'll never stop now," I said quietly. "They see this as some stupid, open challenge to their manhood, so they won't back down. The only way to get them to back down is by force. By proving I'm stronger and no matter how they try, they will not win. They'll bring guns next time. They'll go for the kill, and I'll have to—"

"Enough for today, then," she said, lowering her voice until she was whispering. "You're going to kill one of them."

"That doesn't sound like a bad thing to me," I said, glaring at the retreating aggressors. "They've got it coming. They even want it, a death match. That's how this will end. It's the only way this will end."

I felt Tessie pound my chest with her fist. "Don't even joke about that," she said through clenched teeth.

"I'm with the big guy on this one, T," Val said, watching their retreat with the same dark and angry look I had. Here eyes were bright with tears, but I could also see the same resigned acceptance in her eyes that I felt.

"Stop, Val," Tessie said angrily. "He'll do it. Look at him! He'd do it now." Val looked at my face and stepped back, wary. It looked like I wasn't the only one with a troubled past. I looked away from her, struggling not to run after Chad and his gang of thugs.

"Let's go," I said. "But you guys are going to have to let go. I'm going to look a little funny with you hanging off me."

Reluctantly, I felt the hands begin to loosen. I could hear Sharon and Kristie whispering as they turned to walk away. I could feel Val's eyes on me, studying my features, probably debating on just how dangerous her friend's boyfriend was. Out of all of Tessie's friends, she seemed to be the one who knew danger, had seen it in real life. Looking at me, she probably saw it in a place too close to her friend. I looked in her eyes and I could see the conflict: she knew I was right, knew that what I said was true, and part of her wanted to help me or at least be there when it happened; but she didn't want her friend anywhere near it.

Tessie never let go. She was still trembling as she frantically tried to pull me away. "Let's go," she said. "Come on."

I sighed and looked at her as she kept tugging at me. "I never got to explain," I said as I watched her three friends walk away in the fading afternoon sunlight. I walked into the shadows of the trees with Tessie at my side.

For now, at least.

Later

Tessie decided to go home with her three friends, so I drove myself home, ignoring speed limits and taking the long way home, winding the engine up and trying to work out some of the extra aggression that I hadn't gotten rid of in the altercation. I slid sideways around corners, making the tires scream in protest and the engine growl. I drove that way until it occurred to me that I could cause an accident. Hit some innocent bystander or run over someone in the road. So I slowed down, gaining control; the last thing I wanted to do was bring home a broken person to Devin and create another me.

After I'd pulled into the garage, I sighed, looking at the dashboard for answers. With the customizations I'd had done to the car, I needed a lot of gauges. Tachometer, oil pressure, water temperature, amps, volts, and on and on. So many gauges, one of them had to tell me whether I was right or wrong. Or give me an idea of what Tessie's mood would be like – although I could probably guess. After the shock wore off, she'd probably be frightened out of her wits.

I opened the door to the car and didn't bother going inside – I wasn't ready to talk to Devin yet, although I knew he'd want to look me over after he heard about the knife. And he'd probably have to make a call to the cops again. Although it was five on one and they did have weapons, it was still a one-sided fight and I'd gotten carried away. Arguments could be made about self-defense, but I was starting to become a trouble magnet.

I walked out into the backyard, not even looking toward the lab. I stared straight ahead through the trees as I walked into the welcoming shadows again.

"Breathe deep, the gathering gloom," I sighed to myself, remembering the rest of the Moody Blues' lyrics. How fitting and apt.

As I walked through the pines, scraping my hands along them, I tried to imagine what I would say to Tessie, how our conversation would go. And I was coming up empty.

I slowed my pace as I got closer to their backyard, wondering how the night would play out. I debated on turning back and putting it off, but I wasn't that cowardly. Sure, I could face five thugs any day of the week, but a 120-pound young woman with an axe to grind? Forget it...

I sighed and walked into the backyard and I saw her, waiting.

"Would you have killed him?" Tessie was sitting on her deck, staring at me. She had known I was coming. She was curled up in her favorite chair, wrapped in an over-sized hooded sweatshirt, her eyes still red and a little wet.

"I don't know," I answered honestly, standing in the grass, unsure if I were welcome or not. I had known this was coming for a while: the gulf was widening between us.

"Look, I know Chad is a jerk and he needs to be put in his place, but he doesn't deserve to die."

"Are you sure? Do you know what men like him really are? They're predators! They prey on the weak. They exploit people who can't stand up to them. Men like him grow up to abuse their wives and children, if they have any. If they don't, they abuse the women who spend time with them."

"You don't know what he'll grow up to be! People change! And besides, you can't just kill him," she said, clearly stressed. I could see she was upset, but there was more to her tears than just being scared or remorseful over someone being hurt. There was a real sadness to it, like she had lost something she would never get back. "You can't."

"Someone has to stop him," I said. "He can't stop himself. Not that he *won't*; he *can't*. It's like a sickness, a disease that he has. And there's no cure. Nor does he want one. Someone has to stop him, any way possible."

"Yes, but why you? I really like you," she said. "Val was right, I usually don't fall for guys. But I think I've fallen for you. And I don't want to lose that. Sit." I stepped up onto the deck and sat in the oversized Adirondack. She got up and crossed the deck, sitting on my lap.

"Fallen for me?" I looked at her, raising my eyebrows. "Are you sure?"

She looked at me quietly, shyly. She nodded and then laid her head on my shoulder.

"That's unfortunate. For you, I mean. I guess you could say I've fallen for you, too, but that's like calling a diamond a shiny rock," I said, smiling.

"And why is it unfortunate that I fell for you?"

"Well…I'm not sure where to start."

"It's me," she whispered, sitting up a little so she could look into my eyes. She pulled one of my large hands into both of her small ones. "Yes I'm upset and a little more than angry with you, but we can always talk. You can talk to me."

I sighed, looking into her innocent eyes. And realized, once again, how different I was. How far away from her world I was and how much further I was getting every day. The changes Devin's…*compounds*…had created were the catalyst. They took something fundamental from me and Devin feels guilty for it. I was no closer to understanding what was in the "compounds", but I'll bet it wasn't strictly legal. I'm sure that was part of Devin's guilt. But whatever the nature of those compounds was, the effect it created was obvious: I was moving further and further away from humanity every day.

And did I want to tell Tessie?

"Here it goes," I said.

"I've got a lot of darkness in my life. And I'm not just talking about now. Yes, I have a lot of inner demons and issues I'm struggling with, but I'm talking about my past, too. The flashes I'm getting could be memories, which means I'm remembering a violent past. When I was…beating…on Chad and his four friends, I kept getting flashes of a man beating a woman. And it made me angrier. It was feeding my violence. So who knows what those past experiences have created in me or how they've shaped who I am?

"Beyond that, I'm angry all the time. When I feel that anger peak, I lash out at parking meters and motorists and put people in the hospital. And who knows who might get hurt? Innocent bystanders? People I love? I have violent tendencies and don't hesitate to act on those tendencies, no matter how small the provocation. Anger is like breathing for me. As cold as I am, my anger is one thousand times colder. Most people equate anger with heat, but for me, it's cold.

"And I live in fear. Fear of what I've done, fear of what I'm becoming. Fear of what my future holds if I continue down this path into darkness. I'm getting bigger and stronger. My development doesn't appear to be slowing at all, so I'm afraid of what that means when it gets combined with my anger. I truly live in fear. Fear of what I *might* do. What I'm capable of.

"If my anger truly gets uncontrollable, will I hurt Devin? Will I hurt you? I get angry over stupid things, so would I…would I…hit…you, if we argued and you said something that made me angry? I don't know…"

I looked up and her eyes were wide with shock. She was speechless.

"So that's why I think it's unfortunate that you've chosen someone like me," I said, looking at my hands, lost.

"Hey," Tessie said, putting her hands on both sides of my face and pulling my head up so she could look in my eyes. "It's OK. Really. I'll be here."

"But what if..."

"No one can see the future," she said, cutting me off. "You're afraid of what you might become, but there's nothing saying that you need to follow that path. You can change."

I nodded. It made sense, but she was wrong. Just as Chad could never change, neither could I. I couldn't just let go of the anger and ignore things that made me angry. I couldn't try to reason with those things that made me angry the most: people. The way they waste their lives, the way they take advantage of the weak, the way they take, take, take. The fear in their eyes as I approached them; the shrinking and flinching when I spoke; the shock when they first saw me: all of that and more made me angry, angry, angry.

And as much as I wanted to believe Tessie's dream, that I could change and that I could be with her, I was worried. I was worried that she still made a poor choice of a guy to fall in love with...

Revelation

"Well, I think that does it," Devin said, dropping his pen and pad on the lab table. "Six feet, eleven inches. Three hundred pounds. I think we need to schedule the surgery very soon. At this rate, within a few weeks you'll be over seven feet tall and close to 330 pounds."

I nodded. "I'm ready when you are. We knew this was coming, Devin."

He sighed, nodding his head. "Yes, I just didn't think this soon. I suppose I should start developing a larger pump, too. Just in case you continue to grow. I've continued to try to work on the compounds to counteract the growth, but it seems that the original injections...well, they may have kick-started a latency in you that—" He broke off and seemed at a loss as to how to proceed. "Well, let's just say the pendulum was set in motion and there doesn't appear to be a way to stop it."

I nodded. The compounds again. But this time, something new: a *latency*. Hmmm...

"A latency?"

"Yes," Devin said, obviously hoping to move past the topic. But I wasn't ready to.

"You mention the compound that you use, but you've never fully explained what it is. I know it saved my life, but I've never been clear on exactly what it does or what it's made up of. Is it a drug? A steroid? Some type of hormone?"

"Well, it's extremely technical," Devin said, looking very uncomfortable. "It's very experimental at this point and not something available on the open market. It's not illegal in the strictest sense, but it does border on some gray areas of the law, so to speak."

"Meaning…"

"I could get into trouble for using it," Devin said simply.

"And by trouble, you mean prison," I said.

"Possibly," Devin said. "But given my devotion to science and healing, I could probably get a decent plea bargain. I doubt I'd ever be allowed near another lab, but…"

"So what's so illegal about this compound? And what kind of latency are you talking about?" I asked, my interest peaked.

"Well, the compound has, as you suggested, components of steroids and hormones. Some natural components and some synthetic."

"So which one makes it illegal?"

"A few components you didn't mention, combined in unnatural ways," Devin said quietly. "Recombinant DNA, mostly. What I created functions like a virus. The hormones and steroids serve as a sort of fertilizer to keep the viruses going. I developed it to help repair damaged tissue and organs. Because it had…military applications, we'll say…I made it just shy of lethal. It had to be very strong, but I think the viral parts somehow spun out of control."

"And my latency?"

Devin shook his head. "That's a part I really don't understand much at all. Something in your physical makeup meshes with the virus."

"Meshes with the virus?" I asked.

"Some people can carry a virus and never display symptoms," he explained. "But even though they don't have the symptoms, they still carry the virus. And there are times that a virus can be awakened from a dormant state. With you, I think you had something latent in your makeup that was kick-started with the virus. When the virus combined with whatever it was in your body that was dormant…"

He sighed and sat down. "Well, it was the perfect combination for disaster. Somehow, your body and the virus formed a symbiotic relationship. Your body is giving the virus what it needs to survive and in turn, the virus is helping your body to grow. We can only hope that a balance might be reached where your growth will taper off."

I pushed forward, filing away the information to consider later. "OK, so we know I'm growing. Have you worked on any projections? My growth rate seems to be an average of two to three inches every measurement, but it's decelerating."

"It is," Devin agreed. "But still, by this time next year, you could be nearly eight feet tall. If it continues to decelerate, you may only be seven and a half. Still a strain on the pump's original design."

"How much will the new pump support?"

"As much as nine feet, but if you continue to grow, it could only be a couple of years before that one begins to be strained."

"Eventually," I sighed, "I should consider staying inside. No human would ever be nine feet tall. And if I don't stop growing…"

Devin looked at me sadly. "I can probably keep building pumps for you—"

"But what if I'm 25 feet tall? Even if you could build a pump that would support me, I wouldn't fit in the lab. I'm barely human as it is—"

"You are human, Theodore. Relax," Devin said, standing up and putting his hand on my shoulder. "I'll figure out something."

"I know you will, Devin," I said, sighing. "I'm sorry. I just get a little down sometimes, that's all."

"Perfectly understandable," he said, chuckling.

"Let's do it as soon as possible. I'll tell Tessie tomorrow. I mentioned it to her on our..."

"Date?" He looked at me over his glasses with his hands clasped behind his back.

"Yeah," I said. "She seemed OK with it, but still a little concerned."

"After she saw you guzzle almost a gallon of pesticide and half a gallon of drain cleaner, I can't see why," he said, laughing. He looked up at me and I saw that haggard look on his face, the one he gets when he's worked too long without a break. "Do you want to talk about the episode in the park?"

I looked at my hands and shook my head. "I can't, Devin."

"Yes you can," he said. "After I explained what happened to the police, they were confident that no judge would hear the case. Knowing Chad – and his family – you'd probably be given some type of medal. I promise I won't judge you. I'm here to support you, to help you. I promise I won't be critical."

I nodded. "Still, I think it best if you knew as little as possible," I said. "It will be easier. Later."

He frowned, looking at me critically, sending off waves of scrutiny. "Theodore, if you're planning something—"

"I'm not," I said. "Honestly, I'm not. But I know Chad and I know he has the feeling that he needs to even the score. And I know what people like him do..."

"Based on these images you keep seeing?"

I merely nodded.

"But we don't even know what those are," he said. "They could just as easily be scenes from a movie you saw. You don't know they're from your life."

"Yes I do," with leaden conviction. "I know." The words were heavy and burned through me like molten pig iron as I spoke them.

"Just, please don't throw your life away," he pleaded. "Not over someone like him. Or something like this."

"Like what? A schoolboy crush? Is that what you think this is?" I raised my voice and stood, towering over him. "Is that what you think this is about? I'm trying to protect my girlfriend from a common school bully?"

"Easy," Devin said, resting his hand gently on my arm. "Of course I don't think this is trivial."

"Devin, you don't know what's at stake here. He brought a bat. And one of his friends had a knife. Next time..."

"It could be a gun. Or several guns," Devin said, sighing. "I know. And I do know what's at stake. What I mean is, don't throw your life away over a situation like this involving someone like him. He's not worth it. And he will end up in a bad way, without your help. Trust me."

"But before he hurts how many people?" I asked. "Do you know how I'll feel if he hurts more people?"

"But that's why we have police and courts and district attorneys," Devin said. "You can't take this responsibility on yourself. You can't be judge, jury, and executioner."

"I will if that's what he demands," I said, turning to go to my room.

I walked up the stairs and into the darkened hallway that led to my room. I quietly closed the door, then grabbed a set of headphones, flicking on my stereo and pushing play on any random CD. Metallica this time: 'And Justice For All', ironically enough. I cranked the volume as far as it would go. I closed my eyes and stood back in the middle of room, enjoying the maelstrom of sound that assaulted my ears, obliterating all thought.

Fair Warning

I was awake early again. I was concerned about how Tessie would take the news about my impending operation. With the concern she showed when I mentioned the procedure before, I was worried about how she'd take it when she found out it would be soon – sooner than Devin and I originally thought.

I walked out into the backyard, the early morning sun just appearing through the trees. There were a few birds in the trees above me conversing back and forth. I smiled a little, still concerned but feeling peaceful. I managed to push thoughts of Chad away, for the time being. That was one bright side of the operation I was looking forward to: it would push away all of the negativity from my encounter with Chad and his thugs for a while.

I walked out of the sunlight and into the darkness of the woods. As I neared Tessie's house, I sat on the ground with my back against a tree, waiting for Tessie to wake up. I had no sooner sat down than I heard the sliding door on the deck open.

"Ted?" Tessie was peering into the woods.

"Yeah, it's me," I said, standing and walking into her backyard.

"I saw you in the woods," she said as she waved me up onto the deck, "so I thought I'd get up, get my day started, and meet you out here. What's up?"

"What do you mean?" I said, doing my best to look puzzled.

"Nice try, Giant Boy," she said, "but there must be a reason you were planning to wait outside waiting for me."

"OK, you caught me. I needed to talk to you about something."

"Oh? Are you planning on drinking sulfuric acid today?"

"No," I said. "Hydrochloric."

"Ah. OK, so what's new?"

"I'm still growing. In fact, I've grown an extra five inches and gained 40 pounds."

She looked at me with concern, twining her hands together and twisting them nervously. "Wow."

I nodded. "Nearly seven feet tall and 330 pounds."

"Then I think I know where this is headed," she said, looking anxious. "You're going to have a new pump put in, aren't you?" She was nearly whispering.

"Yes," I said simply. "I told Devin we should schedule it as soon as possible. My growth rate is starting to slow a bit, but it's not tapering off. Devin's done some calculations and by this time next year, I could be anywhere from seven and half to eight feet tall." She nodded, biting her lip. "Tessie, I'll be fine."

"But," she said quietly. "You're having your heart replaced!"

"I technically don't have a heart," he said. "It's a pump. So think of it as taking your car in to have the fuel pump replaced. It's pretty much the same thing."

"Not it's not! You're a live person! You're—"

"Not alive," I corrected. "A thinking, active being, but not technically alive."

"Technically," she said, throwing her hands up in the air.

"Devin has pumps that will continue to cycle my...ah...fluid, through my veins."

"But if it stops, you could—"

"Not die," I pointed out. "First of all, I'm not living, remember? Second, I can probably survive for a couple of hours without circulating fluid."

She stared at me.

"Seriously. Of course, Devin doesn't want to test that theory, but he's confident that it's not a matter of minutes."

She continued to stare.

"Are you going to talk?" I frowned at her and put my hands on her shoulders.

She shook her head briskly. "Sorry, I kind of spaced out a little. Short-circuited the brain a little. Did you say a couple of hours?"

"Yeah, but like I said—"

"Devin's not confident," she said faintly, "right." She continued to stare at me for a couple of minutes.

"Something wrong?"

"Oh, no," she said, her voice suddenly an octave higher. "No problem here! You're getting a new pump and you don't need to circulate fluid for days! No problems! Routine as an oil change!"

"Tessie," I said, getting up and kneeling next to her chair. "It's really going to be OK. I've had one already under less than ideal conditions and pulled through fine. This time, I'm healthy and strong."

"But—"

"—nothing," I said, rubbing her arm gently. "I'll be fine. Trust me."

She sighed and her eyes were misting up. "Can I come see you?"

"Of course," I said, puzzled. "I'd be offended if you didn't. Just promise me something."

"What?" she asked, wiping her eyes.

"No teddy bears?"

She laughed weakly and nodded. "Deal."

The Morning After

Confused.

Again.

Not as bad this time. Least I can think.

I think.

Pain. Or something like it. Again not as bad. What is that sound.

THUD...THUD...THUD

"That's the new pump," Devin said quietly, as if he were reading my mind. "I'm sorry it's so loud. I didn't have much time to design and test this time, so it's a little noisier. You won't be able to hear it under normal circumstances."

"Good. To know." Oh. I can talk. But I feel like lead again. Gravity on the surface of the sun heavy. Except the sun isn't as cold as me. Maybe gravity on the dark side of Jupiter. Closer. "How long."

"How long?" I could see Devin's face hovering over me. Like a balloon head, floating over top of me.

"How long. Out." Why couldn't I think clearly? It was like the beginning all over again. The sluggish thought, the inability to speak, confusion. Wait...

"There were some complications," Devin said in a near whisper. "I'd say I nearly lost you, but that's not quite right. We both know that phrase really doesn't apply. Obviously I didn't have to have you hooked to a respirator, but I did have a machine circulating your fluid. But something went wrong."

I heard him sigh as he sat down. I was thinking of what I wanted to say, but all I could manage was "how long" again.

"You were out for three days. But you were without circulating fluid for nearly twelve hours toward the end.

226

Halfway through the first day, I needed to exchange your fluid again. Something happened and it began to coagulate, clogging the external pump I was using. I'm still trying to figure out what happened – exposure to air, I think. A hole in the line or something, but it couldn't be because I was so careful."

Troubled, he floated away and I couldn't focus on anything. Everything was not just blurry at the edges – it was blurry *everywhere*. "Devin," I called out weakly.

"Sorry, I'm still here. Your vision will improve with time," he said as he moved back into view and resumed his story. "I had trouble getting the new heart pump in you and working. It was almost too large and there were some small defects that I had to correct during the operation. Trying to correct defects in my design while trying to get it in you…well, let's just say it created delays. The second day went about the same way, except that the external pump began to show signs of impending failure."

He sat down heavily and I tried to sit up. I was strapped to the table. Again. Just like when this all started. I tried hard to think through a coherent question.

"Strapped?"

"I thought you might need to be. You've been dreaming, I think. Some of your movements have been violent and I've had to replace the straps a few times, too."

"O. K. What. Happened?"

"Sorry? You're very weak and I didn't hear you," Devin said, moving closer to me.

"What…happened…"

"The external pump eventually failed. I exchanged your fluid the third time, hoping that would be the last. I've run out. I wasn't expecting to need so much. On the third day, the pump burned out. And I had no more fluid. The

227

fluid you have now is coagulated and taxing the new pump. I have more fluid preparing now and it should be ready in a few hours. Once we have some new fluid in you, you should be thinking more clearly and able to talk better."

Thinking through sludge. Ah, that would do it.

"What. Else."

"Not now," Devin said kindly but firmly. "You have to rest. We can talk later. Anyway, I've got a surprise for you," he said quietly. He stepped back and I could hear him talking to someone. Who?

"Ted."

Tessie. Of course.

"Ted, it's me, Tessie," she said.

"Tessie," I whispered. "Who else. Would it be."

"Yeah, it's me," she said, sniffing. I could hear her crying.

"I'm. Fine. Stop," I said, trying to reach up and touch her face. Couldn't. Strapped again.

"Don't move," she said, whispering frantically, putting a hand on my shoulder to restrain me even more. She put her other hand against my face, stroking it gently.

"Therese," Devin said gently, "he's not going to break. In fact, he'll probably be out of bed and walking around tomorrow after the transfusion I give him today. I have no doubt that he could break through those straps right now if he chose to."

"I know, but what you said about the fluid!" She was nearly hysterical now. "And the scalpel—"

"I haven't told him yet," Devin broke in softly. "Tomorrow."

"OK," she said. "Can I stay? Please? I know I only live a couple hundred feet away, but I promise I won't get in the way!"

Devin chuckled. "I wouldn't think of asking you to leave. There's a spare room at the top of the stairs next to Ted's. I doubt there's anything of his that would fit you, but some of his smaller stuff is in boxes at the bottom of the closet in the hall. It will still be huge, but—"

"That's OK. I can always go back home and grab some stuff, but I don't...really want to be away," she finished quietly.

"He'll be fine," Devin said, patting my arm. "Despite the challenges and complications, he'll really be fine."

"OK," she said. "I'm going to take a short nap. Wake me up if anything...changes?"

"I have to do the transfusion once the new batch is prepared. If you're not up after that, I'll come get you. Now, you really should take care of yourself. You've been up for nearly 36 hours!"

"OK. I'll be back, Ted," she said, kissing my lips softly. "I'll only be one room away."

The Night

What the…

I woke up and couldn't move. I have to admit, I panicked a little. I still wasn't thinking too clearly and I forgot what had happened. I snapped through the straps and sat up, shoving the bed out of the way and standing ready for action. The bed slid across the floor and banged into the wall, making huge dents in it.

"Easy, son," Devin said. I looked across the lab and saw him sitting behind a flat screen monitor. "It's OK. You're probably a little disoriented, but you're OK. You're fine."

I felt something pulling at my chest and looked down. There was a vertical line of what looked like staples in my chest. I could see some blue fluid gummed at the edges. Devin typed a few keys and stood, hesitating a little.

"How do you feel?" he asked.

"OK," I said, shaking my head. "Still a little groggy, but much better than before. Sorry about that. Must have had a bad dream."

Devin nodded and motioned toward the bed. "Have a seat – I'll take out those staples," he said, yawning a little.

"Would you rather wait until tomorrow?" I asked, sitting down.

"That's OK," he said, waving away my concern. "I'll just do this and then get to bed." He walked forward with what looked like a pair of pliers. "Sorry if I seemed a little skittish when you first woke, but you startled me. I couldn't be sure if you were fully awake and I didn't want to take a chance—"

"On getting attacked," I said, chuckling a little. "Kind of like being in the same cage with a lion, huh?"

"Something like that," Devin said. "But it's an acceptable risk."

I sat in silence as he pulled out the last of the staples. He pulled out a box of antiseptic wipes and started cleaning up the wound a little, but I stopped him, gently pulling away the wipes.

"I can get this, Devin," I said quietly. "Why don't you go get some rest."

"It's no trouble, really," Devin said urgently. "I can take care of you…I mean, take care of it."

"You've taken care of me enough. More than you should have to," I said.

"But you don't understand," he said, with the same urgent note in his voice. "I *need* to do this. I'm the reason you're like this. I'm responsible for your injuries, for all of our pain. For taking away…"

"No, you're not," I said firmly. "What happened to me was an accident. And what continues to happen to me was born of a good deed. You tried to heal me. You had no idea this would happen, that I would wind up in this state."

"But—"

"No," I said more firmly. "You had said there was something latent in my makeup that caused the compound to perform differently than you expected. Well, what if this *latency* is what caused this? What if the compound works perfectly fine in millions of normal patients, but I'm the one in millions that it won't? You can't continue to blame yourself; it's not healthy."

"And so the patient becomes the doctor," Devin chuckled, raising his eyebrows.

"If needed," I said. "You could use a kick in the pants once in a while, too, you know."

He chuckled again, nodding. He handed me the box of wipes as I continued to mop up the gummed goo.

"And I'll tell you something else," I said. "You need to let go of the guilt, Devin."

He didn't respond, so I looked away from the incision. He was staring at me.

"How can you say that," Devin said, amazed. "After what I've done to you. I'm supposed to just live with the consequences and not feel any responsibility?"

"Yes," I said. "You've more than made up for it. You're living with the consequences and you've more than taken responsibility. You're human, Devin. You made a mistake. Even if you were taken to court, you probably wouldn't have served time. After everything you've accomplished and the work you've done, the *good* you've done, let alone all of the time and effort you've spent trying to help me get back to normal, no judge in the country would send you to prison. It was a simple, honest mistake. You probably weren't even speeding."

"I wasn't," Devin said quickly. "But I was groggy. That's at least negligent—"

"That may be," I agreed, stopping my mopping up to rest my hand on his shoulder. "But that's the most it is. It's not criminal negligence and you weren't driving to endanger. You weren't impaired. You said yourself I was standing in the middle of the street. What was I doing there at that time of night?"

"It doesn't mean you deserved…this."

"And *our* accident doesn't mean you deserve a lifetime of guilt and remorse," I countered. I finished mopping up and got off the table. I started putting on a t-shirt and jeans, feeling even better with clothing on.

"Besides," I said, turning to Devin. "I'm glad this happened. I would have never met you, Devin Boroughs. And I'm better for it."

I could see tears in his eyes, his hands trembling as he pulled off his glasses. He stood up and held out his arms as he stumbled toward me. I caught him and held him tightly as he sobbed against my chest.

"I've never had to forgive you for anything," I whispered to him. "But you need to forgive yourself."

He stepped back, nodding and smiling weakly. "Sorry, I'm a little overtired. It's been a little stressful, as you can probably imagine."

I nodded, smiling myself. "Off to bed with you," I said in my best Devin voice.

"OK," he growled, trying to imitate mine. I laughed as he walked off toward his bedroom.

After he disappeared, I looked toward the steps, knowing that Tessie was in the room next to mine. I debated for a while – should I let her sleep or go to her? Was she awake, wondering if I were OK?

I started up the steps quietly, hoping to check in on her without her waking if she were asleep. As I lightly tread on each stair, I was thankful Devin had Louie hire a carpenter to reinforce the staircase a bit and to get the squeaks out. After he was done, there wasn't any noise, but I wanted to be careful anyway.

I got to the landing and approached the door quietly. It was open only a crack, but I could see moonlight spilling into the room. I could barely make out Tessie huddled in the middle of a twist of sheets, blankets, and pillows. As I surveyed the mess, a chuckle fell out of me and she stirred a little. I saw her head lift off the pillow.

I knocked quietly and whispered, "Tess."

"Devin," she said groggily. "Is that you? What's happened? Is Ted OK?" She tried to free herself from the tangled mess of sheets and blankets, but she was barely awake. In her panic, though, she was starting to wake a little.

"No, it's Ted," I said. "May I come in?"

"Ted? Really?"

"Yes, it's really me."

"Yeah, come in," she said, sitting up. "What time is it?"

"Still night. Or early morning. Just wanted to let you know that I'm OK," I said, pushing open the door and walking in.

"You're OK?" she asked, still a little fuzzy. She rubbed her face and squinted toward me. "You can turn on a light if you want. But you're not allowed to make fun of my hair or what I'm wearing."

"That's OK," I said. "Lay back down and go to sleep. I just wanted to let you know—"

"Don't go," she said, trying to get out of bed.

"OK, OK," I said, gently pushing her back into bed. "Have a seat." I knelt by the bed and looked at her. As she sat she turned a little, the moon lighting her face. Her eyes were barely open and I laughed quietly. "Why don't you lay back down?"

"'Kay," she said sleepily, still looking at me. As she laid back down, I saw she was wearing one of my sweatshirts and a pair of my sweatpants. She had the sleeves rolled up into ridiculous balls as well as the legs of the sweatpants.

"Nice sleepwear," I said quietly.

"Funny," she said, smiling. "I told you not to make fun. Are you really OK? I mean, what are you doing up? Does Devin know?"

"Yes," I said. "Relax. Devin knows I'm OK – I just sent him to bed. You should get back to sleep, too."

"Fine, but I don't want you to go," she said, reaching out to me and tugging on my arm.

I leaned forward and put my massive hand on her shoulder. Actually, since it was so large, it covered a bit more than that, my fingers wrapping around her back a little. "I don't think your mother – or Devin, for that matter – would approve of us sleeping in the same room," I said quietly.

"We're adults. Besides, I wasn't thinking of...you know...doing anything," she said quickly. And I'll bet she was blushing right now. "I just want you near me."

"OK," I said, lightly stroking her hair as she slowly closed her eyes again. "By the way, I can actually hear you blushing."

"Shut up," she whispered, laughing.

"Sleep," I said quietly, still stroking her hair.

"That feels good," she murmured as she closed her eyes.

I put my palm lightly against her cheek and looked at her, lying so peacefully, breathing so quietly. She shivered and laughed softly. "Your hand is cold."

"And you feel like you're burning up," I said as I pulled the sheets and blankets up around her shoulders.

"Hmm," she sighed contentedly. "It's been years since I was tucked in." She opened her eyes and smiled at me.

"I'll be right over here," I said, standing and walking over to a recliner in the corner.

"Don't you need to sleep?" she asked, her voice getting softer and weaker.

"I might sleep a little," I admitted. "But you look so peaceful now. I might stay up, just to be this close to you."

"'Kay," she said.

"Tess?"

"Yeah," she said, her eyes fluttering open a little.

"I love you," I said awkwardly.

She smiled and I thought she was waking up a little more. "Wow," she said. "Big step for you. Ted?"

"Yeah?"

"Love you too," she said, smiling as she drifted off again.

Tomorrow

"Showoff," Tessie yawned as I stepped onto the patio.

"Telling my secrets?" I asked Devin weakly as I hobbled to sit in one of the wrought iron chairs. It creaked under my weight. "We may need an upgrade to our patio furniture," I whispered, wincing at the sound of my voice, sounding more ruined than ever after my surgery. I could think again, now that the fluid was flowing better.

I had slept in the chair in the spare room and when I woke up, I had a blanket draped over me. There was a note sitting on top of it that said, 'Good morning Giant – on the patio with Devin'. I slept more hours than I have in months and even though I was awake, alert, and better, I still felt a little off.

"Diet," Tessie said, throwing a bagel piece at me.

"And exercise," I said, chucking it back at her.

"No exercise! You're already a giant."

I smiled and flexed my biceps.

"Easy, my dear boy," Devin laughed. "Don't strain yourself so soon after your operation."

"Ha. Strain, he says. Actually, I think I might need a nap. I'm tired. I stayed up a little too much last night," I finished with a meaningful look at Tessie.

"Are you feeling OK?" Tessie asked, looking up at me with concern, her cheeks a little pink.

"Actually, it feels like someone ripped open my chest and stuck a chugging motor in it. Oh, wait, that's right, that's exactly what happened," I said, standing. I laughed again and shook my head. "I am a little off today, I think."

"Ha, ha," she said, chucking another bagel piece at me. Showing off my quick reflexes, I tipped it up in the air with the back of my hand, bounced it on my palm a couple of times, then flicked it with my index finger in midair right back at her.

"Don't pick on the girl," she said, ducking.

"Don't throw stuff at the patient," I said, hobbling back over to her. "Thanks for staying." I kissed the top of her head in a rare show of affection (for me at least).

She blushed a little more deeply, not having recovered from the previous episode. "You must be feeling better if you're practicing on public displays of affection."

"Well, my recent operation has given me a deeper appreciation of you. And if I can't say stuff like that in front of Devin, then I should just become a potted plant," I explained as she looked at me with her jaw hanging loose. "I'll be inside on the couch if anyone wants me."

I shuffled inside and eased myself onto the couch. It was odd – I felt something like pain, but it wasn't really pain. I was getting the signals from my chest that something was awry, but it wasn't a sharp stinging or a dull ache. It was just…pressure.

I closed my eyes and tried to sleep, but all I could do is rest. And listen to the metallic thud-thud-thud in my chest. It was fading into the background a bit – Devin was right: it was easy to get used to.

I heard the door open and knew it was Tessie.

"Are you asleep?"

"No, just resting," I said, opening my eyes. "I'd considered going upstairs to get some dignity while I lay down, but couldn't be bothered."

She laughed and sat in one of Devin's rolling stools. She wheeled her way over to me and leaned over me, but hesitated.

"You're not going to hurt me," I said, chuckling.

She leaned over again, wrapping her arms awkwardly around me and resting her head on my shoulder. "Get better soon. Our deck needs more work."

"I'll be breaking things by the end of this week," I said. "Trust me. I just need the incision to heal a little more. No fluid leaking since last night, but I don't want to risk anything."

"Do you think you're up to a visit from the girls?"

"I'd rather they not see me like this – maybe tomorrow?"

"Are you that vain?" She sat up and looked at me, smiling slyly.

"Maybe. But I think it would also be a bit of a shock, at least to Sharon. I'm also afraid that Val would use this against me at some point, trying to prove that I'm not so tough."

"I think you're right; Sharon would definitely be upset. But I don't think Val would use it…at least not soon," she said, laughing. She put her head back down on my shoulder and repositioned her arms a little.

"Still, I feel…vulnerable…right now. And I'm not very comfortable with people seeing that," I replied, glancing at her out of the corner of my eye. She caught on.

"But I'm different?"

"Yes. I don't feel that I need to be the tough guy, at least around you."

"I'm impressed," she said. "An enlightened Neanderthal."

"Funny, another giant joke," I said, smirking at her.

"It wasn't that big, just a teeny one," she said, laughing.

"Visitors are welcome, but let's not mention my vulnerability. I'm still not ready to share that with anyone else," I said.

"Neither am I," she said quietly, kissing my cheek. "Sleep. Or at least close your eyes."

"Are you staying? Please?"

"Of course," she said, smiling at me.

We were both quiet for a while, but something was bothering me. The comment Devin made about the scalpel.

"I was thinking about the scalpel," I said, lowering my voice. "I know Devin doesn't want to upset me, but I could tell he's concerned. Worried."

"Well..."

"I'll get him to tell me, but I want to be able to control my reaction, based on how bad the news is," I said trying to sit up. "I don't want to overreact if he's going to be upset about it to begin with.

"Lie still," Tessie said, putting her hand in the middle of my chest. She giggled a little. "That's going to take some getting used to. That pump must be massive! I can feel it thumping in your chest!"

"I know. I'm still working on tuning it out..."

"The scalpel. Devin had said he had a hard time using the scalpel on you – even the special one he uses," she said in a hushed voice. "He was able to cut through, but it damaged the scalpel. He has to find a stronger material or figure out a different way to make incisions. Plus, you started to heal so quickly, the incision starting closing up pretty fast."

"Wow. How did he keep it open?"

"He used a pair of clamps, I think he called them. And a spreader? Something like that to keep the cut open and the two…pieces…away from each other so they couldn't heal."

"Ruined the scalpel. That's not good."

"Because it will be harder the next time?"

I looked at her and could see the hope in her eyes. She believed there was a next time for me. And why wouldn't she? To her, Devin could just keep making more pumps, bigger and better.

I didn't want to tell her that there probably wouldn't be a next time. I knew Devin could develop another pump, but how big would it have to be? And if the next operation is as tough as this, what will I be like if the fluid does congeal and it never circulates again? Judging how difficult it is to think and speak clearly when it's a little congealed, I might become an inanimate object incapable of speech and thought with a few errant electrical currents occasionally circulating through my brain.

I didn't think there would be a next time. Time was like me: a manually wound clock that was running down.

Visitors

The next morning I was up at my usual time and the tightness in my chest was almost gone. I wasn't feeling nearly as out of it as the day before. I dressed in a pair of jeans and a dark green t-shirt (knowing it was Tessie's favorite color on me), then started getting ready for my visitors.

Val, Sharon, and Kristie had never been to the house before, so I wanted to straighten my room up a bit to make it presentable to them, in case I needed to do a house tour. I'm not a slob, so I didn't have dirty laundry hanging all over the furniture; I don't eat, so there weren't empty soda bottles and food wrappers lying around, either. But I have been known to leave books and CDs lying all over my room, so I started to stack and reshelf things.

I looked around my room and felt better about the way it looked. I started down the stairs and checked for piles of my stuff; Devin's subtle hint to get me cleaning up is to leave stacks of my stuff on the stairs leading up to the loft that serves as my bedroom.

I don't leave clothes or shoes around the lab, but I do leave books on end tables, countertops, and workbenches. I also leave CD cases around the stereo system, too. Devin has a very nice central sound system, with speakers in every room. When he's not around (which isn't very often), I pop in what Devin calls my "guttural inhuman screeching" – metal. At its loudest. I usually try to clean up those, mostly so Devin doesn't get disturbed about what I'm listening to. But I occasionally lapse.

There weren't any stacks of books or CDs, so I continued down the stairs to the foyer, checking for newspapers and magazines that usually get left on the antique secretary and matching credenza. I pushed a stack further into the secretary and closed it to hide the mess. The credenza had a small pile of magazines on it that I shoved into a drawer.

I continued through the sitting room (immaculate, since we never used it) and the kitchen (always spotless). Satisfied, I moved on to the library, the den, the game room, and a few other rooms my guests were likely to spend time in. I didn't bother with the laboratory – like the kitchen, Devin always kept it spotless and all signs of my non-human condition were always stowed away under lock and key.

Out of pure paranoia, though, I checked for any signs of needles, test equipment, or anything else that might not look like normal paraphernalia for a doctor to have to treat a sick *live* patient. Tessie was well aware of my condition, but she had kept her friends in the dark. And I intended it to stay that way.

Just as I had finished my walk-through, I heard a tap at the back door. Tessie.

"Good morning," I said, opening the door and stepping aside.

"Hi," she said. "I thought I'd stop by early to see if you're up for the company. I could always tell the girls—"

"I'm fine," I said, easily lifting her off the ground.

"Easy, you're going to hurt yourself," she said, clearly enjoying herself.

"Admit it, you missed this," I gloated, spinning her around.

"OK, I did."

"Thought so." I set her down gently. "And the girls?"

"Right outside in the—"

"Hey Shug," I heard Val's voice calling. "Look at you, all up and walking. Didn't Devin just open your chest and replace your ticker a few days ago?"

"Devin's an amazing surgeon," I explained. "And I heal fast. Come on in, I was just getting some stuff together for brunch out on the deck for you guys."

"My, my, Mr. Host," Val purred, rubbing my shoulder. "You do look good. Still a little off color, but you always are."

"Hi Ted," Kristie said coming through the door.

"Hi Kristie. Hey Sharon," I said, waving them on in. "If you guys would like to follow me to the kitchen, you can help me carry the spread out if you don't mind."

"Don't worry about it," Tessie said, "just point us in the right direction and we'll get it. Like I said, don't—"

"Strain myself," I said, laughing. "OK, this way to the kitchen."

Of course, they oohed and aahed over the kitchen. I finally clapped my hands together to get them to focus and pointed them toward the refrigerator. We were laughing and joking as we made our way out to the patio when Sharon said, "Ted, remember what you said when you told me Devin owned a Murcielago?"

I laughed out loud. "Of course! Which is why I got all of this stuff out: I figured the others could enjoy themselves while I took you for a spin."

She clapped her hands together, literally jumping up and down, waving to the others while she dragged me to the garage.

"Wow!" Her mouth hung open for almost a full minute while she surveyed the garage.

"That's what Tessie said, and she's not even into cars."

"A Judge!"

"That's mine, and I like to drive that when Tessie and I go out, but Tessie doesn't like the noise. That's a fall-winter car for her, so we can ride with the windows closed."

"Well, you'll have to take me out in that as well. Looks like it's had a few upgrades," she said, admiring the interior.

"Ahh, eyes on the prize," I said, flipping a switch on the wall. The spotlight over the Murcielago came on and she gasped.

"Let's go," she said, sprinting over to the car.

I tossed her the keys and walked over to the passenger's side, smiling.

"No way," she nearly shrieked.

"Just try to keep it under 190," I said, folding myself into the passenger's seat.

"You're sure Devin won't mind?"

"He won't. Besides," I said, grimacing a little, "I can't really fit in the driver's seat anymore."

———

After we got back, Sharon was intoxicated with the ride. She couldn't stop giggling and shrieking.

"It's a *car*," Tessie said, shaking her head.

"Girls," Sharon said, rolling her eyes.

"Shug, I still say you're looking pretty spry for someone who just had their ticker changed out," Val said, sitting on my lap and eyeing Tessie.

"Hands off, woman," Tessie said. Val wrapped her arms around me and kissed me loudly on the cheek. "That's it." Tessie wrenched Val's arms behind her back and pulled her off me while Val laughed hysterically.

"Who knew you were the jealous type," she said.

Tessie batted her eyelashes at Val and sat on my lap.

"So Ted," Kristen said, "how do you feel? I mean, you look great, but I can't believe it was only a few days ago—"

"I feel great," I replied. "Like I said before, Devin is a gifted surgeon. He's done the operation before under much worse circumstances."

"You are healthy as a horse," Kristen said shaking her head.

"And nearly the size of one," Tessie said, tousling my hair.

"Nice, make fun of the freak when he's recovering."

"Oh, give it a rest," Tessie said, lightly punching my arm. "Girls, he was up and around yesterday before I was even out of bed. He's probably just playing it up right now to get sympathy from you. He's healthy enough for another round with Chad."

"Hmph," Val said. "I doubt Chad is going to be up for another round. You got him good last time, so I think he'll be out of commission a bit more. But I don't think you stopped him."

"Or his uncle," Kristie said quietly. Everyone turned to look at her. "Donnie Lawson might not like Chad much, but he's still a blood relative."

"And you definitely stepped in it after you tattooed his nephew, poor excuse for a human that he is," Val said.

"So you think I'm on Donnie's radar?"

"They don't know that," Tessie said. But she still looked worried.

"Donnie will come," Sharon said quietly, looking at me. She looked more scared than I'd ever seen her, even during the altercations with Chad.

The Deck

A few days after the girls visited, I was sitting in the Adirondack, watching Tessie. She didn't look happy.

"You're worried," I said.

"You should be, too," Tessie said, frowning. "You know, Donnie Lawson might not be able to hurt you, but he can hurt the people close to you."

I shook my head. "He wouldn't. He knows that would only make me angrier. Make me more violent and dangerous."

"He doesn't care! He lives for violence!" She got up and stomped across the deck.

"No, he doesn't," I said. "People like him live for money, leisure, and theft. Violence is only a means to an end for men like him."

"What do you know about men like him?" Tessie demanded, anger flashing in her eyes.

"More than you think." I looked at her, remembering the flashes I kept getting.

"How?"

I shook my head again. "I don't know. I just do. I've...I don't know...I've seen it somewhere before."

"Before. You mean..."

"I don't know what I mean," I said, getting out of the chair, which creaked. Sounded like the garden crew needed to build a bigger one. Again. "It's like a song that you keep hearing in your head that you can't name. Or words from a book that you can't remember reading. There's something just out of reach. Something that tells me I know Donnie. Or knew him from before."

"You said you don't remember your past."

"I don't, but—"

"Then how can you know what Donnie is like?" Tessie said.

"I don't know how I know, but I do. I haven't met him, but I know what men like him are like. What *he's* like."

"From the flashes you get?"

I nodded. "The guy in them is violent. Every time I see the images, he's pounding on some poor woman. But there's a look in his eyes. But it's not the violence he's enjoying. It's the power. The rush of making someone grovel and feel small." I clenched my fist tightly and gritted my teeth. "That's what men like Donnie are like."

Uncle Donnie

A few days later, I was sitting in the lab reading a book when I heard a knock at the door. I put the book aside and walked to the door. Had I known who was there, I never would have answered.

I opened the door and a short man with black hair surveyed me while loudly smacking a piece of gum. "Holy crap, Chad wasn't kidding! You are a giant freak," the man said chuckling. His hard eyes flashed at me as he stuck out one hairy-knuckled hand. "Don Lawson. Nice to meet you. Don't take any offense about the freak comment. His words, not mine."

I shook his hand, gripping firmly. The only reason I shook his hand was to give him the sense that he was dealing with someone – some*thing* – a little different. I frowned at the two beefy friends standing behind him. They were taller and meatier, but definitely not as dangerous as Don. The bald one had a tattoo crawling up his neck to the back of his head. The fidgeting one looked like he was expecting to be jumped by a band of roving thugs at any minute; he kept adjusting the cuffs on his shirt and glancing out the door at the driveway.

"That's a strong grip you've got there! No wonder you tore Chad up. He's a daisy. My associates," Don said, waving at his henchmen absent-mindedly and smoothing the sleeves of his silk shirt. Or was it rayon? "They're harmless. As long as you are."

His eyes flashed again, along with a hard smile that showed blinding white teeth with flat canines.

He's a chewer, I thought.

"Can I come in?" He asked this as he ducked in past me.

"Can I help you?" I frowned, wondering what he wanted and why he welcomed himself in.

"Sorry," Don said, "I—holy cow, look at this place!" He whistled through his teeth shaking his head. "I'm a self-made man as well, but this place is amazing. Live here with Devin, do you? Where is he?"

"Wait a second," I said, walking toward him, "who are you, why are you here, and what do you want?"

As I advanced on him, Baldy grabbed my arm.

"Slow down, pal," the man said, smiling smugly as he grabbed my arm. His smile faltered a little as I flexed my forearm and pulled it out of his grip. He frowned and looked around me at his boss. "He's a big one, Don. Maybe we should do this outside."

"Nonsense, we're friends," Don said, patting me on the back. "Whoa, Hercules! My name is—"

"Don Lawson, I got that part. And you're related to Chad, unfortunately for you. But what—"

"I know," Don said, sighing. "Chad is a bit of a disappointment to his mother. My kid sister, that is. And he's not a great nephew, but he is family. Which brings me to why I'm here and what *we* want. Not just I."

"We?" I folded my arms.

"Yeah, you and me. We both want peace, right?"

"Peace?"

He sighed again, sitting on the edge of the credenza in the foyer.

"Chad is a little hasty with the ladies, I know. He doesn't have the patience his suave uncle has…"

He smoothed his graying hair theatrically and smoothed on his sleeves again. He stopped smiling, though, as his eyes flashed dangerously. Looking angry.

"Regardless, I can't have you busting him up every time he makes a pass at one of your friends."

"The last time he made a 'pass' at one of my friends, he was in the process of assaulting her."

He waved his hand. "'He-said-she-said' is what it amounts to. Never hold up in court."

"And the second time," I said softly, unfolding my arms and clenching my fists, cracking the tendons and ligaments in my hands and forearms loudly. "He had a few friends. And a couple of weapons including a knife and a bat."

"Yeah, I know," Don said, looking sad. "The kid can't handle himself. And he's not a good leader. Weak genes from his father, I guess. You know you put him in the hospital?"

"He's lucky it wasn't a grave."

"Broken jaw and cheekbone. Broken collarbone, ribs, breastbone." Don started talking more loudly as he walked toward me, jabbing his finger at me. "You broke his upper arm and dislocated his shoulder. He was in the hospital two weeks. And I had to see my baby sister bawling like her world was coming to an end. And I had to lie to her *again* about how good *her baby* is, how this was some sick and twisted thug looking to settle a score after Chad stole his girlfriend. And you did that to him. And, by extension, to me."

"He would have had worse than that if my friends weren't there," I said, stepping up to him and staring down. "He had four friends, one of whom pulled a knife, or did you forget that part?"

"Which I hear you snapped in half like it was a plastic comb, without even bleeding," Don said, looking impressed and angry at the same time. "Want to tell me how?"

"I have thick skin," I said, smiling at him.

He nodded, sitting on the credenza again, waving off his buddies one more time.

"It's OK, relax," he said to them. "Lost my temper. Sorry, Ted, I got upset."

"Right," I said, walking toward a chair and sitting in it. I stretched out my legs and crossed my arms. "What now?"

"A truce," he said, holding his hands in front of him and smiling, smacking his gum again. "Let's just go on the way things were before."

"That's it?"

"What did you think?" Don asked. "That I was going to break your legs?"

"I thought you'd try," I said, looking at his buddies and smiling.

"As a younger man I might have, but I've mellowed," Don said. "Chad stays away from you and your friends and you leave him alone. Deal?"

"I'd like to make a small amendment to that," I said, putting my hands behind my head and lacing my fingers together.

"Oh," Don said, frowning. A dangerous look crossed his face for a second before it smoothed out again. Probably shades of the younger Donnie. "I'm not used to making more concessions than I get, so I can't wait to hear this."

"Chad leaves everyone in town alone," I said. "Not just my friends. He's a nuisance and eventually, he'll push one girl too far and he'll get his. Jail, angry father, angry boyfriend or husband, something. But he'll also eventually hurt someone. You know that as well as I do."

Don frowned, nodding. "You're right. Eventually, he's going to do something stupid and get caught. But you don't want to be the person doing the hurting."

"As I said, as long as he doesn't hurt anyone—"

"I guarantee he won't hurt you or your friends," Don said, standing and raising his voice. "What more do you want?"

"Your guarantee that he won't hurt anyone else," I said, standing so suddenly his buddies stepped forward and uncrossed their arms, tensing. "Those four that he bothers all the time aren't my only friends in town."

"I can't guarantee the safety of everyone in town," Don said. "This is a free country! Chad can do whatever he wants—"

"And anyone he hurts is going to become my best friend in the world," I said, stepping forward. His buddies stepped in front of me and put their hands on my chest to hold me back. Not that it did a lot of good. "Chad's bullying days are over."

Don eyed me as he watched his buddies struggle to keep me back. His face broke into a smile. "Interested in a job? The way you push these boys around, I'm sure I could find you a good spot in my company."

I glowered at him, pushing his buddies back even further without raising my arms.

"OK, OK, that's enough," Don said, putting his hands on the shoulders of Baldy and Twitchy. "Let's go. I think he got the message."

"I'm not sure you got mine, but just to be clear: the next person Chad hurts is going to become my best friend," I said, leveling my finger at Don's face. "Got it."

"I hear you," Don sighed. "And I know we haven't met for the last time. Shake?" He held out his hand.

Looking at it like it was the foulest piece of garbage I'd ever seen, I pointed to the door and simply said, "Out."

"OK," Don said, walking toward the door. "Think about what I said, though. Very carefully. We might not be able to hurt you directly, but there are always indirect means."

I advanced on him so quickly his buddies never had a chance. I put my hand on his shoulder and stuck my finger in his face. "You'll be on my list, too."

"No one touches Donnie," Baldy said as he punched the side of my head. As he howled in pain, shaking his hand, I grabbed him by the throat and lifted him off the ground. He was stuck between amazement at being suspended in midair and the crushing pressure I was putting on his throat. I launched him across the foyer toward the front door with one arm. He flew through one of the glass panes framing the door, shattering it and spraying the steps with broken glass.

Twitchy jumped on my back and put his arm around my throat, pulling on his arm with his free hand, trying to choke me. I grabbed the elbow he had at my neck and squeezed until I heard a crack – he shrieked in agony. I spun him around to face me and shoved him with both hands into the roll top desk, flattening it and putting holes in the drywall behind it.

Don stared at his buddies and looked at me with something like fear as his eyes darted side to side, looking for an escape route or a weapon.

"Out," I said quietly. "And take this trash with you."

Don yanked on the collar of Twitchy, who was still screaming in agony. "Get in the car, you moron!" Baldy was picking himself up gingerly off the broken glass and shattered pieces of wood around him, dripping blood on the front porch. "Both of you!"

The three of them ran back to the car and climbed in. Don pulled away before the doors were even closed.

I sighed, looking at the ruined foyer.

"Friends of yours," I heard Devin ask quietly from the lab.

I turned quickly, looking at him guiltily. "I'm sorry Devin, I never—"

He held up a hand, smiling sadly. "No need to apologize. I should be thanking you, actually. Those appeared to be very bad men. I can't imagine what would have happened if you weren't here. I suppose they would have given me some severe injuries."

I nodded. "We'll need to get the security system upgraded. And hire personal guards for you and the house."

"Might not be a bad idea to hire some for your friends as well," Devin suggested.

I shook my head. "Chad wouldn't be that stupid. Well, at least Don wouldn't," I said as Devin raised his eyebrows.

"You know," Devin said delicately. "You may want to rethink your approach to some things. I know men like Don only know one way – the way of violence. But you—"

"I have to respond in kind, Devin," I said, frustrated. "I hate it, I really do. But there is no other way, not with Chad and Don."

"I suppose," Devin said, shrugging his shoulders. "But please, please try."

"I will," I nodded. "But if Chad crosses the line…"

"Son," Devin said quietly. "You can't save the world. I hate to say it, but you can't even save the whole town, much as you'd like to. Chad and people like him—"

"Deserve to die!" I yelled at him, suddenly furious. I pointed out the ruined front door. "What gives them the right to take? Chad and Donnie and their endless line of thugs? What gives them the right to *be*?"

"Ted, please," Devin said, resting his hand on my shoulder.

"People like him degrade humanity by simply drawing breath," I said, my voice getting louder. "They throw away their human dignity and everyone else's! They discard the chance to be something I can't..."

Devin's shoulders slumped as he nodded his head. "Some people do, yes," he said quietly. He took of his glasses and rubbed his eyes.

"I hate them, Devin," I said, lowering my voice. It was still full of rage, glutted with poisonous anger that felt something like madness. "Chad and everyone like him. Don and his thugs. If I had a way—"

"You'd turn to murder," Devin said, stating a fact he could see in my face, no matter how much he didn't want to believe it. "You really would throw away everything?"

"I..." I gritted my teeth and seethed, clenching my fists and wrestling with my anger, rage, violence...

"Ted," I heard a voice whisper.

Tessie.

I looked at her, shocked to see her standing there. "I heard your voice and thought you were in trouble. There were noises—"

Devin stepped aside and let Tessie into the foyer. Her eyes widened as she saw the ruins of the secretary and the demolished side pane by the front door.

"I'm fine," I said quietly. "Here, I'll walk you home." I pulled her arm gently and headed toward the back door.

"What's going on?" she almost whispered as we stepped out the back door and into the yard.

"Nothing. Just a visit from Chad's uncle, that's all," I said, walking slowly into the woods.

"Wait, Chad's uncle?" Tessie stopped in the middle of the woods and yanked her arm out of my hand.

"Uncle Donnie paid me a visit."

She stared at me, mouth open. She knew this was going to happen, but must have tricked herself into thinking it wouldn't.

"What's the big deal?" I gently pulled her arm but she yanked it back again.

"He's a crook," she said, suddenly furious. "A mob boss. And dangerous. What did you do?"

"I didn't do anything," I said, frowning and walking the rest of the way through the woods into her yard.

"Then what was with the foyer?"

"Our negotiations got a little…heated," I answered, shrugging my shoulders. "So I straightened them out."

"'Straightened them out'? Donnie Lawson is a killer, Ted," she said, throwing her hands up and raising her voice. "What were you thinking?"

"What I was thinking," I said, getting a little loud myself, "was that he and his friends muscled their way into Devin's house and threatened him. And they threatened everyone I value in this world."

She shook her head and flopped into one of the deck chairs. She was quiet for a few minutes, opening her mouth a few times to speak, but so flabbergasted that she couldn't.

"Ted, he could kill Devin, you know," she said loudly. "You shouldn't have hurt Chad like that."

"So what would you have done?" I asked, leaning against the rail. "Tell me."

"You didn't have to hurt him so badly," she said, standing up and folding her arms.

"So what should I have done, let him brain me a few more times with the bat? Let his buddy carve up my shirt? And when they're done with me, let them have their fun with you and the girls? Just let all of those useless thugs walk all over—"

"Stop," she nearly shrieked. "No, you shouldn't have done that, but you didn't have to put him in traction, either!"

"What are you two arguing about?" Tessie's mother asked innocently as she closed the screen door behind her. She looked concerned, but not scared.

"Ted challenged Donnie Lawson to a duel," Tessie huffed, sitting in a chair abruptly.

"Donnie? Ted, tell me you didn't!"

"I didn't!"

"You may as well have, after beating up two of his bodyguards," Tessie countered.

"Two of his...Ted, Donnie is a dangerous man! He could hurt you and Devin," she said, almost collapsing in a chair herself.

"He doesn't care," Tessie said scathingly. "As long as he gets to satisfy his need for what he thinks is justice. He's on the side of truth, justice, and the American way, so—"

"STOP IT!" I shouted. Both Tessie and her mother cringed into their chairs. It hurt me in a fundamental way to see that. Watching them cower back from the force of my shout, seeing them shrink away from me, made me feel as though I were building one final wall between me and the rest of the world. Before now, it seemed like I had a bridge to the rest of the world – Devin, Lilly, Tessie and her friends. But now I could see that bridge started to smoke a little, the prelude to a huge inferno that would burn it down.

I sighed and lowered my voice a little. A little. "Chad was going to hurt Sharon, probably Kristie as well! I stopped him. When he caught up with me that day in the park, what do you think he might have done after he was through with me? Five guys and four females, four females, by the way, who would have witnessed a brutal beating if they could have managed it!"

"Tessie," her mother whispered. "What's he talking about?"

Before she could answer, I jumped in. "We ran into Chad one night months ago and he was basically assaulting Sharon and he shoved Kristie to the ground. I stopped him from hurting them. Then a little while ago he and four of his friends came after me in the park. I stopped him and his friends—again."

"And put Chad in the hospital for a couple of weeks," Tessie said. "And now Donnie visited."

"Tessie, I don't want you going out with those girls any more—"

"Mom, they're my friends!"

"And you're my daughter. Ted, I'm glad you helped protect Tessie, but as for those other girls…"

"My *friends*." Tessie looked furious.

Her mother sighed and suddenly looked old and weary. "I'm sorry Tessie, but you're my only responsibility. I love those girls, you know that. But given the choice, I'd rather have you safe than—"

"Stop," Tessie said shortly. "I don't want to hear it." She stormed in the house and banged the door.

"I'm sorry, Lilly," I said. "But Donnie showed up at the house with two of his goons."

"But Donnie Lawson! Ted, he's a monster," Lilly said in a small voice.

"I know, but...Chad couldn't just be allowed to do what he was doing," I said, lowering my voice. "Not to Sharon. You didn't see what he was doing—"

"I can imagine," Lilly said. "Donnie wasn't very nice in his day, either. Everyone steered clear of him."

"Well, age hasn't cooled him any, despite what he says."

"I know you did what you had to," Lilly said. "But Ted, Tessie is all I have. I can't..." She dropped her head. "I can't lose her, too." She finished quietly, putting her face in her hands.

"I'd better go," I said awkwardly as I turned my back and walked into the darkened woods alone.

Friends

"So, are you going to tell them or should I?" Tessie said, finally getting around to what was bothering her. Our last few meetings were tense and just that—meetings. We didn't do anything fun, just discussed my current situation with Donnie Lawson.

"You seem so eager, please do," I growled, flopping onto the couch in the lab.

"Hmm, trouble in paradise," Val said, squeezing onto the couch next to me.

"More than that. Ted's being hunted by a murdering psychopath."

Val laughed. "Is that what's got you so worried? Look at the boy, T! He's more than a giant now – he's a *god*! I can't imagine anyone who could hurt him, I mean—"

"How about Donnie Lawson," Tessie said quietly.

Val stopped her joking and frowned. Kristie and Sharon gasped audibly. "I know he's Chad's uncle," Val said, "but I didn't think they were close."

"Apparently now they are since Ted put Chad in the hospital. Donnie stopped by with two of his henchmen to see Ted. That's why the foyer is such a mess."

Absolute silence followed the announcement. Kristie looked at me as if she were more frightened of me than she was of Chad. No one said anything for a while.

"So what happened?" Val asked.

"Ted basically disabled the two henchmen and told Donnie to split. So now Ted has a target on his back."

"You don't know that," I said, frustrated.

"Yes, I do! The last guy that crossed Donnie was found in the lake at the park, wrapped in chains with the initials 'DL' carved into his forehead," Tessie said vehemently.

"Tessie, I didn't go looking for this! Why do you keep acting like I actively sought this guy out and spit in his face?"

"Because you did when you hurt Chad!" She came over to the couch and pointed her finger in my face. "It's your fault!"

"It is not," I said, standing up and towering over her. "Chad asked for it when he grabbed Sharon."

"That's just an excuse," Tessie said, "and you know it! You wanted to hurt him because he made you angry. You lost your temper and he was a convenient outlet."

"How dare you say that!" I stepped forward and Val was on her feet in an instant, stepping between us, putting a hand on my chest and looking at her friend, concerned. "He was going to hurt Sharon! What did you expect me to do?"

"Easy big boy," Val said huskily in a calm voice I'd never heard her use before. It was firm and powerful, commanding. And it meant business. "We're all friends here."

I looked down at her stern face, embarrassed. I'd seen her like this before – she clearly had to deal with violence and diffusing volatile situations before. I nodded and breathed in deeply.

"Tessie, he's right," Sharon said, speaking quietly. "Chad had to be stopped. I don't like it any more than you do, but Chad had to be stopped. And Ted is unfortunately the one who had to do it."

Tessie calmed down and looked at Sharon, softening a bit. "But Sharon—"

"No," Sharon said. "I know what I'm talking about. You remember my brother?"

Val looked at the floor, embarrassed; Tessie winced. Kristie looked out the window, biting her lip. Silence ensued for what seemed like eons.

"Yes," Tessie finally whispered, resigned.

Sharon turned to me and sighed. "My older brother was a bad seed. He wasn't just a joker or a class clown; he was a bad man and he did lots of bad things. He was a small town hoodlum, but he started getting into big league trouble early on in his life. He sold drugs in school, stole from people. He hurt people, too, like Chad was trying to hurt me. He took advantage of just about everyone around him.

"One night, he tried to rob a gas station on Rauhut Street. He shoved the clerk to the ground and the man started having a heart attack. On the surveillance video, you could see my brother laughing at the man as he...died...trying to catch his breath and wrapping his arms around his chest. Billy just stood over him and watched him die, laughing in his face.

"A few days later, the cops caught up with Billy. They shot and killed Billy in the middle of the street in broad daylight. Like a rabid dog. He was shot seven times by three different police officers."

"I'm sorry," I said immediately, putting one hand on her shoulder and using the other to brush the tears off her cheeks.

"I'm not," she said, looking up at me, anger in her eyes. "Billy was a horrible person who needed to be stopped. He was responsible for that clerk's death and he would probably have killed more if he hadn't been stopped."

"But this is different," Tessie said. "Chad is—"

"Harmless?" Val turned to Tessie and put her hands on her hips. "Is that what you think?"

"No, but Ted didn't have to escalate it to this! He could have...worked it out..." she said, trailing off lamely, clearly unsure of how to continue her line of argument.

Val snorted. "Yeah, worked it out with a psycho."

"So now what! Now Ted walks around waiting for Donnie to find him after Ted beats Chad up again?" Tessie threw her hands up in the air.

"No," I said firmly. "I'll flush him out."

"That's suicide," Tessie said.

I shook my head. "Chad will go after someone else, easy prey. I know he will. I told Donnie that Chad better not touch anyone in town. I know Chad can't stop himself, so eventually he'll slip up. And I told Donnie that person would become my new best friend. I would take the attack personally."

"Brave old soul," Val said, crossing her arms and looking at me.

"Stupid," Tessie said quietly.

"I don't think so," Kristie said. "I agree with Val and Sharon."

"Of course, I'm the bad guy," Tessie said.

"No, you're practical," Kristie said. "And so am I."

She walked toward me and put her arms around my waist, her head level with where my diaphragm used to be. She hugged me hard and I could feel her chest hitching.

"I'm sorry Ted," she said, her voice unsteady. She looked up at me, tears forming in her eyes. "I don't want to do this, but I'm not strong enough. I feel very close to you now, but—I can't—" Her voice dissolved into tears as she started to cry harder, burying her head in my midsection again.

"But you have to go," I said, putting my arms around her.

"Yes," she whispered. "I can't be around you, not when you're in so much danger..."

Tessie looked up in shock. Val looked at the floor sadly and Sharon just stared at her.

"You're right. I have to go," she said. "I'm sorry I'm such a coward, but—"

"You're not a coward," I said, holding her more tightly. "And stop worrying. This is probably the safest..." I couldn't finish, knowing Tessie might be thinking the same thing.

"I'm sorry," she said again as she rushed out of the house.

"Kristie—" Tessie turned to follow her, but I gently pulled her back.

"Let her go," I said. "It's the best thing for her. I don't want her to feel unsafe and being near me right now...well..."

The three of them looked at me sadly. Val and Sharon turned to go after Kristie. Tessie stayed behind, her eyes tearing up as she watched me angrily. I could see the rage building.

"Go ahead. Tell me," I said, sighing.

"This is why I didn't want you to get involved! This is why I wanted you to walk away! Because now..." She sobbed and hid her hands in her face.

"Now you have to choose between me or your friends," I said.

She shook her head slowly. "No. Because now I have to leave you, too. That's why I'm so angry with you! Because of what you've done, my mom...doesn't want me to see you any more..."

It hit me like a sledgehammer. I wasn't prepared for that at all. I never considered that I'd never have Tessie in my life.

"But Tessie, you're practically an adult! You can make your own decisions!"

"And break my mom's heart? Make her sick with worry, wondering if I won't come home after a date?" She shook her head again. "I can't do that."

We stood there looking at each other. I couldn't believe it, but I felt the rage building again. Heaping layer upon layer of ice-laden anger. Chad was taking everything from me and he hadn't done a thing. It was me, this time. Me and my anger.

"When this is over—"

"It will never be over," she said quickly, lunging at me and wrapping her arms around me, hugging me fiercely. "It will always be this way. And if it's not Chad and Donnie, it will be someone or something else. You're always so angry, so willing to fight! It's as if...you go looking for trouble. I know you don't and I know Chad started everything, but...it takes two..."

I nodded and held her more tightly, kissing the top of her head. "I'm sorry. I really screwed things up. But when it's straightened out—"

"No," she said firmly, stepping back. "I wish I could believe you, but no. There is no straightening this out. And even if there is, the way you'd do it... And what happens after Chad? Who's next? Do you start on the kids stealing from their mother's wallets? It will never end for you, Ted, I can see that. There will always be a fight or a last stand. I'm sorry, but this is goodbye for me, too."

"But Tessie, I—"

"Goodbye Ted," she said as she ran from the lab and out the back door. I watched her go, feeling more empty than ever...

Last One

"Seven feet, four inches," Devin whispered, slumping and collapsing onto his stool. "And 375 pounds. Your body is becoming more dense and you're growing, still growing."

"The new pump?"

"Nowhere near completed," Devin said. "If I worked on it every day for the next six months, it could be ready, but…"

"I probably don't have that long, do I? At this rate, I'll be at eight feet in a couple of months, probably stressing the pump beyond its limits. I know you said it's supposed to last me until I'm at least nine feet, but I can hear it struggling."

"You're right. It's not as good a design or as strong as the first one, plus it was strained trying to pump the fluid that had congealed during the operation. And the sheer volume that has to be moved…well, it's a lot of stress on the pump. You probably don't have six months. Less," Devin said, even more quietly. "I've failed you, son." He took off his glasses and put them on the lab table, burying his face in his hands.

"Devin," I said gently, putting my hands on his shoulders. "You gave me new life. I met Tessie and experienced real love. I made wonderful friends. All because of you."

"But what did I take from you?" he sobbed quietly. "I'm the one who caused this with the accident. And then by trying to correct it, I instilled anger and frustration in you. I teased you with the promise of life, only to take it away and make you feel less than human! You found someone you made a real connection with, but I took it away. Me and my miracle cure."

"And I'd do it all again," I said, wrapping my arms around him. "By becoming less human physically, I became more human in other ways. You helped me."

"But now you'll lose everything," Devin said breathlessly. "If Donald Lawson doesn't find you first, you'll die!"

"I know," I said, standing. My voice hardened as I clenched my fists. "That's why I'm going to find Chad. Before it's too late."

Before Devin could answer, I walked quickly to the garage and got into The Judge, not letting up on the accelerator one inch as I drove off.

Hunting

I drove to town, windows down and radio blasting Lamb of God. The radio station I normally listen to was celebrating their upcoming concert in Greensboro by playing all of their albums, back-to-back. I was listening to "Omerta", realizing that Uncle Donnie probably knew a lot about that particular law – the law of silence. I earned a few nasty looks from other drivers with the level of volume, but most of them looked the other way when I stared them down. The ones that didn't merely put their windows up, shaking their heads.

Knowing that Chad was a regular around Cold Stone Creamery and the movie theater, I thought I'd start with the Cold Stone Creamery manager. I pulled my car into an open spot and gunned the engine before shutting it down. A few people turned around to appreciate the sound, whistling at the car. But when I stepped out, they found interest in something else. I stood by the car, debating whether or not to lock it – usually, my appearance is a good enough theft deterrent. I thought it would work again tonight, so I left it unlocked.

I looked up in the moonless night sky. I took comfort in that, the darkness of a moonless night. I could feel the breeze blowing past me, spreading the smell of fresh, crisp fall air. Most people were walking the streets in groups, coats wrapped around them against the wind. But I was walking around in a black t-shirt, alone, of course. My enormous stature drew a lot of attention, but most people looked away as I got closer and looked them in the eye.

I could see people laughing, huddled together, holding hands or walking with their arms around each other. The feeling of friendship and love was almost palpable, almost visible in the cold night air. But I felt outside it, beneath it, being crushed by its weight. I might as well have been a tree in the dark, with dead leaves blowing around me under the cold starlight. Everyone seemed to have someone – everyone but me.

What did I expect? After all, wasn't I playing the role of outsider? I wasn't making any attempt to hide my unnatural appearance. I could have worn a jacket to cover up my gray skin, a hat to hide my face in shadows, but shrugged the idea off – why fit in? And hadn't I alienated the only people who had accepted me? Having been marked by Donnie, hadn't I accepted banishment from the only friends I had? And since I decided not to hide my appearance or mask it, why was I surprised to feel outside humanity?

So why was I feeling so isolated... and angry about it? It was a natural outcome of my decisions and actions, so why should I be angry? I fought the anger as I walked across the street to Cold Stone Creamery and opened the door. I heard the manager gasp and say "Oh crap" as he exhaled. I smiled at him, but it was more like a grimace.

"Don't worry, I'm not going to break anything," I said as I approached the counter.

"Holy crow," the manager squeaked. "Did you *grow* since the last time I saw you?"

"You recognize me," I joked. "I wasn't sure you would."

"Right," the guy laughed. "We always get guys like you coming in. So, can I get you anything?"

"Actually, I'm hunting," I said, looking around the shop. "I'm looking for someone and wondering if anyone has been looking for me."

Several people hurriedly looked back to their desserts or suddenly became very interested in looking out the windows. I continued to stare at them, and, sure enough, one of them looked up again. I met his eyes with what I hoped was a menacing stare. He looked away, nervously fidgeting and whispering to his friends.

"Looking for anyone in particular?" He looked around me. "I don't see your friends anywhere."

"I'm not looking for them," I said. The guy I had stared down got up and motioned for his friends to follow him out the door.

"You're scaring away customers," the manager said, nodding toward the door.

"One of the perks of being me," I said, shrugging. "Like I asked before as part of my initial question, do you know if anyone else has been looking for me?"

"Well, there are some cute young women over there by the door that can't take their eyes off you," he said.

"Probably because they're repulsed by my horrid appearance."

"They aren't looks of repulsion. More like interest."

"Good to know," I said, looking over my shoulder and catching a glance from a redhead sitting at the table. She nervously looked down at her hands. "Actually, I was looking for someone else."

"Chad?"

"How did you guess?"

"Well," he started, "you don't look happy. And you certainly don't look like you're looking for company. Since you said you were hunting and it wasn't for your friends, it made sense. Remembering what happened the last time I saw you – you look the same way, by the way – I thought you might be looking for him."

"Good guess," I said, nodding. "So, have you seen him?"

"Look, I know you're bigger than the average bear and all, but that might not be good for your health."

I just stared at him, waiting, drumming my fingers loudly on the counter. He cleared his throat and fidgeted a little.

"Right. Well, he's been around, but not much since you tuned him up in the park. Oh yeah," he said as I frowned, confused, "that's been around the town for a while. A lot of people were happy about it, the mystery man who cleaned up the town."

"When did you last see Chad?"

"Not since the episode in the park," he said, nodding his head over to the end of the counter. "Come over here; I don't want anyone to hear this part."

Intrigued, I did as he said and leaned over the counter when he motioned with his index finger. In a hushed voice, he continued.

"The redhead that was looking at you – wait, is still looking at you – anyway, he was hitting on her the last time. After you scared him away from your friends, he latched on to her. But she definitely wasn't appreciating the attention."

"I'll bet. Anyone else?"

"Nope, just her. Hey, you're not going to start any trouble, are you?"

"No," I said. "I'm going to finish some. Thanks for the tip."

I turned to walk out the door and slowed a little when I got near the table the redhead was sitting at. With my freakishly fast thinking, I started weighing my options.

Option 1: nod, smile, and continue walking, then try to catch up with her later.

Option 2: walk on by and ignore her, then follow her and try to catch Chad in the act.

Option 3: make her my new best friend, and then smite Chad with my righteous anger.

I liked Option 3.

She looked up, smiling shyly, and I smiled at her, finally stopping.

"Hey," I said.

"Oh! Hi," she said, shaking a little. "You scared me!"

"I know I look a little scary, but I promise I don't bite," I said, chuckling.

"I'm sorry," she said, covering her eyes in embarrassment.

"Nice one, Ash," her friend said.

"Ash. Is that short for Ashley?"

"Yes," the friend said. "And I'm Trish."

"Ted," I said, realizing that the name I gave was the one Devin created for someone special. My first attempt at making friends. I pushed that thought away and held out my hand, hoping this one wouldn't be as much of a disaster as the last.

"Wow," Trish said, "your hands are huge!"

"Trish," Ashley said sternly, holding out her hand to shake mine. "Nice to meet you Ted."

"Nice to meet you – is it Ashley or Ash?"

"You can call me Ash," she said, giggling, "everyone else does."

"Oh my God, can you get any more pathetic," Trish said. "See, this is why guys take advantage of you!"

"I promise I won't," I said immediately, looking at Trish sincerely.

Even though I had an agenda making friends with Ash, I didn't want to take advantage of her. Although if I were being honest with myself, wasn't I still using her? I ignored that thought for the moment.

"Look, I know this probably sounds like a pick-up line, but I'm a nice guy."

"Sorry," Trish said, wincing. "You probably are, I just hate to see—"

"—me get taken advantage of," Ash said, sighing. "Thanks, Mom. Ever think *that's* why I can never get a date on Saturday night?"

"That's odd. Neither can I," I said, smiling. "What are you doing this Saturday?"

Both Ash and Trish laughed out loud, barely controlling themselves.

"OK, so that did sound like a pick-up line," I said.

"Maybe a little," Ash said, wiping tears from her eyes as she kept laughing harder. "But I'm not doing anything. What did you have in mind?"

"I thought we'd start off slow – like a morning walk in the park."

"I don't know," she said softly, peeking at me from under her red eyelashes.

"Please," I said, trying my best to smile. "I'll get down on my knees and beg if you want."

"Do it!" Trish was practically jumping up and down in her seat.

"No!" Ash shook her head and her hair slipped out of place into her face. She nervously pushed it back, looking around at the staring faces.

"OK, I won't. But will you be there Saturday?"

"Mind if I bring a chaperone?" Ash asked, looking at me shyly.

"Not at all," I said. "Not a bad idea, since you don't know me at all. By the way, that's one of the reasons I picked a public place in daylight."

"Sensitive," Trish said, eyeing me appreciatively. "Tall, dark, and sensitive."

"*Trish!*"

"That's me," I said. "I'll meet you and your chaperone at 10 by the duck pond. Sound good?"

"OK," Ash said quietly. She smiled and brushed her hair out of her eyes. Green eyes. And the blush on her pale, freckled skin looked good with her red hair.

"See you then," I said. "Let me give you my number." I knelt on the floor, but still had to bend down a little to write on a napkin on the table.

"Be still my beating heart," Trish said, fanning herself with her hand. "Down on bended knee, even."

"Is she going to be the chaperone?" I asked, eyeing Trish with what I hoped was an evil smile.

"I'll bring duct tape," Ash promised.

"I'll supply the gag," I said, pushing the napkin over to her. "Have a good night."

"You too," she said softly, biting her bottom lip.

"And don't worry," I said. "I might look like an enormous ogre, but I'm not bad once you get to know me."

"OK, Shrekenstein," Trish said. "I promise I'll be on my best behavior."

"Right. I'll believe that when I see it," I said skeptically.

"She will, I promise," Ash said, scowling at her friend, then breaking into laughter.

Alone

I walked out of the shop, looking at Ash as I walked away, a smile on my face. She waved a little and smiled shyly. I smiled back and laughed a little, giving her a wave of my own.

I turned away from her to walk toward my car and the smile slipped from my face, a grimace forming to replace it. I felt pathetic. And conniving, cruel, scheming, and every other horrible adjective I could think of. I was using Ash to get to Chad and she would figure it out soon enough. I hated myself for what I was doing, but I knew it was the only way. I was laying a trap for Chad, just waiting for him to come back to Ash.

If I were totally honest with myself, I'd admit that Ash was attractive. Beyond that, she seemed sweet, if a little naïve. And Trish definitely had some of the qualities that Tessie's friends had. Although they'd never replace my original friends, I could still see that it would be fun to hang out with them. But is that what I wanted to do, look for replacements for what I had lost? Did I really want to treat people like substitutes?

I tried not to think about how much I was using Ash, tried to think it was for the greater good. I knew I'd never let anything happen to her or Trish for that matter: Chad would never hurt another innocent woman again.

I turned the corner and walked toward the theater, looking at the crowd as it emptied. I moved back into an alley and leaned against the wall, watching them as they walked out of the darkened theater and into the light, laughing, joking, not a care in the world. Sheep. They never saw the world as it truly was, the one where wolves like Chad lived on the fringe and picked off the sheep.

As I stood there, dead leaves blew into the alley, across my feet. I turned my back to the entrance and looked down the bleak, dark alley. I realized I was on the fringe, too. But I wasn't a wolf. I was a hunter, using unsuspecting sheep to lure the wolf into the open to get a clear shot.

I walked out of the alley and started back to my car. I glanced at the crowd as I walked to my car, then stopped short. I saw Tessie walking out of the theater – followed by Val, Kristie, and Sharon. She turned back to them and said something that made them all laugh. Watching them, I realized this would be my life – living in shadows and darkness, a voyeur at best, a mere witness to life.

Life. I smiled at the irony of that.

Even the charade I was planning with Ash and Trish was nothing. It was me playing at life, not really living it. Yes, I'd probably have fun with them, but I knew they would be short-lived friends. Especially once they found out what I had been planning when I first met them. I only hoped I could make up for it over the next few weeks or months...

Tessie turned in my direction and it was her turn to stop short. She spotted me – and her friends followed her gaze. I abruptly turned my back and walked quickly to my car, practically jogging. I could hear my name, but didn't know which one of them was calling it. I ignored them as all of them started calling to me.

I jumped in the car and savagely turned the ignition, nearly ripping it off the steering column. I cranked the radio and roared out of the parking spot, speeding down the street a little sideways as my rear tires left plumes of smoke behind me. I looked in my rearview mirror. I could see them still running after me, slowing as they ran into the middle of the street.

I drove into the darkness and away from them.

Interlude

After I had put my car in the garage, I stomped into the kitchen. I stopped momentarily to calm down before going to my room, sitting on a stainless steel barstool. I could hear Devin walking into the kitchen hesitantly.

"Tessie called," Devin began quietly.

I ignored the comment.

"She saw you by the theater," he continued. "She said she and her friends called to you, but you didn't hear them."

I ignored that one, too.

"Ted, you should call."

"No, I shouldn't. It's not safe for any of them. Their decision was the right one, even if it does hurt. I'm not angry with them. I can't be part of their lives – especially given what I have to do."

"But you don't," Devin said, raising his voice. "You don't need to do this!"

"Devin, I'm not going to argue. I've made my decision."

"But you should at least allow her to apologize. She feels awful for the way she left things and wants to talk. Lilly says she cries herself to sleep most nights."

"It's hard, I know," I admitted. "It's not easy for me, either. Tessie was the closest thing to a real life that I've had. But I can't be selfish." I cringed, realizing that's exactly what I was doing with Ash.

"You don't need to take such a fatalist attitude!"

"Yes, I do," I said. "This is the way it has to be." I got up and went to my room quickly, trying to drown out my thoughts with Slipknot's shrieking lyrics and blistering guitars.

Saturday

"So, did you bring the duct tape?" I whispered to Ash as we watched Trish duck-walking around the pond, following the real ducks walking away from her.

"Forgot it, sorry," Ash said, smiling sweetly.

"You certainly are an odd duck," I said loudly to Trish.

"Look who's talking," Trish said.

"*Trish!* Ted, I'm sorry, I—"

"Don't worry," I said, waving her apology away. "My feelings aren't hurt."

"I'm just kidding," Trish said, standing up. "Lighten up, Ash."

"Maybe the reason I can't keep a man is you, you web-footed freak," Ash said, picking up an acorn and chucking it at Trish.

"'Keep a man'. Hmm, what exactly did you have in mind? Are you looking for a proposal?" I nudged her gently with my elbow.

"Easy with that thing," she said, chuckling and rubbing her side. "You could break a rib."

"You haven't answered my question."

"Well..." she looked at me, obviously embarrassed. "No, I'm not looking for a proposal. I don't even think I'm looking for a serious relationship." She even framed the words 'serious relationship' in air quotes. "I just want to have fun."

"Ditto," I said. "Friends?"

"Absolutely," she said.

"Good. Can I have him?" Trish stepped up and hooked her arm through mine. "On second thought, maybe not. My skin tone clashes with yours."

"Do you know how to swim?" I asked innocently.

"Yes—wait, don't you dare!" Trish started to run away and I laughed at her, lumbering after her.

"Come on," I yelled after her, "I'm sure the water isn't that cold!"

We walked toward the refreshment stand so Ash and Trish could get something to drink. I, of course, declined.

"I've got a lot of food allergies," I said lamely. We walked to the edge of the park, near the woods, and sat down on a bench.

"So..." I started. "I have to commend both of you on your manners. Your parents must be exceptionally proud."

Trish and Ash looked at each other, shrugging.

"OK, neither of us have a clue," Trish said. "What are you talking about?"

"My appearance," I said. Both of them exchanged extremely uncomfortable glances. "You guys haven't asked one question or made one weird comment or given me any stares or looks. OK, maybe Trish made some weird comments, but she seems to make those a lot."

"Well, you're right, it's not polite," Ash said.

"Yeah, we figured you'd tell us – if you wanted to," Trish said, shrugging.

"You're not curious? The two of you must have talked."

"Of course!" Both of them said it at once and giggled nervously.

"It's no big secret," I said naturally enough. "I was hit by a car. Most of the injuries – like the scars and the skin color – are the result of the injuries and the treatments I had to heal."

"Were you always this big?" Trish took a long sip of her soda, raising her eyebrows.

"Not exactly," I answered, chuckling. "Something sparked my growth. Maybe the treatments. Or maybe the accident damaged my pituitary or something. There have been cases where external stresses or events have caused accelerated growth in people." It was a good thing I couldn't blush – I was doing my best to keep a poker face, but I felt awful about lying to them.

"Mystery explained," Ash said, smiling. "I thought maybe you were an alien."

"Ha," I said, folding my arms.

"OK," Trish said, pointing at my arms. "Those? Are huge. You look like you are *ripped* my friend."

"Maybe a little," I said, flexing my arms a bit, groaning when I heard a seam rip. "Great, I think I just ruined my shirt."

"Wow-wee!" Trish reached over and lifted the sleeve of my shirt to look at the seam. "And as long as I'm this close," she said as she gave my arm a squeeze. "It feels like steel! And about as cold! Aren't you freezing?"

"Not really," I said, shrugging. "My body temp has always run a little low since the accident."

"And I think your nerve endings must have been damaged if you don't feel cold," Trish said.

"Let me feel," Ash said, running her hand along my arm. "Wow," she said laughing, "Trish is right; you feel like you should be freezing."

"Well, you know what they say," I said, smiling. "Cold biceps, warm heart."

———

I took Ash and Trish for a ride in the car after our excursion in the park. Ash really liked the way it looked and wanted to see if it felt as cool as it looked. Trish was game, so I took them for a spin around Burlington, out onto the highway to crank the engine up, than back onto Huffman Mill Road toward the city again.

"OK, that was awesome," Trish said as she climbed out of the back of the car. "Rick would love that."

"Rick?" I asked.

"Trish's boyfriend," Ash answered. "He's a real car nut. You two would get along well."

"Hey, maybe the four of use could get together," Trish said. "That way, Ash and I could talk while Rick drools over the car."

"What about you?" I asked Ash. "Isn't there anyone you'd like to invite?"

"Well, there is this tall giant gray guy, but he's just a friend," Ash said.

"She's kind of sworn off guys," Trish said.

"For a while, anyway."

"Want to talk about it?" I asked casually.

"Not really," Ash said, shaking her head and frowning. "The last guy I dated turned out to be a loser. And the only other guy besides you to show any interest...well..."

"Chad," Trish said in disgust. "I heard he got the crud stomped out of him. By a guy who matches your description."

"Yeah," I said sighing. "Unfortunately, I showed some weakness toward the end or I really would have given him a good beating."

"High five on that," Trish said holding out her hand as I smacked it. "OK, lighten up, dude. It's like smacking a rock."

"Sooo..." I started.

"Want to do this again sometime?" Ash asked, smiling at me.

"I would. Even with the chaperone, if necessary," I said, bowing deferentially (and mockingly) to Trish.

"Thank you," she said, mimicking a curtsey.

"OK. I'll give you a call later in the week?"

"Sounds good," I said, stepping toward her and giving her an awkward hug.

"Aw, ain't that sweet," Trish said, batting her eyes.

"That was a friend hug," I said, "you're getting one, too." I swept her up in my arms and spun her around, laughing as she tottered a little when I set her back down.

She giggled, trying to catch her breath – and her balance. "Wow! You have to give me a warning or something next time!"

"Talk to you later this week," I said winking at Ash and walking back to my car. Of course, I turned to make sure she was looking and gave her a little wave. She waved back, beaming at me.

I got in my car and looked at my reflection in the rearview mirror. I sighed, looking through the windshield at the other sheep, thinking about how I was leading Ash – and Trish – around by the nose, just waiting for Chad to show the first sign of any attention.

I looked up at my reflection again and with a snarl, yanked the mirror off the windshield, cracking the windshield in the process. I restrained the urge to explode, putting the rearview mirror on the passenger's seat next to me. I exhaled slowly, and drove home – carefully.

Devin

As I drove up the long driveway to the house, looking through the cracked windshield, I knew I'd have questions from Devin. Where I had been, who I was with, what I was doing. Probably more emphasis on the latter question.

I pulled into the garage and parked the Judge, making a mental note to call Monday to get the windshield replaced. I turned off the car and unfolded myself from the driver's seat, thinking I'd have to check into a way to have the front seat customized to move it a little further back from the dashboard.

Which was why I was surprised when I opened the door and Devin was standing there in the doorway, looking at me with his eyebrows up and his arms folded. I thought I'd at least have a chance to get through the door.

Uh-oh.

"Hi," I said, moving to walk around him. He stepped in front of me.

"Where were you?" he asked quietly.

I knew this was coming, but knowing didn't help how I felt about it.

"Out with some friends," I said, not looking him in the eye.

"Friends? Who?"

"No one you know," I said as he stepped back and allowed me into the house.

"And do they know you? I mean, really know you? Or do they just know the version you want them to know?" Devin uncrossed his arms and clasped them behind his back, looking very much like a strict school teacher upbraiding an errant student.

"Devin, we've been through this. Of course they don't know the real me."

"Then how can you call them friends? Or have you made it routine to lie to friends now?" he asked, raising his voice.

"It's easier this way," I said, hanging up my keys and turning to face him again.

"Of course it is."

"Stop it," I said, raising my voice to match his volume. "You don't know how I feel about this. You can't know how conflicted I feel, how horrible."

"Then stop," Devin said gently. "It's an easy solution. Just stop. Tell them the truth and they'll probably forgive you. Even if they don't, at least you'd stop the pain you're in."

"I can't just stop. If I want to stop Chad—"

"But it shouldn't be up to you," Devin said. "That's the point. You've appointed yourself the protector of this town, but that's a job for the courts and the police."

"The courts and cops can't stop him. It has to be me. And I have to do it anyway possible. I have to trap him."

"Regardless of the cost," Devin said firmly. "Is that what you really believe? No cost is too high?"

"I don't know," I answered honestly. "I don't want Ash or Trish to get hurt. I'm almost positive they won't—"

"Almost positive," he interrupted. "But not certain."

I shrugged my shoulders, not answering. There was no way I could answer.

"And how about how these girls will feel when you're through with them? How about what you're doing to them? What Chad does is worse, yes, but you are using them, aren't you?"

I didn't answer.

"Aren't you?" he asked, tugging at my arm gently. "I know your intentions are good. And I know you'll protect them and even continue your friendship. That is, if they'll still have you. You're asking an awful lot of new friends, Ted."

"I know that. And yes, I'm planning to continue our friendship if I can. I hope they'll understand. But I need to do this. I feel like I was *made* for this."

Devin recoiled as if I had slapped him. He slowly sat down on a stool, looking winded. "Made? I didn't make you."

"That's not what I meant," I said. "Circumstances made me for this. You saved me, but something larger – call it fate or whatever – *made* me into this."

"So you feel like an instrument of fate," Devin said, looking at me carefully. "Why?"

"How can you ask me that?" I asked quietly. "You of all people. You, the only one who knows how truly unique I am. How can you ask me that?"

"I'm trying to understand," Devin said.

"I'm stronger than almost any human on the planet. I don't injure. The compound you developed uniquely fits my physical makeup. You yourself said there was a latency in me that responded in a way you hadn't anticipated. I don't require hardly any sleep, almost no nourishment, and you are the closest thing I have to a relative. I have no identity, no loose ends. Circumstances – fate – whatever – put me in this position for a reason. I was thrown into your path for a reason, literally. I was standing in that road for a reason. And what you've done for me makes me the perfect fit for this. I'm an instrument of reckoning."

"Stop," Devin said, standing. He was shaking. "I never meant for this to happen, any of this. I didn't want to make a tool of vengeance and retribution."

"I know," I said, putting my hand on his shoulder. "You wanted to give me a second chance. *I'm* the one who is twisting that second chance into something you never intended."

"But you think fate did intend for this to happen? You think fate...pushed me into this," Devin said, a statement more than a question.

"Yes," I answered, putting my other hand on his shoulder. "I think I've finally found my purpose in the second chance I've been given."

I could feel Devin's shoulders slump as he sat back down on the stool. More like collapsed.

"My God," he said, whispering, "what have I done."

"It's not you," I said, sitting next to him and putting my arm around him. "It's not your fault. You did what you thought was right. I'm the one who bears responsibility for what I'm doing now. Not you. I still have freedom, Devin; freedom to choose my own path, no matter how twisted or perverted from what you intended."

"But you don't need to—"

"Yes, I do," I said. "It's my choice, a choice I know you wouldn't take away from me even if you could. End of discussion. I'm sorry."

I got up and walked toward the stairs. I hesitated, then turned back. Devin was still sitting on the stool, looking after me. The light over the stove lit only half his face, showing an aged, haunted look – the look of a creator who has unleashed a monster on the world. The other half of his face was shrouded in darkness, featureless.

"I'm sorry," I said again, turning away and heading up the stairs.

Ash

I was spending a couple of days a week with Ash – sometimes both Trish and Ash, but mostly just Ash. She was sweet, fun to be with, and so innocent that I almost fell into the trap the rest of the population (who are sheep) believe – that the world is a good place with people who are generally good, doing mostly good things.

A few weeks after our first meeting, I drove over to her house for a "TV night". AMC was airing a run of National Lampoon movies that she wanted to watch.

"Haven't you seen most of them before?" I had asked a couple of days before the "date".

"Yes. But not with you," she said. "Movies can be different experience each time, depending on who you watch them with. Besides, I thought we could get to know each other a little better watching a comedy."

"Good choice," I said. "I'm partial to Mel Brooks movies myself – History of the World Part I, Spaceballs, you know. But I like National Lampoon's stuff, too."

"Spaceballs. Really?"

"Yeah," I said. "Pizza the Hut is my favorite character. Makes me look like a model."

"Oh yuck, that creeped me out. I couldn't eat pizza for a month after watching that scene," she said, wrinkling her nose in disgust.

———

I pulled up in front of her house, making sure to park in the street so I wouldn't block her parents in the driveway if they were going out. And I had a feeling Ash would contrive a way to be alone with me. I frowned as I got out of the car, not sure how I felt about being alone with her.

I was wondering if I'd feel the same spark I felt with Tessie, hoping I wouldn't, realizing it would be more painful to do it all over again. But I didn't need to worry – I wasn't attracted to her the way I was to Tessie. And it turned out that Ash wasn't interested in a more serious relationship. We did like spending time together, but it was purely a friendship. For now, at least.

Thankfully, her parents weren't overly concerned about her spending time with me. I got to meet her parents earlier – which was almost a disaster.

"Good thing she's not interested in you," her father said, lowering his voice so she couldn't hear me. "None of my threats of doing you bodily harm if you hurt my little girl would do any good." He laughed and clapped me on the shoulder, shaking his head at my massive size.

Her mom insisted on feeding me, even after I tried to explain that I really couldn't eat anything.

"How on earth do you grow, then?" she asked after trying to ply me with oatmeal cookies.

"Special nutritive drinks," I explained. "Honestly, I don't quite understand how they work, but Devin – my father, or adoptive father – is a genius. He's keeping me healthy, despite all my allergies."

I smiled as I got to the front door because before I could knock, it opened and her father was standing there with his hand extended.

"Ted," he said, nodding at me as he shook my hand. "Watch your head on the doorframe, big boy. Whew, you keep growing and I'm going to have to move the TV to the garage."

"Dad!" Ash came around the corner, hands on her hips. She was wearing a baggy sweatshirt and sweatpants. "Ease up, will you?"

"It's OK Ash," I said, shaking his hand lightly (but still seeing a little wince). "Sorry – I tried to go light!"

"No problem," he said. "Good to know my little girl is in the care of such strong hands. I don't have to set the alarm with you around!"

"Stop making fun of his size," Ash said, looking truly mortified.

"He's not making fun," I said and I could see her dad's mischievous grin. "Maybe a little. But I'm OK with it. He's not hurting my feelings, honest."

"Behave, Dan," Ash's mother said as she walked in from the kitchen. "Hi Ted, good to see you again."

"Good to see you, too," I said, nodding politely.

"We'll be over at the Martins'," her mom said. "You know the number—"

"Mom, I'm not a kid," Ash said, sighing.

"She's right, Pat," her father said. "Besides, what do you think could happen that Andre the Giant couldn't handle?"

"Go! Now!" Ash put her hands on her dad's back and pushed him toward the door. I laughed and stepped out of the way as she shooed her parents out, closing the door with her back and leaning on it. "How embarrassing. Sorry about that."

"Don't worry," I said, chuckling and waving it off.

"OK. But to make amends, you can pick your spot on the couch," she said, grabbing my arm and trying to drag me into the TV room. "You're going to have to play along and pretend that I'm dragging you. You weigh like three times what I weigh."

"Got it," I said, walking into the TV room with her. I sat down on the couch and looked around. "Where are you going to sit?"

"Very funny," she said, slapping my leg and moving me over as best she could. She picked up a bowl of popcorn off the coffee table and leaned in against me. "It's like leaning against cold steel," she said, pulling the blanket down off the back of the couch and wrapping up in it before leaning against me again. Sighing with exasperation, she then grabbed a pillow and stuck it between us. "Better."

I pretended to yawn and stretched my arm out behind her. She started giggling, then laughing right out loud. "So nonchalant."

"I know, not very subtle," I admitted. "I'm trying to practice on you for a real date, if I ever go on one. But then again, you can't be very subtle when you're over seven-four and weigh 375 pounds."

She whistled softly. "I'm not sure the couch is rated for that."

"I'll get your folks a new one if it breaks," I said. "So, what are we really doing tonight?"

"I don't know what you're talking about," she said. "We're watching movies."

"Which you admitted you've seen about a dozen times each. So I ask again: what are we really doing? Nothing too naughty, I hope."

"Funny. Especially since you know I've sworn off guys and from what I've been able to pick up, you've sworn off girls."

"Agreed then. We'll behave ourselves while your parents are gone. But what are we really going to be doing?"

"Talking," she said. "You caught me. I wanted to get you alone so I could talk to you."

"About?" I asked, very wary. Ash was smart. I knew my lame excuses for not eating and vague descriptions of my conditions and treatment would only last so long.

"A few things," she said. "Like first, what's really going on with you?"

"What do you mean?"

"I mean you don't eat and you grow like a weed. Your body temp is way below normal, but you're never cold. You're probably stronger than three grown men and your arms feel like they're made of iron." She was ticking off each point on her fingers, her voice getting quieter with each word she said.

"I take vitamins," I said, smiling.

"And you're...well...*gray*. I mean, I know people have skin conditions and issues, but your skin is like leather."

"Does that bother you?" I asked, leaning in a little.

She smiled a little and shook her head. "No, I just think there's more to it than you're telling me."

"You think I'm lying to you."

"Not exactly. Just not telling the whole story," she said, shrugging her shoulders.

"A lie of omission."

"I don't like the word 'lie'," she said. "I'm sure there's a reason you're not telling me everything. I just wanted to find out if there is more."

Damn. She caught me. And she was deftly avoiding an argument by not calling me a liar (which I really deserved). I knew she was observant, but she's a lot more forward than Tessie. I couldn't be as honest with her as I was with Tessie. I cringed from my callous decision, but I needed Ash. I couldn't afford to have her scared away by the truth.

"There is," I admitted. "But I can't tell you."

"Why? Are you afraid I'll tell Trish?" she asked, slapping me lightly on the chest with the back of her hand.

"No," I said earnestly. "But I can't tell you everything."

"OK, but why?"

"I'm afraid," I said quietly. Telling her the truth – but again, not the whole truth. "I'm afraid you'll walk away."

"I won't," she said, grabbing my hand. "Look, I know we're not exactly dating, but I still care about you. We might only be friends, but that doesn't mean I stop thinking about you or caring about you when I'm not with you."

"I know," I said, smiling. "But it's hard. I promise I'll tell you everything. Just not yet." And I meant it. After I got to Chad, I would tell her everything. Then I'd deal with her anger and feelings of betrayal, of being used.

"OK. So how about the growth and strength. Is there anything you can tell me there?"

"Well," I started. "Not really. And that's only because I really don't understand what's happening, which translates to 'Devin doesn't understand what's happening'. Devin isn't sure when – or if – it will taper off."

"What does that mean, though? How big could you get?"

"He has no idea. There have been people with pituitary disorders that get much taller than I am. But they usually also have physical problems which I don't have."

"That doesn't sound encouraging," she said, picking up a few pieces of popcorn and tossing them into her mouth.

"Well, Devin thinks it won't be an issue," I said evasively. "My body is growing proportionately and I don't have any physical ailments with the growth. Besides, there are guys that are taller than me."

"Yes, but they're in the NBA," she pointed out. "And they aren't anywhere near as wide and solid as you are."

293

"Yeah, but I can't dunk," I said chuckling. "I've got no vertical leap."

She sniggered and picked some more popcorn out of the bowl.

"Anything else?" I said, cringing internally. I wasn't sure I wanted to dance around anymore issues.

"Well, what about the body temp and your skin? I'm sorry I'm being so blunt, but…"

"I know, you've been burned before," I finished for her. "To be honest, you'd have to ask Devin. Something about the treatments I get makes my skin feel and look the way it does. He's tried explaining it a few times, but I honestly feel like deciphering the US tax code written in Sanskrit or ancient Greek would be easier."

She laughed and nodded. "Fair enough. My science is OK, but not exactly my strong suit. How about the temp?"

"I know I always feel cold," I admitted. "I think it's my circulation. I remember Devin mentioned something about that last time we talked about the treatments. I have poor circulation, which makes me feel colder and lowers my temp a little. I also don't feel cold the way everyone else does."

"Like a reptile," she said, tossing popcorn at me.

"Funny," I said, chucking the popcorn back in the bowl.

"OK, how about the strength," she said, glancing back at the TV and laughing at Chevy Chase and his antics.

"The guy cracks me up, too. The strength is actually more natural than you'd think. I work out a lot." Bold-faced lie, but how could I tell her the truth?

"I thought so," she said smugly. "So, how much and how often?"

"Usually every day," I lied, trying to keep my voice even. "But I do skip a day once in a while."

"You lift?"

"Yes," I lied again. "Free weights mostly, plus some cardio and boxing."

"Boxing?"

"Yeah. Devin used to box and I just kind of picked it up. It helps with my anger issues."

"Anger issues? About what?"

"Does this mean we're done with the physical inquisition portion and we're moving on to the mental and emotional parts?"

"Sorry," she said, smiling sadly. "I know I'm not being very polite, but I feel like I hardly know you."

"That's OK," I said, relaxing a little now that I could move closer to the truth. "I get angry about a lot of things..." And I started in with the same speech(es) I had given Tessie: people wasting their lives, taking advantage of other people, etc., etc...

I could answer those questions more easily and be more honest. Even the questions about Chad. I danced away from questions about my "love life", but did answer a few questions about Tessie and her friends.

"Irreconcilable differences," I said shrugging my shoulders. "We didn't see eye to eye on a lot of things, so we kind of drifted apart."

"Sorry," she said, rubbing my arm. "I didn't mean to open old wounds."

"Actually, it's good to talk about it," I admitted honestly. "I can't really talk to Devin and I don't know any other people."

"Any time," Ash said, smiling and putting a hand on my shoulder. "So...irreconcilable differences..."

"Something like that," I said. "I viewed myself one way, she saw me another."

"Oh. How do you view yourself?"

I sighed and shook my head. "Are you sure you want to hear it?"

"I promise I won't judge you on your opinion of yourself," she said, barely containing a smile. "But I reserve the right to disagree."

"I don't really feel part of your world," I said honestly. I thought she deserved that much. "Besides my anger issues and my obvious difference in appearance, I just don't feel like part of life."

"I don't think you're the only one that feels that way," she said softly.

"Probably not," I admitted, "but I feel that way not just because of my appearance or how different I am from everyone else. I feel that way because there's a dark side to my past, even though I don't remember it all. And I just feel...so alone some times. And angry."

"Anger doesn't make you different. If anything, it makes you more like everyone else than you think."

"But it's how I feel when I'm angry."

"Besides angry? OK, now I'm confused."

I debated, but decided to push on. At least I could claim I tried to tip her off when my house of cards collapses. "Part of the reason I box is to work off the anger. But I can't get rid of the thoughts."

"The thoughts?"

"Violent thoughts. Thoughts of revenge and vengeance."

"Like an avenger," she said. At first I thought she was kidding, but the expression on her face was serious enough.

"I guess, but I've never seen myself as a superhero."

"Well, this might come as a surprise but you're not the first to have thoughts of violence and revenge, either," she said, patting my leg softly. "You shouldn't be so hard on yourself."

I looked at her and smiled. She was wrong, but I smiled anyway. "Maybe it's the music I listen to."

"That I can believe," she said, rolling her eyes. "The noise you listen to would make charter members of PETA think about clubbing baby seals."

I laughed so loud she actually jumped a little, then started laughing herself.

"That's a good one!"

"Stick around," she said, tossing a few more pieces of popcorn in her mouth, "I got a million of 'em."

Chad – Again

Things were going OK for a while. I spent some more time with Ash and truly felt that we were friends. I always declined big parties or get-togethers, but she kept asking anyway.

"One of these days you'll surprise me and say yes," she said, shrugging her shoulders and smiling.

And just when I was thinking maybe I wouldn't need to play the role of avenger...

It happened again. Chad.

―――――

Ash and I were at a movie and walked right past Tessie and Val. Val looked like she was going to say something, but she saw Ash with me and decided against it, thankfully. I saw Tessie storm into the theater and I met Val's eyes. I could see her sadness.

After the movie started and got really boring (a real chick flick, if there ever was one), I went out to the snack bar to get a drink for Ash. And there was Val, just waiting for me to step out of the movie.

"How did you know I would come out?" I tried to act casual, but she was making me nervous. Out of Tessie and her friends, Val always seemed to be the one that could sense danger. And know when things would get out of control.

"Please," she replied, smiling a little. "You in a movie like that? I'm surprised you lasted that long."

"Me too," I laughed and nodded, shoving my hands in my pockets. I looked at her and could see she wasn't smiling anymore. A long silence followed and I knew she was thinking. Calculating.

"Friend of yours?" Val asked quietly.

"And nothing more," I stressed. "Just a friend, seriously."

"And is she in danger?" Val eyed me critically.

I sighed. "I don't know."

"Yes, you do," she said flatly. "I can see that on your face, Ted. And you're a horrible liar, even if you can't blush."

"Yes, she's in danger," I said evenly, frowning a little. She didn't flinch, even though my frowns usually made people drop what they were holding and start shaking uncontrollably.

"Playing with fire, you know," she said in her low voice. "I know it seems like we're all cowards for staying away—"

"No, you're smart," I interrupted. "And I'm a liar for not saying anything to Ash and her friend Trish. In some ways, I'm not better than Chad."

"Yes you are! Don't even think that!" Val hissed furiously, grabbing my arm tightly, digging her nails into my arm – or at least trying. "Don't compare yourself to that lowlife scum!"

"No, I'm not better than him Val. I befriended Ash because I knew Chad had gone after her, too. I've put just as big a bull's eye on her as I did on you guys. All for my revenge. But I'm doing what I have to."

"We all do, Shug," she said sadly, walking away and shaking her head.

I took Ash her drink and suffered through the rest of the film, mostly in silence. Once it was over, we walked out of the theater and there was Chad, across the street, leaning into his car. Thinking quickly, I hoped I'd be quick enough to get out of sight.

In those quick seconds, I thought of all the reasons not to do it: not to put Ash in harm's way, not to use her as a means to *my* ends, not to debase myself in that way or turn Devin's second chance into something twisted and deranged. I didn't want to expose her to danger. I didn't want to lower myself to Chad's level: he wanted to use Ash for his own sick, personal gratification, but isn't that what I was doing, too?

But I also thought about the reasons to do it. Yes, I was using Ash for my own personal reasons, but I was *right*. What I was doing was right, it was just. It needed to be done, by any means necessary.

And it would help protect Tessie.

And in that moment, I felt myself not just turn toward the darkness, but step into it willingly and embrace it, with the full knowledge of my actions and what that meant for me. What it said about me. I thought of Devin's response to my decision and maybe he was right to question what he had done for me. But I stepped into the abyss anyway.

"Just a second, I wanted to get a flier of coming attractions," I said, moving to go back into the theater lobby. "Something with action and violence that I can subject you to."

"I knew I was going to pay for picking this one," Ash groaned.

I stepped inside and around the corner. I gazed through the window, resting my hand on the handrail in front of me, and watched Chad – sure enough, I hadn't been seen. And he was approaching Ash. I could feel the horrible smile on my face and felt awful, knowing I had put her in danger. I was confident I could save her, but I thought that said more about my arrogance than the level of danger she was in.

Chad gave her a sleazy smile and stepped toward her, grabbing her arms. He was still sporting some of the marks from the previous beating I'd given him. She shrugged him off and jabbed her finger in his chest. After some pushing and shoving (mostly from Ash), I could see it was getting out of hand. And of course, no one stepped in. Just as I was getting ready to walk out and settle an old score, I was frozen in surprise at what happened next.

Val came running out of nowhere, practically launched herself in the air, and slammed Chad in the side of the head with her forearm.

Dazed, Chad stumbled and went down on one knee. As he stood, Val aimed a kick at his crotch, but missed and kicked him in the thigh. Chad stumbled again, limping, but quickly recovered and punched Val in the face. Val fell to the ground holding her bloody nose and Tessie rushed to her side. Chad stepped forward, pointing his finger at Val and yelling, looking furious.

In that moment, the quick flashes of memory returned, so strong they temporarily blotted out all vision, as if I were watching a movie.

...the woman again, her face bleeding and bruised, crying on the couch this time...

...the man, still smiling, jeering at her...

...the child hiding on the landing on the stairs, promising he'd stop this...

...clenching his fists, tears of anger and rage streaming down his face...

...one day...

Tessie walked forward, pointing her finger at Chad and yelling. He pushed her hand away and shoved her aside. He grabbed Ash's wrist and started toward his car, dragging her and yanking her along. And I could see things beginning to spiral out of control. First one friend injured, and now a second being taken away.

A sense of urgency filled me, like I'd never get her back if I didn't do something now. How could I face her mother and father, knowing I'd set this up? How could I look Devin in the eye or look at my own shattered reflection in the mirror? And even worse than all of that were the thoughts of what Chad would do to Ash when he got her alone. The sick, base, horrible things that he had planned for her.

Ignoring the door to the theater, I grabbed the handrail in front of me and ripped it off the wall. Then, I raised my foot and stomped it through the full-length window in front of me, shattering it into a million pieces as I roared as loud as I could, an inarticulate, guttural sound rending the dark night sky.

"LET HER GO!" I could hear my inhuman voice booming across the street. People screamed as I rushed out of the opening I just made in the side of the theater. Chad stopped cold and turned to look at me.

And for once, he was afraid.

Ash wriggled free and ran back toward me. She looked at the broken glass and me.

"My God, are you OK? Ted? *Ted?*"

She glanced back over her shoulder at Chad, like a frightened animal looking for a predator.

"I'm fine," I said in a voice that was amazingly steady, my eyes burning holes into Chad's chest. He still hadn't moved, but I wasn't taking my eyes off him. "Are you OK?"

She nodded, trembling as she brushed the red hair out of her pale face. I could see tears forming in her eyes as I put my massive hands on her shoulders and gently squeezed. I could feel her relax, the trembling almost stopped.

"It will be OK. I will make this OK," I whispered as I kissed her forehead. She frowned, looking at me, clearly confused. "Val, are you OK?"

"My nose hurts like hell," she said, sounding like she had a bad head cold. "Other than that, right as rain."

"Thank you," Ash said, kneeling down next to her. "I'm sorry you got hurt. Is there anything—"

"Don't worry, honey," Val said, patting her arm. "I've been wanting to hit that jerk for ages – you gave me an excuse. Felt good, too. Well worth the price." She smiled up at Ash, who smiled back.

"Chad," I said softly, aware that he hadn't moved and we had drawn a crowd. "Tell your uncle the deal is off. He'll know what I mean."

"You can't. He'll...he'll kill you," Chad said, backing up toward his car, his eyes wide. He looked like all pathetic bullies look when they've met their match: like little boys who have been caught doing something naughty, crying while they are scolded.

"He'll *try*," I said. "He'll *try* to kill me. But he won't be able to. You tell him it's open season. And that goes for anything – human or otherwise – that gets in my way."

Chad ran back to his car and I followed, walking quickly and still managing to keep up with his running.

"Where are you going Chad?" I yelled out to him. "Come on, let's play. You can't just start the fun and leave in the middle of it."

I made it to his car in a few strides and started raining blows on his car. I kicked the driver's side door, denting it inward and nearly springing the hinges, breaking the window.

"Come on," I said, yelling louder than he was. He was practically screeching as he frantically tried to pull his keys out of his pocket. "We'll have so much fun together."

I slammed my fist down on the roof and dented it in a little, then punched the rear quarter panel, pushing it in and buckling the trunk lid. He managed to get the keys in the ignition and the engine started.

"Leaving so soon?" I asked, grabbing the front quarter panel and ripping it off the car. As he stepped on the gas, spinning the rear tires, I kicked the rear bumper and knocked it off the car. As his car fish-tailed away, I picked up the bumper and threw it after him, spearing the rear window with it.

"Monster," I muttered.

"My God, how did you do that? You just demolished his car with your bare hands!" Ash's mouth was open almost as wide as her astonished eyes.

"I work out," I said, shrugging my shoulders and watching the car speed away into the night. And as it disappeared into the night, I realized it was taking my chances at happiness with it. But I accepted that, just as I accepted the consequences when I made my deal with Donnie.

"And what deal are you talking about?" Ash was still kneeling next to Val, looking confused. "What deal did you make with Chad's uncle?"

"The deal where he tries to get killed," Tessie said, looking at me angrily. "Happy?"

"Far from it," I said, frowning at Tessie. I turned back to Ash and shrugged my shoulders. "Ash, I'm sorry."

"Tell her," Tessie said. "Tell her that you're planning to ambush Chad now. And that Donnie Lawson will come after you when you do!"

"What?" Ash was clearly confused. "What does this have to do with that thug?"

Tessie turned from me to face Ash, her voice shaking along with the rest of her. "Donnie paid Ted a visit and Ted gave Donnie an ultimatum: Chad was to stay away from me and my friends, plus anyone else that Ted was friends with. Let me guess, Chad was harassing you at some point?"

"Well, yeah, but he harasses almost everyone. Wait," Ash said. "What's going on? I'm really confused. Ted, who is she and what's she talking about?"

"That's—" I started, but was interrupted by Tessie.

"My name is Tessie. I was…sort of dating Ted," she said uncomfortably, looking at her feet. "I broke things off with Ted after his run-in with Donnie. Let me guess, Ted never said anything before you two started…dating?"

"We're not dating," Ash said, smiling a little and blushing. "We're just really good friends. But Ted never mentioned anything about you or Chad or Donnie?" She frowned and looked at me suspiciously, which hurt me more than I wanted to admit.

"And Ted just happened to 'befriend' you one day, right? And you told him about your run-ins with Chad, right?" Tessie's voice was raising and her eyes sparked as she looked at me.

"Well, yeah," Ash said, "but I'm still not following what that has to do with—"

"Ted picked you to befriend because he knew Chad would come after you." Tessie looked sad all of a sudden, all the anger rushed out.

"What?"

"Ted only wanted to be friends with you because of your problems with Chad," Tessie explained in a soft voice, realizing she was probably destroying a relationship in the process. "Ted's deal with Donnie would be broken if Chad hurt anyone else. And Ted made sure he was making friends with someone Chad had targeted before. To make sure that the deal would get broken. Is that about right, Ted?"

"You only wanted to be friends with me to go after Chad?" Ash stared at me, unbelieving.

"At first," I said quietly. "I'm sorry. But I had fun with you and Trish. I do think of you as a friend."

"A friend of convenience! Is that the only reason you picked me out that day?" She folded her arms and frowned at me. She was trembling a little, clearly livid. Tears of anger were starting to well up in her eyes.

"I could have picked any girl there that day," I said. "And I guarantee each one of them would have been stalked by that..." I stopped myself and looked down the road Chad had just sped down, realizing he was taking everything from me. "Look, it might have started out as a friendship of convenience, but I really do like you."

"But you wanted to be my friend to get to Chad?" She repeated the question as if she couldn't believe the answer she had just heard. But it sounded more like a statement this time.

"At first, yes," I admitted again. "But spending time with you...helped me forget I'm me for a little while."

"And you set me up – you saw him, didn't you?" She was getting angrier, the tears starting to stream down her face, her breath hitching a little. And I could see Tessie starting to tear up as well, looking nearly as miserable as I felt. Clearly, this wasn't as satisfying as she thought it would be.

"Answer me," Ash yelled, slapping me in the chest. "You saw him, didn't you? When you went back into the theater!"

"I did see him, yes. But I would have never let him take you. I was going to stop him, I swear. You were never in any danger."

Ash seemed to slump, still shaking. She wrapped her arms around her chest, her breath still hitching a little. She was barely containing her sobs. "I can't believe you used me like that. You of all people."

"I'm sorry," I said again.

"You already said that," she grumbled, wiping her eyes angrily with the cuffs of her shirt. "Guess Trish was right. I am too trusting, that's why I always get burned."

"Look, I don't know what else to say. I wanted to spend time with you and get to know you. And once I did, I knew I couldn't just walk away. I had to protect you, too."

She looked at me, unsure. It was like she was looking at me for the first time and I suppose she was. I still hurt from Tessie, but Ash's anger hurt, too. It seemed I was doomed to leave a trail of broken people in my wake.

"Why me?" she asked quietly. "Why do you even need a reason? Clearly, you wanted to get Chad so why did you have to use me to do it?"

"He needed provocation," Tessie explained in a monotone. "He wouldn't feel his actions were…*validated*…if he attacked unprovoked after having given Donnie the ultimatum. He wanted to play by the rules he set up so he could say that he kept his word." Tessie looked up at me and raised her eyebrows. "Is that about right?"

I nodded, surprised at how closely she could read me, how much better she knew me than I knew myself.

"So now what?" Ash asked, a little less vehemently.

"Now he goes to kill Chad," Tessie said sadly. "He's got his license to kill."

"No," I said forcefully. "I go *confront* Chad."

"Who will most likely be at his uncle's house," Tessie added. "Surrounded by henchmen and thugs."

"You don't know that," I said quickly.

"So it's kill or be killed, right Ted?" Tessie asked, ignoring my remark.

"Oh no," Ash said, sitting abruptly on the sidewalk, all the strength running out of her legs. "Not because of me!"

I looked at Ash and shook my head. How could I explain what I had to do and why? What needed to be done – no, what *I* needed to do. How could I even begin to make her see? Or any of them?

"It could be because of me, too, you know," Val said, patting Ash's leg. "Chad hurt me more than you. But I don't feel guilty."

"Why not?" Ash asked weakly, very pale now.

"Look at the boy," Val said, a light, knowing smile on her face. "He's a natural. He was *born* for this."

"Val, stop," Tessie said, her voice shaking as she wiped her eyes. "Stop encouraging him."

"I'm not encouraging him, Sugar," she said softly, looking kindly at her. "He's going to do what he's going to do. I thought you knew that by now."

"You're not really going to..." Ash's eyes widened as she began to consider what I was going to do. "That's suicide!"

"No it's not," I said, as the cold anger gripped me. "Val is right, in a way, except that I wasn't *born* for this. I was *made* for this."

Tessie seemed to grow angrier by the second, all of her sadness and remorse forgotten. Something I said sparked her anger – and I was pretty sure I knew what it was.

"So it's back to that again," she said. "Back to the same old reason you've always told me you're different from everyone else. Is that why you think it's not suicide?"

I looked at her, shaking my head minutely, trying to tell her that I hadn't given Ash the whole story. But why should I expect Tessie to keep my secrets now?

"Is that why you think it's not suicide?" she asked again, more loudly. "The reasons you're *different*."

I was wondering how much further she was going to go. She'd never so much as hinted about my real nature to her mother, let alone any of her friends. And now...

Before she could continue, however, Kristie and Sharon came running over.

"Ohmygod," Sharon squealed as she looked at the broken glass and Val's bloody nose. "Ted? What are you doing here? What happened to Val?"

"Chad," I said. Kristie and Sharon exchanged a look and they both paled.

"Look, no matter how huge you or are or how many small cars you can bench press," Ash said weakly, "it's still suicide."

"Suicide doesn't work on the dead," Tessie yelled at me, her voice going up an octave and sounding slightly hysterical. She pounded my chest with a fist, looking desperate. "Does it, Ted? Am I right?"

"Tessie," Kristie said, putting her hand on her arm. "What are you talking about? Calm down."

"No, I won't! Ted, tell them! Tell them why you think this is such a great idea! Tell them why you're invincible, or at least why you think you are," she shouted. She pounded me with both fists this time, practically leaving her feet as she did. The crowd that was gathering started to disperse; apparently people thought it better not to be around. Funny how there seemed to be a large crowd watching the display, but no one bothered to call the cops.

"Tessie," I said quietly. "Stop, please. What are you doing?"

"Something I should have done a long time ago," she snapped, tears streaming down her face. She looked furious and sad at the same time. "Something that might have changed your choices so I wouldn't have to walk out of your life, something that might have saved your life if I'd thought of it sooner." She laughed sarcastically and said, "Oh, that's right, you don't really have a life, do you?"

"Tessie, stop," I said, walking to her quickly, speaking quietly. "You have to stop talking. Now."

"Why?" she asked, quickly walking backward, away from me. "Aren't you tired of lying?"

"What are you guys talking about?" Ash asked, pulling some tissues out of her purse and handing them to Val.

"Yeah," Sharon chimed in. "What do you mean he doesn't really have a life? That's an awful thing to say about him, especially since you know what he's been through and—"

"Ted thinks he's an animated corpse," Tessie said, almost unintelligible through her tears. "He's convinced that he's already dead, so why should a little violence hurt him? According to him, he's not even human, so why should the paltry human laws apply to him anyway?"

Val got up from the ground, holding a tissue against her nose. She put her arm around Tessie. "Tessie, I think you need to go home and rest, baby. You're not making much sense."

"No," Tessie yelled, shrugging Val's arm off. "Ted, tell them! Tell them the truth! All of them! Stop lying to them!"

"Tessie," I pleaded, practically whispering. "I can't. You know how much it took for me to tell you. What it took for me to be honest. You remember that day, don't you?"

"Of course," she said, lowering her voice. "But don't you think my friends and your new friend deserve the truth? You've been living a lie, a lie I helped you live. You asked me to lie to my mother, my friends. And I did. I think it's time to end it."

"Why are you doing this?" I asked, still whispering. I couldn't believe what she was doing, what she was about to do. I was partly worried about the consequences of my secret being known, even by people I cared about and trusted. But a large part of my concern was that I wanted her to be the only one outside of Devin's house who knew my secret. I wanted that to be something only she and I knew – a secret we shared, that would bind us together somehow.

She didn't answer; she just shook her head.

"Please tell me why," I said, hardly speaking the words.

"Because I can't lie for you any more! Because I can't do this anymore," she said, coming undone in front of me. Her voice sounded as weak as she looked, her energy and strength sapped. She would have slumped to the ground if Val hadn't grabbed her arm and Kristie hadn't rushed forward to support her. "I can't do this by myself, knowing what I know, watching you go to what could be your *real* death."

"Baby, what do you mean his 'real' death?" Val asked, looking concerned. "Honey, you're not making any sense."

"Tessie," Sharon said quietly, "I think Val is right, I think you need to rest."

"I think we could all use some downtime," Ash agreed. "I've had enough for one night and I want nothing more than to go home. Can I catch a ride with one of you?"

"Sure," Sharon said. "I can drop you off—"

"NO!" Tessie shouted and practically launched herself at me, grabbing my shirt in her fists and trying to shake me, tearing the neckline a little. "You tell them! Tell them now! Or I will!"

"You seem so intent," I said quietly as I held her arms gently in my huge hands. "You do it. I've already told you I can't."

"Fine!" She breathed deeply and yanked her arms out of mine so forcefully that she stumbled and would have fallen if Ash hadn't grabbed her, putting a supportive arm around her waist. Tessie held onto Ash, wrapping both arms around her, as if holding onto a lifeline.

"You probably all know about the accident," Tessie began, giving me a strange look that I couldn't read. Forgiveness, pity, and love? Or revulsion, frustration, and hate? A little bit of all of them?

"Yes," Ash said hurriedly, "Ted said he was in an accident."

"And you told us it was the injuries and treatments that left Ted the way he is," Val said.

"And Ted said his growth was due to the accident, something to do with his pituitary," Ash continued.

"But that's not what Tessie said," Kristie interrupted. "Tessie, you said it was a side-effect of the growth hormones and steroids Ted was taking."

"Both of which are lies," she said, still staring at me. "Devin developed a compound to help Ted heal, but he's not sure why Ted keeps growing. And the compound that was supposed to heal him actually killed him. You're looking at a corpse."

"You said you didn't believe that," I almost yelled. All of them flinched at my voice. "You said that I had a new life! I was just as human as everyone else! How many times have I heard you tell me about my humanity, how I'm part of life!" My bitter sarcasm was only matched by the growing volume of my voice. "Or was that all lies?"

Tessie ignored me and kept going, divulging my most personal secrets. "The compound actually replaced Ted's blood – he doesn't have any blood in his body. I know how that sounds, but it's true. Ask him. I've seen the lab, the equipment, the…the compounds. I've seen everything. It wasn't a heart Devin replaced; it was a pump. He has a pump in his chest that circulates the fluid, but that's about all he has. He doesn't breathe and he doesn't need to eat. Most of his organs have been removed. Technically, he's an animated corpse. Obviously not really dead, but not exactly alive, either."

The silence spun out for seconds, then minutes. No one moved, no one asked any questions. I felt the gulf between Tessie and me widen further and further. And since no one else was as close to me as Tessie, the rest of humanity – including her friends and Ash – might as well be on another planet.

"Sorry, but you're going to have to explain that again," Ash said evenly. "I'm not sure I caught all of that."

"She's right," I said, controlling my voice. "I'm dead."

"What are you talking about," Kristie said. "You can't be dead! Is this some kind of joke? You're talking, walking, thinking, feeling…"

"But he's not really alive," Tessie said cruelly. "Right, Ted? So you can play the superhero and win the day, since you don't really have a life to risk!"

"I told you that's not what this is about," I said through my teeth.

"Ted," Sharon said quietly. "What Tessie just said – is it true?"

I looked at her, so small and fragile. With my new size, I truly looked like a giant as she walked toward me. I put my hands lightly on her shoulders and they nearly disappeared under my hands.

"Yes. I don't have any blood – it's a compound that's a mix of recombinant DNA, a genetically engineered virus, plus some hormones and steroids. And yes, most of my organs have either been removed or are non-functioning. I have a pump that helps circulate the fluid, but it's not a heart. Obviously my brain still functions and I can see, I can talk. The fluid actually helps me think faster than most people. And my reflexes are quicker, I'm stronger, faster. But my body isn't like a human body. My bones are denser. I heal more quickly. And I have more in common with a corpse than I do with any of you."

I looked from Kristie to Val and from Val to Ash. And finally back at Sharon. "I'm sorry," I nearly whispered. "I'm sorry I lied to all of you."

"Why didn't you tell us?" Sharon asked, getting closer.

"I don't know. I was afraid. Afraid you wouldn't accept me. Afraid I couldn't tell you or that I would screw up if I did try. I haven't yet come to terms with what I am exactly. I was afraid of being even more alone than I am."

Suddenly, she looked angry and she reached up and slapped me in the face. Then she hit me again and again, slapping harder each time, yelling and crying. I knew she must be hurting her hands but she kept it up, anyway, even while Sharon and Val tried to stop her. I waved them off, shaking my head. "Why? Why didn't you tell us? You jerk!"

"I'm sorry," I said as I put out my arms. "I'm sorry."

She eventually stopped hitting me and sobbed against my chest, wrapping her arms around me and hugging me tightly. "You jerk! You should have told us. You're our friend."

"I didn't know how to tell you," I said. "I told Tessie, but asked her not to say anything. She didn't break my confidence because I asked her not to, I made her promise not to say anything. I underestimated you, obviously."

"But Tessie's right," Sharon said in a muffled voice. "You can't just walk into a trap like that. Even if you say you're not alive, you can't just risk yourself like that. Make any technical arguments you want, but you're still you and I don't want you to go."

"I have to, Sharon. Part of my past tells me I need to do this," I said. I lifted her chin and looked into her eyes. "I'm sorry to say this, because I know it will cause you pain, but remember your brother?"

She nodded, tears still falling from her eyes.

"*That's* why I need to do this. Chad is worse, worse than you can imagine. And he's being protected by someone much stronger than Chad himself is."

"But Ted," Kristie said, "you can't just take yourself away from us. Not away from your friends."

"I know I haven't known you that long," Ash broke in, "but I agree. I don't want you to do this, either."

"I told you," Tessie said, that furious look in her eyes. "I told you they'd understand!"

Sharon walked away and Kristie folded her into her arms, rubbing her back. The way they were looking at me made me want to reconsider. I didn't want to throw everything away, but I would be. There was an invisible line I was about to cross, one that I didn't think I'd be able to come back from once I went over it.

"Please," Tessie said, pleading. "None of us can imagine what you've been through, what you've endured. I'm sorry I did this to you, but I want to save you from what you're choosing to do. This was the only way I knew how."

And the compassion was too much. I could see it in each face: Ash, Val, Kristie, Sharon, and Tessie. The empathy they were feeling. I know what they just heard hadn't sunk in yet, but I could see they were accepting that I was different. And their instinct was to accept what was different, to value differences. If they began to accept me, then when I had to leave it would be even harder. I knew I had to do it again – keep the break Tessie had made. It would be easier this way.

"I don't need your pity," I said quietly, trying to keep the anger out of my voice. "This has to be done." I started walking away and Tessie shrugged Ash off and grabbed my arm, walking with me.

"Ted, I'm sorry," she said. "I know I betrayed you and—"

"You've had your say," I said stiffly. "You've told them the truth. But it doesn't change what I'm going to do. You've just made it harder because now they feel sorry for me."

"That's not it," she said. "Will you just stop so I can talk to you?"

"I told you, Tessie," I said, finally stopping. "I don't need your pity."

"I'm sorry," she said again quietly. "And I don't pity you. Yes, I feel compassion and it hurts me more than you know that you're in pain, but—"

"Stop," I said, almost pleading, my façade breaking a bit. "I can't do this anymore Tess. Don't you understand? This is hard enough for me to do, to make this break. But I have to. And I can't do it if you keep working against me like this. I'm not strong enough."

With that, I pulled my arm out of her hands and rushed to my car, trying to block out the sound of her tears. She was letting go again.

Showdown

It wasn't hard to find him; it took less than a week. Chad was keeping a low profile and staying away from town. But I hadn't seen him anywhere near his uncle's house. I drove by the house numerous times and saw several cars parked there, none of them Chad's. And there was no sign of Chad anywhere inside (or outside) the house.

The fact that I lacked the need for regular human necessities meant that I could sit outside the house (or near it, at least) without needing to take a break. I didn't need to eat, didn't really need sleep, and didn't even need to stretch my legs. While I conducted my stake-out, I smiled at the thought of a possible career in law enforcement.

During the days I was out looking for Chad, I would stop occasionally at the house to check in with Devin, whose appearance seemed to degrade with every day I kept up my manhunt. We would talk, but not much. He'd check me over and sit on his stool after he was done, looking exhausted. He'd update me on who called and when; I could tell that talking to my six friends (Trish and Ash started calling, too) was taking its toll on him.

"You should call them back," he said. "It's the right thing to do."

"No, it's not," I disagreed. "It will only be more painful when I have to—"

"First of all," Devin interrupted, "there's nothing that you have to do."

"You're wrong," I said.

But he pushed on. "You should at least give Tessie a chance to apologize."

"For betraying a confidence?"

"Yes," Devin said. "She really does feel awful about that and does feel that she betrayed you. She's also still trying to make amends for leaving you in the first place."

"But you agree with what she did."

"I do. She was doing what she thought was necessary to try to get you to change your mind. To get you to see reason, to try to save your life. Besides, do you think it's fair that you make all the decisions of what's painful for your friends? Especially Ash and Trish. They only just got to know you and clearly they like you. Now you're cutting them out of your life and—"

"For their own good," I argued, getting up and walking to the sliding door to look out into our backyard, wondering if I should try the walk into the darkened woods again. I decided against it – like I had said to Devin, it would only delay the pain and sorrow. I leaned my forehead against the sliding glass door and closed my eyes. I couldn't stand to live through the present.

But then there were the memories, which made it tougher to relive the past.

...the woman, rubbing her face with her right hand, her nose bleeding and bottom lip split. She was crying again, holding her left arm around her midsection, bent over a little in pain.

The man was pointing at her, jabbing his finger at her and poking her in the shoulder. The words were just noise, but his features stood out a little better: he had pale skin, a weak chin, and a bushy mustache that twitched when he talked.

The woman's hair shielded her face a little and she cringed with every word he spoke, as if he were lashing her with words...

And the boy is watching, always watching, planning and devising a way to stop the pain for the woman. He gets up and walks down the stairs, the man smiling at him as he comes.

The man slowly smiles, raising his hand to the boy.

And the woman steps in, earning herself another punch that lands her on the ground.

And the boy steps up to the man, angry, yelling...and gets knocked to the floor

The woman launches herself off the floor at the man who shoves her away. She hits her head on the coffee table and doesn't get up this time.

While the man's back is turned, the boy runs, out the door, down the street, away from the man's screams...

And before I knew what I was doing, I was in the garage, getting in my car. I started it up, mashing the accelerator to the floor, making the tires scream against the pavement. I raced toward Donnie's house, barreling through town and pushing the Judge to its limits. Somehow, I knew Chad would be there. Had to be there.

I wouldn't walk away this time.

I slid the car around the corner as I turned onto Donnie's street, hoping to announce my arrival as loudly as possible. I gunned the engine long and loud before turning it off. I stepped out of the car and looked toward the house. I could see Chad's car parked in the driveway as well as a few other cars.

Like it was meant to be.

I walked up the driveway and could hear voices around the side of the house. I walked around the corner and next to Chad's car, I saw his uncle's. I could hear a heated conversation further down the driveway toward the back of the house.

"What did I tell you, huh? I told you he'd come. I told you to lay off, but no, you couldn't do that."

"Aw come on, it's not that bad," I heard Chad's confident voice say.

"Are you stupid? You want the jolly gray giant to come down here and—"

"Relax, Uncle Don," the other voice said. "He's too busy mourning. I've seen Tessie around without him, so she probably split up with him. Now, he's trying to start something up with this other girl, Ash, only because I was with her."

"And based on how your car looks, he did start up something," Donnie said, raising his voice. "Or did you forget? He tore the thing apart with his bare hands!"

"Uncle Don, he's alone right now, probably crying at home in his—"

"Wrong again, Chad," I interrupted quietly as I stepped around the corner. "Hey Donnie, how are you?"

"I'm good," Donnie said, looking at me warily. "Can't say the same for my boys. Frank, the guy you chucked through the window, needed quite a few stitches and a blood transfusion. Sean, the guy whose arm you crushed, has nerve damage and probably won't regain use of his arm."

"That's nothing compared to what I'm going to do to him," I said, pointing at Chad. I punched the front fender of Donnie's car, denting it and rocking the entire car.

"Easy, Ted, easy," Donnie said, stepping up and putting his hands out in a placating gesture. "Look, I'm a business man. I know, Chad screwed up. You warned me what would happen. But maybe we can come to an agreement."

"I don't deal with crooks," I said, shoving him out of the way and grabbing Chad by his jacket. I threw him into the side of Donnie's car, relishing the sound his body made when it hit.

Donnie started shouting names and calling for his people, but it was too late – I had him. I shoved him against his own car, breaking the driver's side window and denting the door. As he slumped to the ground, I grabbed his shirt, yanked him to his feet, and threw him against the side of the house.

I picked Chad up off the ground and slapped his face to wake him up a bit. He started struggling, whimpering and blubbering.

"I'm sorry, I won't do it again," he said. "Please, don't hurt me again."

"Oh, I know you won't do it again after tonight. But as for not hurting you again, too late," I said, throwing him against the side of the house next to his uncle. I pulled him forward and shoved him back again.

And again.

And again.

Someone grabbed my arm, trying to spin me around. I grabbed his hand and crushed it, mangling the fingers, smiling at the sounds of his screams. Another of Donnie's men stepped in front of me and swung a pipe at me. I caught it in my hand, wrenched it out of the guy's hands, and then cracked him on the skull with it. He fell to the ground, convulsing, feet twitching.

Things got a little blurry and out of hand after that...I remember hitting Donnie and Chad with the pipe repeatedly...disabling more henchmen...the blood, the broken bones, the destroyed cars...picking up men after they were unconscious and beating them again and again...the unconscious bodies I threw around...

...I remember feeling demented, demonic. I remember the small voice in the back of my head telling me to stop, this was wrong, this wasn't me...

...but I don't remember when Donnie and Chad drew their last breaths. I don't remember when I killed them or how. Which punch it was, or which shove, or which kick.

I don't remember when I became a murderer.

At some point, I simply stopped. I was standing in the middle of Donnie's driveway, my shirt torn and ripped. There were smears of blood on my hands and arms. My boots. I could see unconscious bodies around me, possibly several dead ones. I knew two that were. They were the most damaged: Donnie and Chad.

And that's when I finally saw what Tessie had seen, what she was fearing for me. Not the knowledge that I would carry with me that I ended two lives – that was acceptable to me. It was the final thing that would cut me off from the outside world. I would need to live on the run, never putting down roots, never getting close to anyone again. For the rest of my life. I was a fugitive, a murderer.

I had finally crossed the line, become what I hated most: a criminal who had wasted what he had.

I had a chance, and I threw it all away.

What Tessie wanted to save me from was what I was facing – a long stretch of nothing spread out ahead of me: no future, no plans, and no one to help me.

Alone, once and for all.

Finally, alone.

Goodbye

I drove home in a daze, not really remembering too much of the evening. I tried to wipe the blood off my hands before getting in the car, but I didn't think I got it all.

I knew I couldn't stay with Devin, even though I wanted to. I thought in some ways this would be easier for him. He wouldn't have to watch me grow and grow until I wore the pump out.

But I needed to see Tessie, one more time. Despite everything I had said about a clean break, I was ignoring what I knew would be the easiest thing to do. I wasn't going to simply walk away. I had to see her, to try to explain one more time, to get her to see what I had done was right – no matter how horrible and terrible it might have been.

I drove quickly, recklessly up the long driveway, got out of the car and ran up the steps. I rushed through the front door and up the stairs.

"Ted," Devin called out.

"Upstairs," I called back as I flew into my room and grabbed a duffle bag. I started shoving clothes into it, then grabbed the loose cash lying around the room, hoping I'd be able to get some from Devin as well.

"Could you come down here a minute," he called.

I grabbed a few more things and headed downstairs.

"Devin, I have to go, look—" I broke off midsentence when I saw Tessie sitting in the lab with her mom. The TV was on and a late-breaking story covering the death of a local criminal, his nephew, and a few associates was being covered...

"What have you done?" Tessie asked quietly, tears streaming down her face.

"I have to go," I said, ignoring the question. "Tell the cops everything – the car I took, the clothes, everything. Don't hold back any information. Tell them I threatened you and stole it. There's no need for you to get into trouble over me."

"Ted," Tessie's mother said, "What are you talking about? Where are you going?"

"Away," I said, looking at Devin, who sadly nodded his head.

"It's done, then?"

"Yes," I said. "Done."

"I was explaining the predicament with your heart pump," Devin said.

"So you know," I said quietly, looking at Tessie.

"Is this why you did it? Because you felt you had nothing to lose," she shook her head in disbelief.

"No," I said, throwing down my duffle bag, still furious even after venting what I thought was all my rage and anger. I wanted to tell her, to make her see. But I was doing it all wrong. "We've been through this before. I did it because it had to be done. Chad never would have stopped and with his uncle protecting him, he was going to become a—"

"Monster," Tessie said, looking at me, hard.

"I was going to say career criminal. A non-human."

Devin and Lily watched us intently, clearly confused.

"So you play the white knight and ride off into the distance," she said. "Leaving your family and friends behind."

"I didn't do this to be a hero," I roared. "How many times do I have to tell you that? Besides, who else was going to do it? WHO? NO ONE!" I slammed my fist on the lab table hard enough to crack the granite top and send a large chunk falling to the floor. I kicked it across the room

325

and it flew through the door leading to the kitchen, breaking it off its hinges and showering the next room in splinters.

"I did this because no one else could," I explained. "I didn't want to! I would have been content to live the rest of my months—maybe only weeks—with you on your back porch, talking to your friends and laughing. But after I was gone, he'd still be around. He'd still go after people like Trish and Ash. Even if you and your friends were safe, innocent people would still get hurt. And he'd still be around. And protected. Did you stop to think of that, or were you too busy trying to make this my fault that you never thought about it?"

I glared at her and I could see a revelation – she hadn't thought of it.

"Ted...I didn't know," she started, standing up and walking quickly toward me.

"You thought this was a macho trip?"

She nodded, tentatively reaching out for my hand. I grasped it and frowned at my hand, easily covering hers, hiding it.

"Something like that," she said. "You, saving the damsels in distress, saving the day. Even though you said that wasn't the reason, I thought you'd convinced yourself it wasn't the reason."

"I should have tried to explain," I said. I looked her in the eyes, cupping her small, fragile face in my monstrous hand.

"And I shouldn't have come back here," she said, sobbing. "It would have made the goodbye easier."

I wrapped my arms around her and looked at Devin, helpless. He reached into a cabinet and pulled out a strongbox.

"Take this, you'll need it. It's enough cash to get you wherever you want to go. I'll send more if you'll call me and tell me where to send it. Please call when you can," he said, looking hopefully.

"I'll try," I said.

"Take me," Tessie suddenly said. "Please take me."

"Tessie," her mother said breathlessly, "what are you saying?"

"Mom, he's not going to be…around forever. But I want be there for whatever time he has left."

And I was tempted. Even if only for half a year, I would have her all to myself. But I couldn't continue torturing her like that. I couldn't do that to her. It would be great for me, but then she would have to settle back into life, for the rest of *her* life.

"I can't," I answered. "You can't go where I'm going. I'm a fugitive and I won't ruin your life, too. Besides, if you know about the pump, then you know there's not much time left for me anyway. Even after I'm gone, you'd still be accountable for aiding a fugitive."

"But Ted," Lily said. "Why not give yourself up? The law will have to see your side of it!"

"I can't," I said. "I can't live the rest of what little time I have in and out of court rooms and jail cells."

The three of them looked at me helplessly. Another choice that was made for me. An impossible, painful situation. I tried a smile, but it felt horrible.

"I'm sorry, but I have to go. Now."

I turned my back and walked quickly out the door to the car. I could hear Tessie calling, begging me to take her, but I jumped in the car and gunned it, drowning out her pleas, driving into the darkness one last time...

Highway

Another state. Another sunrise.

I'd lost track of all of them after a few days, but I was somewhere in the Midwest, driving through big open skies. I couldn't remember all the state signs I'd passed or which one I'm in on any given day.

I called Devin, but didn't tell him where I was. Just that I was traveling. And I was feeling fine, to let all of my...friends...know I was OK. I didn't feel the need to tell him that I could almost feel myself growing at this point or that the clothes that fit the day before seemed a little tighter the next.

I even called Tessie. I knew it was probably cruel, but I couldn't stand the goodbye. I wanted her to know I was still out there, still alive...or something like it. I wanted to hear her voice again. When she answered the phone, I couldn't say anything. Besides, I didn't know what to say. So I just held the phone to my chest so she could hear my pump, still going. I heard her crying out "I love you" as I replaced the phone in the cradle.

———

I stop off the highway once in a while to see the sites, breathe the fresh air so to speak. It gives me time to reflect on the borrowed time that Devin gave me. I'm hoping he feels I made the best of it, but I know I failed miserably.

As I breezed through town after town, I stopped in one little burg to fill my tank and grabbed the small local newspaper. I could see the headline regarding a couple of local hoods and some problems they caused – bar fights, stolen cars, a home invasion of a family in which the mother and oldest daughter were killed. The two were out on bail.

"Just passing through," the old man at the cash register commented. He hardly noticed my size, the practiced look of a man who tries not to notice details, who would make a lousy eyewitness to a crime.

"Well," I said, eyeing the headline about the two thugs. "Maybe it wouldn't hurt to stay a few days."

I smiled at him. I looked through the story again as I walked to my car...

A Word (or Several Words) of Thanks From the Author

Almost every book has a thank-you page and this one is no exception. Part of the reason I feel compelled to have one is because I could not have written this without my life experience. If you read this book and you know me, you've had a hand in getting this created. The other reason for a thank-you page is because this book has been a humbling experience: most people probably know this, but writing is extremely hard. And although I'm the author, I certainly didn't do this alone. I'll try to not be overly sentimental or expansive.

First, thank you for taking the time to read my book. I wrote this over a period of four years and during that time, I vacillated between feeling as though I were wasting time and feeling as though I were embarking on a great adventure. Thanks for joining me on that adventure and (possibly) paying for the journey.

Second, a huge thanks to my family:

Dillon – the Peter Pan of the family who keeps me a kid at heart, provides me an excuse to play video games, and gives me daily reminders of the power of daydreaming

Taylor – my artistic director, editor, and gentle critic, a talented writer who will someday amaze us all

Karen – the chief editor, scientific advisor, and not-so-gentle critic who gave me a swift kick when I needed it, her bravery gave me the courage to publish this

Otis (the English bulldog) and Yawkey (the some-sort-of-terrier mix) – the unwavering fan club, probably because I feed them most often

Third, I want to thank the people who had a positive impact on my life (there goes the expansive limitation). It sounds cliché, but they need to be mentioned. I can't mention everyone by name, so please don't be offended if you don't see it below. And don't be offended that you're listed below the pets.

My parents, Bob and BJ, are at the top of the list along with my big brother, Rob (a.k.a Boo). Next on the very long list is my extended family of aunts, uncles, and cousins in South Jersey and everywhere else. There are too many to name. I blame it on my mother's side of the family and their need to populate the United States with descendants from the Kennard and Master families.

I would be remiss if I didn't mention friends, starting with those I made in LAC Elementary, Salem High School, Lebanon Valley College, and into my adult life. Again, the list would be very long as would be the list of teachers and professors who gave me the crazy idea that I would see my work published someday.

So to the friends and family who've touched my life, whether you're still among us or not (and there goes the sentimental limitation) – thank you.

I hope I haven't disappointed anyone...

www.ingramcontent.com/pod-product-compliance
Lightning Source LLC
Chambersburg PA
CBHW062026170626
46813CB00001B/310